Cinnamo

'Underest...
Mosley . . . is almost as fatal a mistake as crossing Mouse . . .
Easy's investigations . . . allow Mosley to fuse his peerless
crime-writing skills with a penetrating social commentary on
American society, and the black experience of it, which has
organically evolved with each novel . . . there are few writers
working within the crime genre who recreate time and place
with Mosley's effortless exactness, even fewer who can repli-
cate his masterfully sustained sense of danger, and virtually
none who possess his burning social conscience'

Trevor Lewis, *Sunday Times*

'You don't need to be familiar with Mosley's previous series,
starring Easy Rawlins Private Investigator, to enjoy this story set
in San Francisco at the height of the hippy movement . . . An
undercurrent of racism percolates steadily throughout and
America's battle between reactionary conservatism and the
head elixir of 1960s liberalism is well rendered. Combined
with convincing characterisation, they combine to create a
oughly enjoyable romp'

Martin Tierney, *Herald*

Scarlet

Scarlet is a masterwork. Walter Mosley is one of
rica's most exciting, inclusive writers'   George Pelecanos

'Mosley has a unique voice that remains fresh, and he tells a
damn good story. *Little Scarlet* is a compelling portrait of a
painful era, peopled by living, breathing, unforgettable characters. This may be Walter Mosley's best'   Jonathan Kellerman

Walter Mosley is the author, among other works, of the acclaimed Easy Rawlins series of mysteries, and a collection of short stories featuring Socrates Fortlow, *Always Outnumbered, Always Outgunned*, for which he received the Anisfield-Wolf Award. He is also the author of two science fiction books, *Blue Light* and *Futureland*. His books have been translated into twenty languages. Born in Los Angeles, Walter Mosley has been a potter, a computer programmer and a poet; he currently lives in New York. For more information visit www.waltermosley.com and sign up for the Walter Mosley eNewsletter at www.twbookmark.com.

By Walter Mosley

CINNAMON KISS

Walter Mosley

PHOENIX

A PHOENIX PAPERBACK

First published in Great Britain in 2005
by Weidenfeld & Nicolson
This paperback edition published in 2006
by Phoenix,
an imprint of Orion Books Ltd,
Orion House, 5 Upper St Martin's Lane,
London WC2H 9EA

First published in the United States by
Little, Brown & Co. in 2005

1 3 5 7 9 10 8 6 4 2

A CIP catalogue record for this book
is available from the British Library.

ISBN-13 978-0-7538-2107-7
ISBN-10 0-7538-2107-9

Printed and bound in Great Britain by
Clays Ltd, St Ives plc

The Orion Publishing Group's policy is to use papers that
are natural, renewable and recyclable products and
made from wood grown in sustainable forests. The logging
and manufacturing processes are expected to conform to
the environmental regulations of the country of origin.

www.orionbooks.co.uk

For Ossie Davis,
our shining king

1

S o it's real simple," Mouse was saying. When he grinned
the diamond set in his front tooth sparkled in the gloom.

Cox Bar was always dark, even on a sunny April afternoon.
The dim light and empty chairs made it a perfect place for our
kind of business.

". . . We just be there at about four-thirty in the mornin' an'
wait," Mouse continued. "When the mothahfuckahs show up
you put a pistol to the back of the neck of the one come in last.
He the one wit' the shotgun. Tell 'im to drop it —"

"What if he gets brave?" I asked.

"He won't."

"What if he flinches and the gun goes off?"

"It won't."

"How the fuck you know that, Raymond?" I asked my lifelong

friend. "How do you know what a finger in Palestine, Texas, gonna do three weeks from now?"

"You boys need sumpin' for your tongues?" Ginny Wright asked. There was a leer in the bar owner's voice.

It was a surprise to see such a large woman appear out of the darkness of the empty saloon.

Ginny was dark-skinned, wearing a wig of gold-colored hair. Not blond, gold like the metal.

She was asking if we needed something to drink but Ginny could make a sexual innuendo out of garlic salt if she was talking to men.

"Coke," I said softly, wondering if she had overheard Mouse's plan.

"An' rye whiskey in a frozen glass for Mr. Alexander," Ginny added, knowing her best customer's usual. She kept five squat liquor glasses in her freezer at all times — ready for his pleasure.

"Thanks, Gin," Mouse said, letting his one-carat filling ignite for her.

"Maybe we should talk about this someplace else," I suggested as Ginny moved off to fix our drinks.

"Shit," he uttered. "This my office jes' like the one you got on Central, Easy. You ain't got to worry 'bout Ginny. She don't hear nuttin' an' she don't say nuttin'."

Ginny Wright was past sixty. When she was a young woman she'd been a prostitute in Houston. Raymond and I both knew her back then. She had a soft spot for the younger Mouse all those years. Now he was her closest friend. You got the feeling, when she looked at him, that she wanted more. But Ginny satisfied herself by making room in her nest for Raymond to do his business.

On this afternoon she'd put up her special sign on the front door: CLOSED FOR A PRIVATE FUNCTION. That sign would stay up until my soul was sold for a bagful of stolen money.

Ginny brought our drinks and then went back to the high table that she used as a bar.

Mouse was still grinning. His light skin and gray eyes made him appear wraithlike in the darkness.

"Don't worry, Ease," he said. "We got this suckah flat-footed an' blind."

"All I'm sayin' is that you don't know how a man holding a shotgun's gonna react when you sneak up behind him and put a cold gun barrel to his neck."

"To begin wit'," Mouse said, "Rayford will not have any buck-shot in his shooter that day an' the on'y thing he gonna be thinkin' 'bout is you comin' up behind him. 'Cause he know that the minute you get the drop on 'im that Jack Minor, his partner, gonna swivel t' see what's what. An' jest when he do that, I'ma bop old Jackie good an' then you an' me got some heavy totin' to do. They gonna have a two hunnert fi'ty thousand minimum in that armored car — half of it ours."

"You might think it's all good and well that you know these guys' names," I said, raising my voice more than I wanted. "But if you know them then they know you."

"They don't know me, Easy," Mouse said. He looped his arm around the back of his chair. "An' even if they did, they don't know you."

"You know me."

That took the smug smile off of Raymond's lips. He leaned forward and clasped his hands. Many men who knew my murder-ous friend would have quailed at that gesture. But I wasn't afraid. It's not that I'm such a courageous man that I can't know fear in the face of certain death. And Raymond "Mouse" Alexander was certainly death personified. But right then I had problems that went far beyond me and my mortality.

"I ain't sayin' that you'd turn me in, Ray," I said. "But the cops know we run together. If I go down to Texas and rob this armored car with you an' Rayford sings, then they gonna know to come after me. That's all I'm sayin'."

I remember his eyebrows rising, maybe a quarter of an inch. When you're facing that kind of peril you notice small gestures. I had seen Raymond in action. He could kill a man and then go take a catnap without the slightest concern.

The eyebrows meant that his feelings were assuaged, that he wouldn't have to lose his temper.

"Rayford never met me," he said, sitting back again. "He don't know my name or where I'm from or where I'll be goin' after takin' the money."

"And so why he trust you?" I asked, noticing that I was talking the way I did when I was a young tough in Fifth Ward, Houston, Texas. Maybe in my heart I felt that the bravado would see me through.

"Remembah when I was in the can ovah that manslaughter thing?" he asked.

He'd spent five years in maximum security.

"That was *hard* time, man," he said. "You know I never wanna be back there again. I mean the cops would have to kill me before I go back there. But even though it was bad some good come out of it."

Mouse slugged back the triple shot of chilled rye and held up his glass. I could hear Ginny hustling about for his next free drink.

"You know I found out about a very special group when I was up in there. It was what you call a syndicate."

"You mean like the Mafia?" I asked.

"Naw, man. That's just a club. This here is straight business. There's a brother in Chicago that has men goin' around the country scopin' out possibilities. Banks, armored cars, private poker games — anything that's got to do wit' large amounts of cash, two hunnert fi'ty thousand or more. This dude sends his boys in to make the contacts and then he give the job to somebody he could trust." Mouse smiled again. It was said that that diamond was given to him by a rich white movie star that he helped out of a jam.

"Here you go, baby," Ginny said, placing his frosty glass on the pitted round table between us. "You need anything else, Easy?"

"No thanks," I said and she moved away. Her footfalls were silent. All you could hear was the rustle of her black cotton trousers.

"So this guy knows you?" I asked.

"Easy," Mouse said in an exasperated whine. "You the one come to me an' said that you might need up t' fi'ty thousand, right? Well — here it is, prob'ly more. After I lay out Jack Minor, Rayford gonna let you hit him in the head. We take the money an' that's that. I give you your share that very afternoon."

My tongue went dry at that moment. I drank the entire glass of cola in one swig but it didn't touch that dryness. I took an ice cube into my mouth but it was like I was licking it with a leather strip instead of living flesh.

"How does Rayford get paid?" I asked, the words warbling around the ice.

"What you care about him?"

"I wanna know why we trust him."

Mouse shook his head and then laughed. It was a real laugh, friendly and amused. For a moment he looked like a normal person instead of the supercool ghetto bad man who came off so hard that he rarely seemed ruffled or human at all.

"The man in Chi always pick somebody got somethin' t' hide. He gets shit on 'em and then he pay 'em for their part up front. An' he let 'em know that if they turn rat they be dead."

It was a perfect puzzle. Every piece fit. Mouse had all the bases covered, any question I had he had the answer. And why not? He was the perfect criminal. A killer without a conscience, a warrior without fear — his IQ might have been off the charts for all I knew, but even if it wasn't, his whole mind paid such close attention to his profession that there were few who could outthink him when it came to breaking the law.

"I don't want anybody gettin' killed behind this, Raymond."

"Nobody gonna die, Ease. Just a couple'a headaches, that's all."

"What if Rayford's a fool and starts spendin' money like water?" I asked. "What if the cops think he's in on it?"

"What if the Russians drop the A-bomb on L.A.?" he asked back. "What if you drive your car on the Pacific Coast Highway, get a heart attack, and go flyin' off a cliff? Shit, Easy. I could 'what if' you into the grave but you got to have faith, brother. An' if Rayford's a fool an' wanna do hisself in, that ain't got nuthin' to do with what you got to do."

Of course he was right. What I had to do was why I was there. I didn't want to get caught and I didn't want anybody to get killed, but those were the chances I had to take.

"Lemme think about it, Ray," I said. "I'll call you first thing in the morning."

2

I walked down the small alleyway from Cox Bar and then turned left on Hooper. My car was parked three blocks away because of the nature of that meeting. This wasn't grocery shopping or parking in the lot of the school I worked at. This was serious business, business that gets you put in prison for a child's lifetime.

The sun was bright but there was a slight breeze that cut the heat. The day was beautiful if you didn't look right at the burned-out businesses and boarded-up shops — victims of the Watts riots not yet a year old. The few people walking down the avenue were somber and sour looking. They were mostly poor, either unemployed or married to someone who was, and realizing that California and Mississippi were sister states in the same union, members of the same clan.

I knew how they felt because I had been one of them for more than four and a half decades. Maybe I had done a little more with my life. I didn't live in Watts anymore and I had a regular job. My live-in girlfriend was a stewardess for Air France and my boy owned his own boat. I had been a major success in light of my upbringing but that was all over. I was no more than a specter haunting the streets that were once my home.

I felt as if I had died and that the steps I was taking were the final unerring, unalterable footfalls toward hell. And even though I was a black man, in a country that seemed to be teetering on the edge of a race war, my color and race had nothing to do with my pain.

Every man's hell is a private club, my father used to tell me when I was small. *That's why when I look at these white people sneerin' at me I always smile an' say, "Sure thing, boss."*

He knew that the hammer would fall on them too. He forgot to say that it would also get me one day.

I drove a zigzag side street path back toward the west side of town. At every intersection I remembered people that I'd known in Los Angeles. Many of those same folks I had known in Texas. We'd moved, en masse it seemed, from the Deep South to the haven of California. Joppy the bartender, dead all these years, and Jackson the liar; EttaMae, my first serious love, and Mouse, her man and my best friend. We came here looking for a better life — the reason most people move — and many of us believed that we had found it.

. . . You put a pistol to the back of the neck of the one come in last . . .

I could see myself, unseen by anyone else, with a pistol in my hand, planning to rob a big oil concern of its monthly payroll. Nearly twenty years of trying to be an upright citizen making an honest wage and it all disappears because of a bucketful of bad blood.

With this thought I looked up and realized that a woman pushing a baby carriage, with two small kids at her side, was in the middle of the street not ten feet in front of my bumper. I hit the brake and swerved to the left, in front of a '48 wood-paneled station wagon. He hit his brakes too. Horns were blaring.

The woman screamed, "Oh Lord!" and I pictured one of her babies crushed under the wheel of my Ford.

I jumped out the door, almost before the car came to a stop, and ran around to where the dead child lay in my fears.

But I found the small woman on her knees, hugging her children to her breast. They were crying while she screamed for the Lord.

An older man got out of the station wagon. He was black with silver hair and broad shoulders. He had a limp and wore metal-rimmed glasses. I remember being calmed by the concern in his eyes.

"Mothahfuckah!" the small, walnut-shell-colored woman shouted. "What the fuck is the mattah wit' you? Cain't you see I got babies here?"

The older man, who was at first coming toward me, veered toward the woman. He got down on one knee even though it was difficult because of his bum leg.

"They okay, baby," he said. "Your kids is fine. They fine. But let's get 'em out the street. Out the street before somebody else comes and hits 'em."

The man led the kids and their mother to the curb at Florence and San Pedro. I stood there watching them, unable to move. Cars were backed up on all sides. Some people were getting out to see what had happened. Nobody was honking yet because they thought that maybe someone had been killed.

The silver-haired man walked back to me with a stern look in his eye. I expected to be scolded for my careless behavior. I'm sure I saw the reprimand in his eyes. But when he got close up he saw something in me.

"You okay, mister?" he asked.

I opened my mouth to reply but the words did not come. I looked over at the mother, she was kissing the young girl. I noticed that all of them — the mother, her toddler son, and the six- or seven-year-old girl — were wearing the same color brown pants.

"You bettah watch out, mister," the older man was saying. "It can get to ya sometimes but don't let it get ya."

I nodded and maybe even mumbled something. Then I stumbled back to my car.

The engine was still running. It was in neutral but I hadn't engaged the parking brake.

I was an accident waiting to happen.

For the rest of the ride home I was preoccupied with the image of that woman holding her little girl. When Feather was five and we were at a beach near Redondo she had taken a tumble down a small hill that was full of thorny weeds. She cried as Jesus held her, kissing her brow. When I came up and lifted her into my arms she said, "Don't be mad at Juice, Daddy. He didn't make me fall."

I pulled to the curb so as not to have another accident. I sat there with the admonition in my ears. *It can get to ya sometimes but don't let it get ya.*

3

When I came in the front door I found my adopted son, Jesus, and Benita Flag sitting on the couch in the front room. They looked up at me, both with odd looks on their faces.

"Is she all right?" I asked, feeling my heart do a flip-flop.

"Bonnie's with her," Jesus said.

Benita just nodded and I hurried toward Feather's room, down the small hallway, and through my little girl's door.

Bonnie was sitting there dabbing the light-skinned child's brow with isopropyl alcohol. The evaporation on her skin was meant to cool the fever.

"Daddy," Feather called weakly.

I was reminded of earlier times, when she'd shout my name and then run into me like a small Sherman tank. She was a daddy's girl. She'd been rough and full of guffaws and squeals.

13

But now she lay back with a blood infection that no one on the North American continent knew how to cure.

"The prognosis is not good," Dr. Beihn had said. "Make her comfortable and make sure she drinks lots of liquid . . ."

I would have drained Hoover Dam to save her life.

Bonnie had that strange look in her eye too. She was tall and dark skinned, Caribbean and lovely. She moved like the ocean, surging up out of that chair and into my arms. Her skin felt hot, as if somehow she was trying to draw the fever out of the girl and into her own body.

"I'll go get the aspirin," Bonnie whispered.

I released her and took her place in the folding chair next to my Feather's pink bed. With my right hand I held the sponge against her forehead. She took my left hand in both of hers and squeezed my point finger and baby finger as hard as she could.

"Why am I so sick, Daddy?" she whined.

"It's just a little infection, honey," I said. "You got to wait until it works its way outta your system."

"But it's been so long."

It had been twenty-three days since the diagnosis, a week longer than the doctor thought she'd survive.

"Did anybody come and visit you today?" I asked.

That got her to smile.

"Billy Chipkin did," she said.

The flaxen-haired, bucktoothed white boy was the fifth and final child of a family that had migrated from Iowa after the war. Billy's devotion to my foundling daughter sometimes made my heart swell to the point that it hurt. He was two inches shorter than Feather and came to sit at her side every day after school. He brought her homework and gossip from the playground.

Sometimes, when they thought that no one was looking,

they'd hold hands while discussing some teacher's unfair punishments of their unruly friends.

"What did Billy have to say?"

"He got long division homework and I showed him how to do it," she said proudly. "He don't know it too good, but if you show him he remembers until tomorrow."

I touched Feather's brow with the backs of three fingers. She seemed to be cool at that moment.

"Can I have some of Mama Jo's black tar?" Feather asked.

Even the witch-woman, Mama Jo, had not been able to cure her. But Jo had given us a dozen black gummy balls, each wrapped up in its own eucalyptus leaf.

"If her fevah gets up past one-oh-three give her one'a these here to chew," the tall black witch had said. "But nevah more than one in a day an' aftah these twelve you cain't give her no mo'."

There were only three balls left.

"No, honey," I said. "The fever's down now."

"What you do today, Daddy?" Feather asked.

"I saw Raymond."

"Uncle Mouse?"

"Yeah."

"What did you do with him?"

"We just talked about old times."

I told her about the time, twenty-seven years earlier, when Mouse and I had gone out looking for orange monarch butterflies that he intended to give his girlfriend instead of flowers. We'd gone to a marsh that was full of those regal bugs, but we didn't have a proper net and Raymond brought along some moonshine that Mama Jo made. We got so drunk that both of us had fallen into the muddy water more than once. By the end of the day Mouse had caught only one butterfly. And that night when we got to Mabel's house, all dirty from our antics, she took one look at the orange-and-black monarch in the glass jar and set him free.

"He just too beautiful to be kept locked up in this bottle," she told us.

Mouse was so angry that he stormed out of Mabel's house and didn't talk to her again for a week.

Feather usually laughed at this story, but that afternoon she fell asleep before I got halfway through.

I hated it when she fell asleep because I didn't know if she'd wake up again.

WHEN I GOT BACK to the living room Jesus and Benita were at the door.

"Where you two goin'?" I asked.

"Uh," Juice grunted, "to the store for dinner."

"How you doin', Benita?" I asked the young woman.

She looked at me as if she didn't understand English or as if I'd asked some extremely personal question that no gentleman should ask a lady.

Benny was in her mid-twenties. She'd had an affair with Mouse which broke her heart and led to an attempted suicide. Bonnie and I took her in for a while but now she had her own apartment. She still came by to have a home-cooked meal now and then. Bonnie and she had become friends. And she loved the kids.

Lately it had been good to have Benny around because when Bonnie and I needed to be away she'd stay at Feather's side.

Jesus would have done it if we asked him to, but he was eighteen and loved being out on his homemade sailboat, cruising up and down the Southern California coast. We hadn't told him how sick his sister actually was. They were so close we didn't want to worry him.

"Fine, Mr. Rawlins," she said in a too-high voice. "I got a job in a clothes store on Slauson. Miss Hilda designs everything she sells. She said she was gonna teach me."

"Okay," I said, not really wanting to hear about the young woman's hopeful life. I wanted Feather to be telling me about her adventures and dreams.

When Benny and Jesus were gone Bonnie came out of the kitchen with a bowl full of spicy beef soup.

"Eat this," she said.

"I'm not hungry."

"I didn't ask if you were hungry."

Our living room was so small that we only had space for a love seat instead of a proper couch. I slumped down there and she sat on my lap shoving the first spoonful into my mouth.

It was good.

She fed me for a while, looking into my eyes. I could tell that she was thinking something very serious.

"What?" I asked at last.

"I spoke to the man in Switzerland today," she said.

She waited for me to ask what he said but I didn't. I couldn't hear one more piece of bad news about Feather.

I turned away from her gaze. She touched my neck with four fingertips.

"He tested the blood sample that Vicki brought over," she said. "He thinks that she's a good candidate for the process."

I heard the words but my mind refused to understand them. What if they meant that Feather was going to die? I couldn't take the chance of knowing that.

"He thinks that he can cure her, baby," Bonnie added, understanding the course of my grief. "He has agreed to let her apply to the Bonatelle Clinic."

"Really?"

"Yes."

"In Montreux?"

"Yes."

"But why would they take a little colored girl in there? Didn't you say that the Rockefellers and Kennedys go there?"

"I already told you," Bonnie explained. "I met the doctor on an eight-hour flight from Ghana. I talked to him the whole time about Feather. I guess he felt he had to say yes. I don't know."

"What do we have to do next?"

"It's not free, honey," she said, but I already knew that. The reason I'd met with Mouse was to raise the cash we might need if the doctors agreed to see my little girl.

"They'll need thirty-five thousand dollars before the treatments can start and at least fifteen thousand just to be admitted. It's a hundred and fifty dollars a day to keep her in the hospital, and then the medicines are all unique, made to order based upon her blood, sex, age, body type, and over fifteen other categories. There are five doctors and a nurse for each patient. And the process may take up to four months."

We'd covered it all before but Bonnie found solace in details. She felt that if she dotted every i and crossed every t then everything would turn out fine.

"How do you know that you can trust them?" I asked. "This could just be some scam."

"I've been there, Easy. I visited the hospital. I told you that, baby."

"But maybe they fooled you," I said.

I was afraid to hope. Every day I prayed for a miracle for Feather. But I had lived a life where miracles never happened. In my experience a death sentence was just that.

"I'm no fool, Easy Rawlins."

The certainty of her voice and her stare were the only chances I had.

"Money's no problem," I said, resolute in my conviction to go down to Texas and rob that armored car. I didn't want Rayford or his partner to die. I didn't want to spend a dozen years behind bars. But I'd do that and more to save my little girl.

I went out the back door and into the garage. From the back shelf I pulled down four paint cans labeled Latex Blue. Each was sealed tight and a quarter filled with oiled steel ball bearings to give them the heft of full cans of paint. On top of those pellets, wrapped in plastic, lay four piles of tax-free money I'd come across over the years. It was my children's college fund. Twelve thousand dollars. I brought the money to Bonnie and laid it on her lap.

"What now?" I asked.

"In a few days I'll take a flight with Vicki to Paris and then transfer to Switzerland. I'll take Feather and bring her to Dr. Renee."

I took a deep breath but still felt the suffocation of fear.

"How will you get the rest?" she asked me.

"I'll get it."

4

Jesus, Feather, and I were in a small park in Santa Monica we liked to go to when they were younger. I was holding Feather in my arms while she laughed and played catch with Jesus. Her laughter got louder and louder until it turned to screams and I realized that I was holding her too tightly. I laid her out on the grass but she had passed out.

"You killed her, Dad," Jesus was saying. It wasn't an indictment but merely a statement of fact.

"I know," I said as the grasses surged upward and began swallowing Feather, blending her with their blades into the soil underneath.

I bent down but the grasses worked so quickly that by the time my lips got there, there was only the turf left to kiss.

I felt a buzzing vibration against my lips and jumped back, trying to avoid being stung by a hornet in the grass.

Halfway out of bed I realized that the buzzing was my alarm clock.

It felt as if there was a crease in my heart. I took deep breaths, thinking in my groggy state that the intake of air would somehow inflate the veins and arteries.

"Easy."

"Yeah, baby?"

"What time is it?"

I glanced at the clock with the luminescent turquoise hands. "Four-twenty. Go back to sleep."

"No," Bonnie said, rising up next to me. "I'll go check on Feather."

She knew that I was hesitant to go into Feather's room first thing in the morning. I was afraid to find her dead in there. I hated her sleep and mine. When I was a child I fell asleep once and awoke to find that my mother had passed in the night.

I went to the kitchen counter and plugged in the percolator. I didn't have to check to see if there was water and coffee inside. Bonnie and I had a set pattern by then. She got the coffee urn ready the night before and I turned it on in the morning.

I sat down heavily on a chrome and yellow vinyl dinette chair. The vibrations of the hornet still tickled my lips. I started thinking of what would happen if a bee stung the human tongue. Would it swell up and suffocate the victim? Is that all it would take to end a life?

Bonnie's hand caressed the back of my neck.

"She's sleeping and cool," she whispered.

The first bubble of water jumped up into the glass knob at the top of the percolator. I took in a deep breath and my heart smoothed out.

Bonnie pulled a chair up beside me. She was wearing a white

lace slip that came down to the middle of her dark brown thighs. I wore only briefs.

"I was thinking," I said.

"Yes?"

"I love you and I want to be with you and only you."

When she didn't say anything I put my hand on hers.

"Let's get Feather well first, Easy. You don't want to make these big decisions when you're so upset. You don't have to worry — I'm here."

"But it's not that," I argued.

When she leaned over to nuzzle my neck the coffee urn started its staccato beat in earnest. I got up to make toast and we ate in silence, holding hands.

After we'd eaten I went in and kissed Feather's sleeping face and made it out to my car before the sun was up.

I PULLED INTO the parking lot at five-nineteen, by my watch. There was an orangish-yellow light under a pile of dark clouds rising behind the eastern mountains. I used my key to unlock the pedestrian gate and then relocked it after I'd entered.

I was the supervising senior head custodian of Sojourner Truth Junior High School, an employee in good standing with the LAUSD. I had over a dozen people who reported directly to me and I was also the manager of all the plumbers, painters, carpenters, electricians, locksmiths, and glaziers who came to service our plant. I was the highest-ranking black person on the campus of a school that was eighty percent black. I had read the study plans for almost every class and often played tutor to the boys and girls who would come to me before they'd dream of asking their white teachers for help. If a big boy decided to see if he could intimidate a small woman teacher I dragged him down to the *main* office, where the custodians congregated, and let him know, in no uncertain terms, what would happen to him if I were to lose my temper.

I was on excellent terms with Ada Masters, the diminutive and wealthy principal. Between us we had the school running smooth as satin.

I entered the main building and started my rounds, going down the hallways looking for problems.

A trash can had not been emptied by the night custodian, Miss Arnold, and there were two lights out in the third-floor hallway. The first floor needed mopping. I made meaningless mental notes of the chores and then headed down to the lower campus.

After checking out the yards and bungalows down there I went to the custodians' building to sit and think. I loved that job. It might have seemed like a lowly position to many people, both black and white, but it was a good job and I did many good things while I was there. Often, when parents were having trouble with their kids or the school, I was the first one they went to. Because I came from the South I could translate the rules and expectations of the institution that many southern Negroes just didn't understand. And if the vice principals or teachers overstepped their bounds I could always put in a word with Miss Masters. She listened to me because she knew that I knew what was what among the population of Watts.

"*Ain't* is a valid negative if you use it correctly and have never been told that it isn't proper language," I once said to her when an English teacher, Miss Patterson, dropped a student two whole letter grades just for using *ain't* one time in a report paper.

Miss Masters looked at me as if I had come from some other planet and yet still spoke her tongue.

"You're right," she said in an amazed tone. "Mr. Rawlins, you're right."

"And you're white," I replied, captive to the rhyme and the irony.

We laughed, and from that day on we had weekly meetings where she queried me about what she called my *ghetto pedagogy*.

They paid me nine thousand dollars a year to do that service. Not nearly enough to float a loan for the thirty-five-plus thousand I needed to maybe save my daughter.

I owned two apartment buildings and a small house with a big yard, all in and around Watts. But after the riots, property values in the black neighborhoods had plummeted. I owed more on the mortgages than the places were worth.

In the past few days I had called John and Jackson and Jewelle and the bank. No one but Mouse had come through with an idea. I wondered if at my trial they would take into account all of my good deeds at Truth.

AT ABOUT A QUARTER to seven I went out to finish my rounds. My morning man, Ace, would have been there by then, unlocking the gates and doors for the students, teachers, and staff.

Halfway up the stairs to the upper campus I passed the midway lunch court. I thought I saw a motion in there and took the detour out of habit. A boy and girl were kissing on one of the benches. Their faces were plastered together, his hand was on her knee and her hand was on his. I couldn't tell if she was urging him on or pushing him off. Maybe she didn't know either.

"Good morning," I said cheerily.

Those two kids jumped back from each other as if a powerful spring had been released between them. She was wearing a short plaid skirt and a white blouse under a green sweater. He had the jeans and T-shirt that almost every boy wore. They both looked at me speechlessly — exactly the same way Jesus and Benita had looked.

My shock was almost as great as those kids'. Eighteen-year-old Jesus and Benita in her mid-twenties . . . But my surprise subsided quickly.

"Go on up to your lockers or somethin'," I said to the children.

As they scuttled off I thought about the Mexican boy I had adopted. He'd been a man since the age of ten, taking care of me and Feather like a fierce and silent mama bear. Benita was a lost child and here my boy had a good job at a supermarket and a sailboat he'd made with his own hands.

Thinking of Feather dying in her bed, I couldn't get angry with them for hurrying after love.

The rest of the campus was still empty. I recognized myself in the barren yards and halls and classrooms. Every step I took or door I closed was an exit and a farewell.

"GOOD MORNING, Mr. Rawlins," Ada Masters said when I appeared at her door. "Come in. Come in."

She was sitting on top of her desk, shoes off, rubbing her left foot.

"These damn new shoes hurt just on the walk from my car to the office."

We never stood on ceremony or false manners. Though white and very wealthy, she was like many down-to-earth black women I'd known.

"I'm taking a leave of absence," I said and the crease twisted my heart again.

"For how long?"

"It might be a week or a month," I said. But I was thinking that it might be ten years with good behavior.

"When?"

"Effective right now."

I knew that Ada was hurt by my pronouncement. But she and I respected each other and we came from a generation that did not pry.

"I'll get the paperwork," she said. "And I'll have Kathy send you whatever you have to sign."

"Thanks." I turned to leave.

"Can I be of any help, Mr. Rawlins?" she asked my profile.

She was a rich woman. A very rich woman if I knew my clothes and jewelry. Maybe if I was a different man I could have stayed there by borrowing from her. But at that time in my life I was unable to ask for help. I convinced myself that Ada wouldn't be able to float me that kind of loan. And one more refusal would have sunk me.

"Thanks anyway," I said. "This is somethin' I got to take care of for myself."

Life is such a knotty tangle that I don't know even today whether I made the right decision turning away from her offer.

5

I had changed the sign on my office door from EASY RAWLINS — RESEARCH AND DELIVERY to simply INVESTIGATIONS. I made the switch after the Los Angeles Police Department had granted me a private detective's license for my part in keeping the Watts riots from flaring up again by squelching the ugly rumor that a white man had murdered a black woman in the dark heart of our boiler-pot city.

I went to my fourth-floor office on Central and Eighty-sixth to check the answering machine that Jackson Blue had given me. But I found little hope there. Bonnie had left a message saying that she'd called the clinic in Montreux and they would allow Feather's admission with the understanding that the rest of the money would be forthcoming.

Forthcoming. The people in that neighborhood had heart disease and high blood pressure, cancer of every type, and deep self-loathing for being forced to their knees on a daily basis. There was a war waging overseas, being fought in great part by young black men who had no quarrel with the Vietnamese people. All of that was happening but I didn't have the time to worry about it. I was thinking about a lucky streak in Vegas or that maybe I should go out and rob a bank all on my own.

Forthcoming. The money would be forthcoming all right. Rayford would have a gun at the back of his neck and I'd be sure to have a fully loaded .44 in my sweating hand.

There was one hang-up on the tape. Back then, in 1966, most folks weren't used to answering machines. Few people knew that Jackson Blue had invented that device to compete with the downtown mob's control of the numbers business. The underworld still had a bounty on his head.

The row of buildings across the street were all boarded up — every one of them. The riots had shut down SouthCentral L.A. like a coffin. White businesses had fled and black-owned stores flickered in and out of existence on a weekly basis. All we had left were liquor stores for solace and check-cashing storefronts in place of banks. The few stores that had survived were gated with steel bars that protected armed clerks.

At least here the view matched my inner desolation. The economy of Watts was like Feather's blood infection. Both futures seemed devoid of hope.

I couldn't seem to pull myself from the window. That's because I knew that the next thing I had to do was call Raymond and tell him that I was ready to take a drive down south.

The knock on the door startled me. I suppose that in my grief I felt alone and invisible. But when I looked at the frosted glass I knew who belonged to that silhouette. The big shapeless nose and the slight frame were a dead giveaway.

"Come on in, Saul," I called.

He hesitated. Saul Lynx was a cautious man. But that made sense. He was a Jewish private detective married to a black woman. They had three brown children and the enmity of at least one out of every two people they met.

But we were friends and so he opened the door.

Saul's greatest professional asset was his face — it was almost totally nondescript even with his large nose. He squinted a lot but if he ever opened his eyes wide in surprise or appreciation you got a shot of emerald that can only be described as beautiful.

But Saul was rarely surprised.

"Hey, Easy," he said, giving a quick grin and looking around for anything out of place.

"Saul."

"How's Feather?"

"Pretty bad. But there's this clinic in Switzerland that's had very good results with cases like hers."

Saul made his way to my client's chair. I went behind the desk, realizing as I sat that I could feel my heart beating.

Saul scratched the side of his mouth and moved his shoulder like a stretching cat.

"What is it, Saul?"

"You said that you needed work, right?"

"Yeah. I need it if it pays."

Saul was wearing a dark brown jacket and light brown pants. Brown was his color. He reached into the breast pocket and came out with a tan envelope. This he dropped on the desk.

"Fifteen hundred dollars."

"For what?" I asked, not reaching for the money.

"I put out the word after you called me. Talked to anybody who might need somebody like you on a job."

Like you meant a black man. At one time it might have angered me to be referred to like that but I knew Saul, he was just trying to help.

"At first no one had anything worth your while but then I heard from this cat up in Frisco. He's a strange guy but . . ." Saul hunched his shoulders to finish the sentence. "This fifteen hundred is a down payment on a possible ten grand."

"I'll take it."

"I don't even know what the job is, Easy."

"And I don't need to know," I said. "Ten thousand dollars will put me in shootin' range of what I need. I might even be able to borrow the rest if it comes down to it."

"Might."

"That's all I got, Saul — might."

Saul winced and nodded. He was a good guy.

"His name is Lee," he said. "Robert E. Lee."

"Like the Civil War general?"

Saul nodded. "His parents were Virginia patriots."

"That's okay. I'd meet with the grand wizard of the Ku Klux Klan if this is how he says hello." I picked up the envelope and fanned my face with it.

"I'll be on the job too, Easy. He wants to do it with you answering to me. It's no problem. I won't get in your way."

I put the envelope down and extended that hand. For a moment Saul didn't realize that I wanted to shake with him.

"You can ride on my back if you want to, Saul. All I care about is Feather."

I WENT HOME late that afternoon. While Bonnie made dinner I sat by Feather's side. She was dozing on and off and I wanted to be there whenever she opened her eyes. When she did come awake she always smiled for me.

Jesus and Benny came over and had dinner with Bonnie. I didn't eat. I wasn't hungry. All I thought about was doing a good job for the man named after one of my enemies by descendants of my enemies in the land of my people's enslavement. But none of that mattered. I didn't care if he hated me and my kind. I didn't care if I made him a million dollars by working for him. And if he wanted a black operative to undermine black people, well . . . I'd do that too — if I had to.

AT THREE IN THE MORNING I was still at Feather's side. I sat there all night because Saul was coming at four to drive with me up the coast. I didn't want to leave my little girl. I was afraid she might die in the time I was gone. The only thing I could do was sit there, hoping that my will would keep her breathing.

And it was lucky that I did stay because she started moaning and twisting around in her sleep. Her forehead was burning up. I hurried to the medicine cabinet to get one of Mama Jo's tar balls.

When I got back Feather was sitting up and breathing hard.

"Daddy, you were gone," she whimpered.

I sat beside her and put the tar ball in her mouth.

"Chew, baby," I said. "You got fever."

She hugged my arm and began to chew. She cried and chewed and tried to tell about the dream where I had disappeared. Remembering my own dream I kept from holding her too tightly.

In less than five minutes her fever was down and she was asleep again.

* * *

AT FOUR Bonnie came into the room and said, "It's time, honey."

Just when she said these words there was a knock at the front door. Feather sighed but did not awaken. Bonnie put her hand on my shoulder.

I felt as if every move and gesture had terrible importance. As things turned out I was right.

"I gave her some of Mama Jo's tar," I said. "There's only two left."

"It's okay," Bonnie assured me. "In three days we'll be in Switzerland and Feather will be under a doctor's care twenty-four hours a day."

"She's been sweating," I said as if I had not heard Bonnie's promise. "I haven't changed the sheets because I didn't want to leave her."

Saul knocked again.

I went to the door and let him in. He was wearing brown pants and a russet sweater with a yellow shirt underneath. He had on a green cap made of sewn leather strips.

"You ready?" he asked me.

"Come on in."

We went into the kitchen, where Saul and Bonnie kissed each other's cheeks. Bonnie handed me my coat, a brown shopping bag filled with sandwiches, and a thermos full of coffee.

"I got some fruit in the car," Saul said.

I looked around the house, not wanting to leave.

"Do you have any money, Easy?" Bonnie asked me.

I had given her the fifteen-hundred-dollar invitation.

"I could use a few bucks I guess."

Bonnie took her purse from the back of the chair. She rummaged around for a minute, but she had so much stuff in there that she couldn't locate the cash. So she spilled out the contents on our dinette table.

There was a calfskin clasp-purse but she never kept money there. She had cosmetic cases and a jewelry bag, two paperback books, and a big key ring with almost as many keys as I carried at Truth. Then came a few small cloth bags and an enameled pin or stud. The pin was the size of a quarter, decorated with the image of a white-and-red bird in flight against a bronze background.

If I wasn't already used to the pain I might have broken down and died right then.

"Easy," Bonnie was saying.

She proffered a fold of twenties.

I took the money and headed for the door.

"Easy," Bonnie said again. "Aren't you going to kiss me good-bye?"

I turned back and kissed her, my lips tingling as they had in the dream where the hornet was hiding in Feather's grassy grave.

6

A thin coating of freshly fallen snow hid the ruts in the road and softened the bombed-out buildings on the outskirts of Düsseldorf. The M1 rifle cradled in my arms was fully loaded and my frozen finger was on the trigger. At my right marched Jeremy Wills and Terry Bogaman, two white men that I'd only met that morning.

"Don't get ahead, son," Bogaman said.

Son.

"Yeah, Boots," Wills added. "Try and keep up."

Boots.

General Charles Bitterman had ordered forty-one small groups of men out that morning. Among them were thirteen Negroes. Bitterman didn't want black men forming into groups together. He'd said that we didn't have enough experience, but we all thought that he didn't trust us among the German women we might come across.

"I'm a sergeant, Corporal," I said to Wills.

"Sergeant Boots," he said with a grin.

Jeremy Wills was a fair-looking lad. He had corn-fed features and blond hair, amber-colored eyes, and big white teeth. To some lucky farm girl he might have been a good catch but to me he was repulsive, uglier than the corpses we ran across on the road to America's victory. My numb finger tightened and I gauged my chances of killing both soldiers before Bogaman, who was silently laughing at his friend's joke, could turn and fire.

I hadn't quite decided to let them live when a bullet lifted Wills's helmet and split his skull in two. I saw into his brain before he hit the ground. It was only then that I became aware of the machine-gun reports. When I started firing back Bogaman screamed. He had been hit in the shoulder, chest, and stomach. I fell to the ground and rolled off the road into a ditch. Then I was scuttling on all fours, like a lizard, into the meager shelter of the leafless woods.

Machine-gun fire ripped the bark and the frozen turf around me. I had gone more than fifty yards before I realized that somewhere along the way I'd dropped my rifle. In my mind at the time (and in the dream I was having) I imagined that my hatred for those white men had brought on the German attack.

The rattling roar of their fire proved to me that the Germans were desperate. I didn't think they could see me but they kept firing anyway.

Kids, I thought.

I took out my government-issue .45 and crawled around to the place where I had seen the flashes from their gun. I moved through the sound-softening snow hardly feeling the cold along my belly. I had no hatred for the Germans who tried to kill me out there on the road. I didn't feel that I had to avenge the deaths of the men who had so recently despised and disrespected me. But I knew that if I let the machine gunners live, sooner or later they might get the drop on me.

The Nazis wanted to kill me. That's because the Nazis knew that I was an American even if Bogaman and Wills did not.

I went maybe four hundred yards more through the woods and then I slithered across the road, making it back to the clump of branches that camouflaged the nest. I jumped up without thinking and began firing my pistol, holding it with both hands. I hit the first man in the eye and the second in the gut. They were completely surprised by the attack. I noticed, even in the two short seconds it took me to kill them, that their uniforms were makeshift and their hands were wrapped in rags.

The third soldier in the nest leaped at me with a bayonet in his hand. The impact of his attack knocked the pistol from my grasp. We fell to the ground, each committed to the other's death. I grabbed his wrist with one hand and pressed with all my might. The milky-skinned, gray-eyed youth grimaced and used all of his Aryan strength in an attempt to overwhelm me. But I was a few years older and that much more used to the logic of senseless violence. I grabbed the haft of his bayonet with my other hand while he wasted time hitting me with his free fist. By the time he realized that the tide was turning against him it was too late. He now used both hands to keep the blade from his chest but still it moved unerringly downward. As the seconds crept by, real fear appeared in the teenage soldier's eyes. I wanted to stop but there was no stopping. There we were, two men who had never known each other, working toward that young man's death. He spoke no English, could not beg in words I might understand. After maybe a quarter of a minute the blade passed through his coat and into his flesh, but then it got caught on one of his breastbones. I almost lost heart then but what could I do? It was him or me. I leaned forward with all my weight and the German steel broke the German's bone and plunged deep into his heart.

The most terrible thing was his last gasp, a sudden hot gust of breath into my face. His eyes opened wide as if to see some way out of the finality in his body — and then he was dead.

I jumped up from my sleep in Saul's Rambler. A sign at the side of the road read THE ARTICHOKE CAPITAL OF THE WORLD.

"Bad dream?" Saul asked me.

It was a dream, but everything in it had happened more than twenty years before. It was real. That German boy had died and there wasn't a thing either one of us could do to stop it.

"Yeah," I said. "Just a dream."

"I guess I should tell you a little about this guy Lee," Saul said. "He's not known to the public at large but in certain circles he's the most renowned private detective in the world."

"The world?"

"Yes sir. He does work in Europe and South America and Asia too."

I noticed that he didn't mention Africa. People rarely did when talking about the world in those days.

"Yes sir," Saul Lynx said again. "He has entrée to every law enforcement facility and many government offices. He's a connoisseur of fine wines, women, and food. Speaks Chinese, both Mandarin and Cantonese, Spanish, French, and English, which means that he can converse with at least one person in almost every town, village, or hamlet in the world. He's extremely well read. He thinks that he is the better of every, and any, man regardless of race or rank. And that means that his racism includes the whole human race."

"Sounds like a doozy," I said. "What's he look like?"

"I don't know."

"What do you mean you don't know? I thought that you'd done work for him before."

"I have. But I never met him face-to-face. You see, Bobby Lee doesn't like to sully himself with operatives. He has this woman named Maya Adamant who represents him to most clients and to almost all the PIs that do his legwork. She's one of the most beautiful women I've ever seen. He spends most of his time hidden away in his mansion on Nob Hill."

"Have you ever talked to him, in Chinese or otherwise?" I asked.

Saul shook his head.

"Have you seen his picture?"

"No."

"How do you even know that this man exists?"

"I've met people who've met him — clients mainly. Some of them liked to talk about his talents and eccentricities."

"You should meet with a man you work for," I said.

"People work for Heinz Foods and Ford Motor Company and never meet them," Saul argued.

"But they employ thousands. This dude is a small shop. He needs to at least say hello."

"What difference would that make, Easy?" Saul asked.

"How can you work for a man don't even have the courtesy to come out from his office and nod at you?"

"I received an envelope yesterday morning with twenty-five hundred dollars in it," he said. "I get a thousand dollars just to deliver you your money and take a drive up to Frisco. Sometimes I work two weeks and don't make half that."

"Money isn't everything, Saul."

"It is when your daughter is at death's door and only money can buy her back."

I could see that Saul regretted his words as soon as they came out of his mouth. But I didn't say anything. He was right. I didn't have the luxury of criticizing that white man. Who cared if I ever met him? All I needed was his long green.

7

A beautiful day in San Francisco is the most beautiful day on earth. The sky is blue and white, Michelangelo at his best, and the air is so crystal clear it makes you feel that you can see more detail than you ever have before. The houses are wooden and white with bay windows. There was no trash in the street and the people, at least back then, were as friendly as the citizens of some country town.

If I hadn't had Feather, and that enameled pin, on my mind I would have enjoyed our trip through the city.

On Lower Lombard we passed a peculiar couple walking down the street. The man wore faded red velvet pants with an open sheepskin vest that only partially covered his naked chest. His long brown hair cascaded down upon broad, thin shoulders. The woman next to him wore a loose, floral-patterned dress with nothing underneath. She had light brown hair with a dozen yellow flowers twined into her irregular braids. The two were walking, barefoot and slow, as if they had nowhere to be on that Thursday afternoon.

"Hippies," Saul said.

"Is that what they look like?" I asked, amazed. "What do they do?"

"As little as possible. They smoke marijuana and live a dozen to a room, they call 'em crash pads. And they move around from place to place saying that owning property is wrong."

"Like communists?" I asked. I had just finished reading *Das Kapital* when Feather got weak. I wanted to get at the truth about our enemies from the horse's mouth but I didn't have enough history to really understand.

"No," Saul said, "not communists. They're more like dropouts from life. They say they believe in free love."

"Free love? Is that like they say, 'That ain't my baby, baby'?"

Saul laughed and we began the ascent to Nob Hill.

Near the top of that exclusive mount is a street called Cushman. Saul took a right turn there, drove one block, and parked in front of a four-story mansion that rose up on a slope behind the sidewalk.

The walls were so white that it made me squint just looking at them. The windows seemed larger than others on the block and the conical turrets at the top were painted metallic gold. The first floor of the manor was a good fifteen feet above street level — the entrance was barred by a wrought iron gate.

Saul pushed a button and waited.

I looked out toward the city and appreciated the view. Then I felt the pang of guilt, knowing that Feather lay dying four hundred miles to the south.

"Yes?" a sultry woman's voice asked over an invisible intercom.

"It's Saul and Mr. Rawlins."

A buzzer sounded. Saul pulled open the gate and we entered onto an iron platform. The elevator vestibule was carved into the rock beneath the house. As soon as Saul closed the gate the platform began to move upward toward an opening at the first-floor level of the imposing structure. As we moved into the aperture a panel above us slid aside and we ascended into a large, well-appointed room.

The walls were mahogany bookshelves from floor to ceiling — and the ceiling was at least sixteen feet high. Beautifully bound books took up every space. I was reminded of Jackson Blue's beach house, which had cheap shelves everywhere. His books for the most part were ratty and soiled, but they were well read and his library was probably larger.

Appearing before us as we rose was a white woman with tanned skin and copper hair. She wore a Chinese-style dress made of royal blue silk. It fitted her form and had no sleeves. Her eyes were somewhere between defiant and taunting and her bare arms had the strength of a woman who did things for herself. Her face was full and she had a black woman's lips. The bones of her face made her features point downward like a lovely, earthward-bound arrowhead. Her eyes were light brown and a smile flitted around her lips as she regarded me regarding her beauty.

She would have been tall even if she were a man — nearly six feet. But unlike most tall women of that day, she didn't let her shoulders slump and her backbone was erect. I made up my mind then and there that I would get on naked terms with her if it was at all possible.

She nodded and smiled and I believe she read the intentions in my gaze.

"Maya Adamant," Saul Lynx said, "this is Ezekiel Rawlins."

"Easy," I said, extending a hand.

She held my hand a moment longer than necessary and then moved back so that we could step off of the platform.

"Saul," she said. "Come in. Would you like a drink?"

"No, Maya. We're in kind of a hurry. Easy's daughter is sick and we need to get back as soon as possible."

"Oh," she said with a frown. "I hope it's not serious."

"It's a blood condition," I said, not intending to be so honest. "Not quite an infection but it really isn't a virus either. The doctors in L.A. don't know what to do."

"There's a clinic in Switzerland . . . ," she said, searching for the name.

"The Bonatelle," I added.

Her smile broadened, as if I had just passed some kind of test. "Yes. That's it. Have you spoken to them?"

"That's why I'm here, Miss Adamant. The clinic needs cash and so I need to work."

Her chest expanded then and an expression of delight came over her face.

"Come with me," she said.

She led us toward a wide, carpeted staircase that stood at the far end of the library.

Saul looked at me and hunched his shoulders.

"I've never been above this floor before," he whispered.

THE ROOM ABOVE was just as large as the one we had left. But where the library was dark with no windows, this room had a nearly white pine floor and three bay windows along each wall.

There were maybe a dozen large tables in this sun-drenched space. On each was a battle scene from the Civil War. In each tableau there were scores of small, hand-carved wooden fig-urines engaged in battle. The individual soldiers — tending can-non, engaged in hand-to-hand combat, down and wounded, down and dead — were compelling. The figurines had been carved for maximum emotional effect. On one table there was a platoon of Negro Union soldiers engaging a Confederate band.

"Amazing, aren't they?" Maya asked from behind me. "Mr. Lee carves each one in a workroom in the attic. He has studied every aspect of the Civil War and has written a dozen mono-graphs on the subject. He owns thousands of original documents from that period."

"One wonders when he has time to be a detective with all that," I said.

For a moment there was a deadness in Maya's expression. I felt that I had hit a nerve, that maybe Bobby Lee really was a fig-ment of someone's imagination.

"Come into the office, Mr. Rawlins. Saul."

We followed her past the miniature scenes of murder and mayhem made mythic. I wondered if anyone would ever make a carving of me slaughtering that young German soldier in the snow in suburban Düsseldorf.

MAYA LED US through a hand-carved yellow door that was painted with images of a naked island woman.

"Gauguin," I said as she pushed the gaudy door open. "Your boss does paintings too?"

"This door is an original," she said.

"Whoa" came unbidden from my lips.

The office was a nearly empty, windowless room with cherry floors. Along the white walls were a dozen tall lamps with frosted glass globes around the bulbs. These lamps were set before as many floor-to-ceiling cherry beams imbedded in the plaster walls. All the lights were on.

In the center of the room was an antique red lacquered Chinese desk that had four broad-bottomed chairs facing it, with one behind for our absentee host.

"Sit," Maya Adamant said.

She settled in one of the visitors' chairs and Saul and I followed suit.

"We're looking for a woman," she began, all business now.

"Who's we?" I asked.

This brought on a disapproving frown.

"Mr. Lee."

"That's a *he* not a *we,*" I said.

"All right," she acquiesced. "Mr. Lee wants —"

"Do you own this house, Miss Adamant?"

Another frown. "No."

"Easy," Saul warned.

I held up my hand for his silence.

"You know, my mother, before she died, told me that I should never enter a man's house without paying my respects."

"I'll be sure to tell Mr. Lee that you said hello," she told me.

"It was a double thing with my mother," I said, continuing with my train of thought. "On the one hand you didn't want a man thinking that you were in his domicile doing mischief with his property or his wife —"

"Mr. Lee is not married," Maya put in.

"And on the other hand," I went on, "being of the darker persuasion, you wouldn't want to be treated like a nigger or a slave."

"Mr. Lee doesn't meet with anyone who works for him," she informed me.

"Come on, Easy," Saul added. "I told you that."

Ignoring my friend, I said, "And I don't work for anyone I don't meet with."

"You've taken his money," Maya reminded me.

"And I drove four hundred miles to tell him thank you."

"I really don't see the problem, Mr. Rawlins. I can brief you on the job at hand."

"I could sit with you on a southern beach until the earth does a full circle, Miss Adamant. And I'm sure that I'd rather speak to you than to a man named after the number one Rebel general. But you have your orders from him and I got my mother's demands. My mother is dead and so she can't change her mind."

In my peripheral vision I could see Saul throw his hands up in the air.

"I can't take you to him," Maya said with finality.

I stood up from my fine Chinese chair saying, "And I can't raise the dead."

I made ready to leave, knowing that I was being a fool. I needed that money and I knew how powerful white men could act. But still I couldn't help myself. Hell, there was an armored car waiting for me in the state of Texas.

Thinking about the robbery, everything that could go wrong came back to me. So, standing there before my chair, I was torn between walking out and apologizing.

"Hold up there," a man's voice commanded.

I turned to see that a panel in the wall behind the lacquered desk had become a doorway.

A man emerged from the darkness, a very short man.

"I am Robert E. Lee," the little man said.

He wasn't over five feet tall. He might not hav[e]
full sixty inches. He wore navy blue pants and [a]
coat cut in the fashion of a nineteenth-century general's ja[cket.]
He had short black hair and wispy sideburns, a complete[ly]
round head, and the large dark eyes of a baby who had wisdom
past its years.

He marched up to the chair behind the desk and sat with an
air that could only be described as pompous.

It was obvious that he had been watching us since we entered
the office. I suspected that he had probably been monitoring our
conversation from the moment we entered the house. But the
little general wasn't embarrassed by this exposure. He touched
something on his desk and the portal behind him slid shut.

"It's like the house of the future at Disneyland," I said.

WALTER MOSLEY

"I've never been "

made the
a black
cket.

s of

..........able for his actions?"

.... to me as if I weren't there. A moment before, that would have angered me, but now I was amused. His effort was petty. I turned to Maya Adamant and winked.

"I'd trust Ezekiel Rawlins with my life," Saul replied. There was deep certainty in his voice.

"I'm my own man, Mr. Lee," I said. "If you want to work with me, then fine. If not I have things to do in L.A."

"Or in Montreux," he added, proving my suspicions about the eavesdropping devices throughout the house.

"The job," I prodded.

Lee pressed his lips outward and then pulled them in. He looked at me with those infant orbs and came to a decision.

"I have been retained by a wealthy man living outside Danville to discover the whereabouts of a business associate who went missing five days ago. This associate has absconded with a brief-case that contains certain documents that must be returned as soon as possible. If I can locate this man and return the contents of that briefcase before midnight of next Friday I will receive a handsome fee and you, if you are instrumental in the acquisition of that property, will receive ten thousand dollars on top of the monies you've already been paid."

"Who's the client?" I asked.

"His name is unimportant," Lee replied.

I knew from the way he lifted his chin that my potential employer meant to show me who was boss. This was nothing new to me. I had tussled with almost every boss I'd ever had over the state of my employment and the disposition of my dignity.

And almost every boss I'd ever had had been a white man.

"What's in the briefcase?"

"White papers, printed in ink and sealed with red wax."

I turned my head to regard Saul. Beyond him, on the far wall, next to a lamp, was a small framed photograph. I couldn't make out the details from that distance. It was the only decoration on the walls and it was in an odd place.

"Is your client the original owner of these white papers, printed in ink and sealed with red wax?"

"As far as I know my client is the owner of the briefcase in question and its contents."

Lee was biding his time, waiting for something. In my opinion he was acting like a buffoon but those eyes made me wary.

"What is the name of the man who stole the briefcase?"

Lee balked then. He brought his fingers together, forming a triangle.

"I'd like to know a little bit more about you before divulging that information," he said.

I sat back and turned my palms upward. "Shoot."

"Where are you from?"

"A deep dark humanity down in Louisiana, a place where we never knew there was a depression because we never had the jobs to lose."

"Education?"

"I read Mann's *Magic Mountain* last month. The month before that I read *Invisible Man*."

That got a smile.

"H. G. Wells?"

"Ellison," I countered.

"You fought in the war?"

"On both fronts."

Lee frowned and cocked his head. "The European and Japanese theaters?" he asked.

I shook my head and smiled.

"White people took their shots at me," I said. "Most of them were German but there was an American or two in the mix."

"Married?"

"No," I said with maybe a little too much emphasis.

"I see. Are you a licensed PI, Mr. Rawlins?"

"Yes sir, I am."

Holding out a child's hand, he asked, "May I see it?"

"Don't have it with me," I said. "It's in a frame on the wall in my office."

Lee nodded, stopped to consider, and then nodded again — listening to an unseen angel on his right shoulder. Then he rose, barely taller standing than he was seated.

"Good day," he said, making a paltry attempt at a bow.

Now I understood. From the moment I flushed him out of hiding he intended to dismiss my services. What I couldn't understand was why he didn't let me leave when I wanted to the first time.

"Fine with me." I stood up too.

"Mr. Lee," Maya said then. She also rose from her chair. "Please, sir."

Please. The conflict wasn't between me and Lee — it was a fight between him and his assistant.

"He's unlicensed," Lee said, making a gesture like he was tossing something into the trash.

"He's fully licensed," she said. "I spoke with Mayor Yorty himself this morning. He told me that Mr. Rawlins has the complete support of the LAPD."

I sat down.

There was too much information to sift through on my feet. This woman could get the mayor of Los Angeles on the phone, the mayor knew my name, and the Los Angeles cops were willing to say that they trusted me. Not one of those facts did I feel comfortable with.

Lee sighed.

"Mr. Lynx has always been our best operative in Los Angeles," Maya said, "and he brought Mr. Rawlins to us."

"How long ago did you first come to us, Mr. Lynx?" Lee asked.

"Six years ago, I guess."

"And you never tried to extort your way into my presence?"

Saul didn't say anything.

"And why should I put a man I don't know on a case of this much importance?" Lee asked Maya.

"Because he's the only man for the job and therefore he's the best," she said confidently.

"Why don't you call Chief Parker and get him to find the girl?" Lee said.

"To begin with, he's a public official and this is a private matter." I felt that her words carried hidden meaning. "And you know as well as I do that white policemen in white socks and black shoes are never going to find Cargill."

Lee stared at his employee for a moment and then sat down. Maya let out a deep breath and lowered, catlike, into her chair.

Saul was looking at us with his emerald eyes evident. For a deadpan like Saul this was an expression of bewilderment.

Lee was regarding his own clasped hands on the red lacquered desk. I got the feeling that he didn't lose many arguments with the people he deigned to meet. It would take a few moments for him to swallow his pride.

"The man we're looking for is named Axel Bowers," Lee said at last. "He's a liberal lawyer living in Berkeley, from a wealthy family. He has a storefront practice in San Francisco, where he and an associate attempt to help miscreants evade the law. He's the one who stole from my client."

"What's the catch?" I asked.

"Bowers had a colored servant named Philomena Cargill, generally known as Cinnamon — because of the hue of her skin, I am told. This Cinnamon worked for Bowers as a housekeeper at first, but she had some education and started doing secretarial and assistant work also.

"When my client realized that Bowers had stolen from him he

called his home to demand the return of his property. Miss Cargill answered and said that Bowers had left the country.

"The client came to me but by the time my people got there Miss Cargill had fled also. It is known that she came to Berkeley from Los Angeles, that she was raised near Watts. It is also known that she and Axel were very close, unprofessionally so.

"What I need for you to do is find Miss Cargill and locate Bowers and the contents of the briefcase."

"So you want Bowers too?" I asked.

"Yes."

"Why? Doesn't sound like you're planning to prosecute."

"Do you accept the task as I have presented it?" he asked in return.

"I'd like to know where these people live in San Francisco and Berkeley," I said.

"Neither of them is in the Bay Area, I can assure you of that," the little Napoleon said. "Bowers is out of the country and Cargill is in Los Angeles. We've tried to contact her family but all attempts have failed."

"She might have friends here who know where she went," I suggested.

"We are pursuing that avenue, Mr. Rawlins. You are to go to L.A. and search for the girl there."

"Girl," I repeated. "How old is she?"

Lee glanced at Maya.

"Early twenties," the knockout replied.

"Anything else?" Lee asked.

"Family?" I said. "Previous address, photograph, distinguishing habits or features?"

"You're the best in Los Angeles," Lee said. "Mr. Lynx assures us of that. Maya will give you any information she deems necessary. Other than that, I'm sure you will find the answers to all of your questions and ours. Do you accept?"

"Sure," I said. "Why not? Philomena Cargill also known as Cinnamon, somewhere on the streets of L.A."

Robert E. Lee rose from his chair. He turned his back on us and made his way through the hole in the wall. The panel closed behind him.

I turned to Maya Adamant and said, "That's one helluva boss you got there."

"Shall we go?" was her reply.

9

"First I want to check something out," I said.

I crossed the room, approaching the small out-of-the-way frame. It was a partially faded daguerreotype-like photograph, imprinted on a pane of glass. It looked to be the detective's namesake. The general was in full uniform. He had, at some point during the exposure, looked down, maybe at a piece of lint on his magnificent coat. The result was the image of a two-headed man. The more tangible face stared with grim conviction at the lens while the other was peering downward, unaware of history.

I was intrigued by the antique photograph because of its vulnerability. It was as if the detective wanted to honor the past general in both victory and defeat.

"Shall we go, Mr. Rawlins?" Maya Adamant said again.

I realized that she was worried about Lee getting mad if he saw me getting too intimate with his sanctorum.

"Sure."

IN THE LIBRARY Maya gave me a business card.

"These are my numbers," she said, "both at home and at work."

Saul had been forgotten. He'd merely been their, or was it her, pipeline to a Watts connection.

"What's the disagreement between you and your boss?" I asked.

"I don't know what you're talking about."

"Sure you do. He went through that whole song and dance about getting rid of me because he wanted you to beg him. What's that all about?"

"You would be better served, Mr. Rawlins, by using your detecting skills to find Philomena Cargill."

There was an almost physical connection between us. It was like we'd known each other in a most fundamental way — so much so that I nearly leaned forward to kiss her. She saw this and moved her head back half an inch. But even then she smiled.

We went down to the library. I gave her my office phone number.

"When will you be there?" she asked me.

"Doesn't matter."

"You have a secretary?"

"Electronic," I said, more for her master than for her.

"I don't understand."

"I got a tape recorder attached to my phone. It records a message and plays it back when I get in."

* * *

OUTSIDE THE SUN was dazzling. A cool breeze blew over Nob Hill.

"What the hell was that all about?" Saul said as soon as we were back at his car.

"What?"

"I don't know. You choose. Making Lee come out to talk to you. Looking at Maya like that."

"You got to admit that Miss Adamant is a good-looker."

"I have to admit that you need this job."

"Listen, Saul. I won't work for a guy that refuses to meet me face-to-face. You know what'll happen if the cops come breakin' down my door and I can't even say that I ever talked to the man."

"I brought you there, Easy. I wouldn't put you in jeopardy like that."

"*You* wouldn't. I know that because I know you. But hear me, man, that black son'a yours will be out on his own one day. And when he is he will tell you that every other white man he meets will sell an innocent black man down the river before he will turn on a white crook."

That silenced my friend for a moment. I had waited years to be able to slip that piece of intelligence into his ear.

"Well what did you think about Lee?" he asked.

"I don't trust him."

"You think he's bent?"

"I don't know about that but he seems like the kinda fool get you down a dark alley and then forget to send your backup."

"Forget? Bobby Lee doesn't forget a thing. He's one of the smartest men in the world."

"That might be," I replied, "but he thinks he's even smarter than what he is. And you and I both know that if a man is too proud then he's gonna fall. And if I'm right under him . . ."

Saul respected me. I could see in his eye that he was halfway convinced by my argument. Now that he'd met Lee he had reservations of his own.

"Well," he said, "I guess you got to do it anyway, right? I mean that's your little girl."

I nodded and gazed southward at a huge bank of fog descending on the city.

"I guess we better be getting back," Saul said.

"You go on. I'm gonna stick around town and see about these people here."

"But all they need you to do is find Philomena Cargill."

"I don't know that she's in L.A. Neither does Lee."

SAUL HAD TO GET BACK home. He was due to meet with a client the next morning. I had him drop me off at a Hertz rental car lot.

It only took them an hour and a half to call Los Angeles to validate my BankAmericard.

"You always call the bank to check out a credit card?" I asked the blue-suited and white salesman.

"Certainly," he replied. He had a fat face, thinning hair, and a slender frame.

"Seems to defeat the purpose of a credit card."

"You can never be too careful," he told me.

"I look at it the other way around," I said. "The way I see it you can never be careful enough."

The salesman squinted at me then. He understood that I was making fun of him — he just didn't get the joke.

* * *

AN OAKLAND PHONE BOOK at the Hertz office told me that Axel Bowers lived on Berkeley's Derby Street. The Bay Area street map in my glove compartment put it a block or so up from Telegraph. I drove my rented Ford across the Bay Bridge and parked a block away from the alleged thief's house.

Derby was a major education for me. Everything about that block was in transition. But not the way neighborhoods usually change. It wasn't black folks moving in and whites moving out or a downward turn in the local economy so that homes once filled with middle-class families were turning into rooming houses for the working poor.

This neighborhood was transforming as if under a magic spell.

The houses had gone from the standard white and green, blue, and yellow to a wide range of pastels. Pinks, aquas, violets, and fiery oranges. Even the cars were painted like rainbows or with rude images or long speeches etched by madmen. Music of every kind poured from open windows. Some women wore long tie-dyed gowns like fairy princesses and others wore nearly nothing at all. Half of the men were shirtless and almost all of them had long hair like women. Their beards went untrimmed. American flags were plastered into windows and tacked to walls in a decidedly unpatriotic manner. Many of the young women carried babies.

It was the most integrated neighborhood I had ever seen. There were whites and blacks and browns and even one or two Asian faces.

It seemed to me that I had wandered into a country where war had come and all the stores and public services had been shut down; a land where the population was being forced into a more primitive state.

I stopped in front of one big lavender house because I heard something and someone that I recognized. "Show Me Baby," the signature blues song of my old friend Alabama Slim, was blasting from the front door. 'Bama was crooning from the speakers. 'Bama. I didn't think that there were ten white people in the United States who knew his work. But there he was, singing for a street filled with hairy men and women of all races in a country that was no longer the land of his birth.

BOWERS'S HOUSE, a single-story wood box, was the most normal-looking one on the block. Its plank walls were still white, but the trim was a fire-engine red and the front door was decorated with a plaster mosaic set with broken tiles, shards of glass, marbles, trinkets, and various semiprecious stones: rough garnets, pink quartz, and turquoise.

I rang the bell and used the brass skull knocker but no one answered. Then I went down the side of the house, toward the back. There I came across a normal-looking green door that had a pane of glass set in it. Through this window I could see a small room that had a broom leaning in a corner and rubber boots on the floor. A floral-pattern apron hung from a peg on the wall.

I knocked. No answer. I knocked again. When nobody came I took off my left shoe, balled my fist in it, and broke the window.

"Hey, man! What you doin'?" a raspy voice called from up toward the street.

I was unarmed, which was either a good or a bad thing, and caught red-handed. The strange character of the neighborhood had made me feel I could go unnoticed, doing whatever I needed to get the job done. That was a mistake a black man could never afford to make.

I turned to see the man who caught me. He walked the slender, ivy-covered corridor with confidence — as if he were the owner of the house.

He was short, five six or so, with greasy black hair down to his shoulders. Most of his face was covered by short, bristly black hairs. He had on a blood-red shirt that was too large for his thin frame and black jeans. He wore no shoes but his feet were dirty enough to be mistaken for leather. His dark eyes glittered in their sockets. Golden earrings dangled from his ears in a feminine way that made me slightly uncomfortable.

"Yes?" I asked pleasantly, as if addressing an officer of the law.

"What you doin' breakin' into Axel's house?" the sandpaper-toned hippie asked.

"A guy named Manly hired me to find Mr. Bowers," I said. "He called on me because my cousin, Cinnamon, works for him."

"You Philomena's cousin?" the crazy-looking white man asked.

"Yeah. Second cousin. We were raised not six blocks from each other down in L.A."

"So why you breakin' in?" the man asked again. He looked deranged but his question was clear and persistent.

"Like I said. This guy Manly, over in Frisco, asked me to find Bowers. Cinnamon is missing too. I decided to take his money and to see if anything was wrong."

The small man looked me up and down.

"You could be Philomena's blood," he said. "But you know Axel's a friend'a mine and I can't just let you walk in his house like this."

"What's your name?" I asked.

"Dream Dog," he replied without embarrassment or inflection. It was just as if he had said Joe or Frank.

"I'm Dupree," I said and we shook hands. "I'll tell you what, Dream Dog. Why don't you come in with me? That way you can see that I'm just looking to find out where they are."

When the man smiled I could see that he was missing two or three teeth. But instead of making him ugly the spaces reminded me of a child playing pirate with pasted-on whiskers and a costume that his mother made from scraps.

10

"You know about karma, brother?" Dream Dog asked as I snaked my hand down to turn the lock on the doorknob.

"Hindu religion," I said, remembering a talk I'd had with Jackson Blue in which he explained how much he disagreed with the Indian system of the moral interpretation of responsibility.

You know, the undersized genius had said, *ain't no way in the world that black folks could'a done enough bad to call all them centuries'a pain down on our heads.*

Dream Dog smiled. "Yeah. Hindu. All about what you do an' how it comes back to you."

"Is this apron Cinnamon's?" I asked.

We were in the door.

"Sure is. But you know she wasn't really a maid or nuthin' like that. She had a business degree from Berkeley and wanted to get on Wall Street. Oh yeah, that Philomena got her some spunk."

"I knew she was in school," I said. "The whole family is very proud of her. That's why they're so worried. Did she tell you where she was going?"

"Uh-uh," Dream Dog said while he gauged my words.

The utility room led into a long kitchen that had a lengthy butcher block counter with a copper sink on one side and a six-burner stove-oven on the other. It was a well-appointed kitchen with copper pots hanging from the walls and glass cabinets filled with all kinds of canned goods, spices, and fine china. It was very neat and ordered, even the teacup set tidily in the copper sink spoke to the owner's sense of order.

Dream Dog opened a cabinet and pulled down a box of Oreo cookies. He took out three and then placed the box back on the shelf.

"Axel keeps 'em for me," he said. "My mom can't eat 'em on account'a she's got an allergy to coconut oil and sometimes they use coconut oil in these here. But you know I love 'em. An' Axel keeps 'em for me on this shelf right here."

There was a reverence and pride in Dream Dog's words — and something else too.

THE LIVING ROOM had three plush chaise lounges set in a square with one side missing. The backless sofas stood upon at least a dozen Persian rugs. The carpets had been thrown with no particular design one on top of the other and gave the room a definitely Arabian flavor. The smell of incense helped the mood as did the stone mosaics hung upon the walls. These tiled images were obviously old, probably original, coming from Rome and maybe the Middle East. One was of a snarling, long-tongued wolf harrying a naked brown maiden; another one was a scene of a bacchanal with men, women, children, and dogs drinking, dancing, kissing, fornicating, and leaping for joy.

In each of the four corners was a five-foot-high Grecian urn glazed in black and brown-red and festooned with the images of naked men in various competitions.

"I love these couches, man," Dream Dog said to me. He had stretched out on the middle lounger. "They're worth a lotta money. I told Axel that somebody might come in and steal his furniture while he was outta town, and that's when he asked me to look out for him."

"He outta town a lot?"

"Yeah. For the past year he been goin' to Germany and Switzerland and Cairo. You know Cairo's in Egypt and Egypt is part of Africa. I learned that from a brother talks down on the campus before they have the Congo drum line."

"You think he's in Cairo now?" I asked.

"Nah, he's always down at the campus on Sunday talkin' history before the drum line."

"Not the guy at school," I said patiently, "Axel."

Dream Dog bounced off the couch and held an Oreo out to me.

"Cookie?"

I'm not much for sweets but even if I had a sugar tooth the size of Texas I wouldn't have eaten from his filthy claws.

"Watchin' my weight," I said.

On a side table, set at the nexus where two of the loungers met, were two squat liquor glasses. Both had been filled with brandy but the drinks had evaporated, leaving a golden film at the bottom of each glass. Next to the glasses was an ashtray in which a lit cigarette had been set and left to burn down to its filter. There was also a photograph of a man, his arms around an older woman, with them both looking at the camera.

"Who's this?" I asked my companion.

"That's Axel and his mom. She died three years ago," Dream Dog said. "His father passed away from grief a year and a half later."

The younger Bowers couldn't have been over twenty-five, maybe younger. He had light brown hair and a handsome smile. You could tell by his clothes and his mother's jewelry that there was money there. But there was also sorrow in both their smiles and I thought that maybe a poor childhood in southern Louisiana wasn't the worst place that a man could come from.

"I told him that he should open the drapes too," Dream Dog was saying. "I mean God gives sunlight to warm you and to let you see."

"Where's the bedroom?" I asked.

"Axel's cool though," my new friend said as he led me through a double-wide door on the other side of the room. "He comes from money and stuff, but he knows that people are worth more than money and that we got to share the wealth, that a ship made outta gold will sink . . ."

He flipped a wall switch and we found ourselves in a wide, wood-paneled hallway. Down one side of the hall were Japanese woodprints framed in simple cherrywood. Each of these prints (which looked original) had the moon in one aspect or another as part of the subject. There were warriors and poets, fishermen and fine ladies. Down the other side were smaller paintings. I recognized one that I'd seen in an art book at Paris Minton's Florence Avenue Bookshop. It was the work of Paul Klee. Upon closer examination I saw that all of the paintings on that side of the wall were done by him.

"I paint some too," Dream Dog said when I stopped to examine the signature. "Animals mostly. Dogs and cats and ducks. I told Axel that he could have some of my drawings when he got tired'a this stuff."

It was a large bedroom. The oversized bed seemed like a raft on a wide river of blue carpet. The sheets and covers were a jaundiced yellow and the windows looked out under a broad redwood that dominated the backyard.

A newspaper, the *Chronicle,* was folded at the foot of the bed. The date was March 29.

There were whiskey glasses at the side of the unmade bed. They also had the sheen of dried liquor. The pillows smelled sweetly, of a powerful perfume. I had the feeling that vigorous sex had transpired there before the end, but that might have been some leftover feeling I had about Maya Adamant.

The room was so large that it had its own dressing nook. I thought that this was a very feminine touch for a man, but then maybe the previous owners had been a couple and this was the woman's corner.

There was an empty briefcase next to the cushioned brown hassock that sat there between three mirrors. Next to the handle was a shiny brass nameplate that had the initials ANB stamped on it.

There was a bottle of cologne on the little dressing table; it smelled nothing like those pillows.

"Axel entertain a lot?" I asked my hippie guide.

"Oh man," Dream Dog said. "I seen three, four women in here at the same time. Axel gets down. And he shares the wealth too. Sometimes he calls me in and we all get so high that nobody knows who's doin' what to who — if you know what I mean."

I did not really know and felt no need for clarification.

The dressing table had three drawers. One contained two plastic bags of dried leaves, marijuana by the smell of them. Another drawer held condoms and various lubricants. The bottom drawer held a typed letter, with an official heading, from a man named Haffernon. There was also a handwritten envelope with Axel's name scrawled on it. There was no stamp or address or postmark on that letter.

"I'm going to take these letters," I said to my escort. "Maybe I can get to Axel or Cinnamon through somebody here."

"But you're gonna leave the dope?" Dream Dog sounded almost disappointed.

"I'm not a thief, brother."

The little white man smiled and I realized that his attitude toward me was different from that of most whites. He was protecting his friend from invasion, but this had nothing to do with my being black. That was a rare experience for me at that time.

There was an empty teacup on the dressing table too. It was also dried up. From the smell I knew that it had been a very strong brew.

11

When we were back out on the sidewalk I felt as if a weight had been taken off of me. Something about the house, how it seemed as if it were frozen into a snapshot, made me feel that something sudden and violent had occurred.

"You spend a lot of time with Bowers?" I asked the hippie.

"He gives these big old dinners and your cousin's always there with some other straights from over in Frisco. Axel buys real good wine in big bottles and has Hannah's Kitchen make a vegetarian feast."

Dream Dog was around thirty, but he looked older because of the facial hair and skin weathered by many days and nights outside.

I was smoking Parliaments at that time. I offered him one and he took it. I lit us both up and we stood there on Derby surrounded by all kinds of hippies and music and multicolored cars.

"We trip a lot," Dream Dog said.

"What's that?"

"Drop acid."

"What kind of acid?" I asked.

"LSD. Where you from? We drop acid. We trip."

"Oh," I said. "I see. You do drugs together."

"Not drugs, man," Dream Dog said with disdain. "Acid. Drugs close down your mind. They put you to sleep. Acid opens your crown chakra. It lets God leak in — or the devil."

I didn't know very much about psychedelics back then. I'd heard about the "acid test" that they gave at certain clubs up on Sunset Strip but that wasn't my hangout. I knew my share of heroin addicts, glue sniffers, and potheads. But this sounded like something else.

"What happens when you drop?" I asked.

"Trip," he said, correcting my usage.

"Okay. What happens?"

"This one time it was really weird. He played an album by Yusef Lateef. *Rite of Spring* but in a jazz mode. And there was this chick there named Polly or Molly . . . somethin' like that. And we all made love and ate some brownies that she was sellin' door-to-door. I remember this one moment when me and Axel were each suckin' on a nipple and I felt like I was a baby and she was as big as the moon. I started laughin' and I wanted to go off in the corner but I had to crawl because I was a baby and I didn't know how to walk yet."

Dream Dog was back in the hallucination. His snaggletoothed grin was beatific.

"What did Axel do?" I asked.

"That's when his bad trip started," Dream Dog said. His smile faded. "He remembered something about his dad and that made him mad. It was his dad and two of his dad's friends. He called them vulture-men feeding off of carrion. He ran around the ashram swinging this stick. He knocked out this tooth'a mines right here." Dream Dog flipped up his lip and pointed at the gap.

"Why was he so mad?" I asked.

"It's always somethin' inside'a you," the hippie explained. "I mean it's always there but you never look at it, or maybe on the trip you see what you always knew in a new way.

"After he knocked me down Polly put her arms around him and kissed his head. She kept tellin' him that things were gonna be fine, that he could chase the vultures away and bury the dead . . ."

"And he calmed down?"

"He went into a birth trip, man. All the way back to the fetus in the womb. He went through the whole trip just like as if he was being born again. He came out and started cryin' and me and Polly held him. But then she an' me were holdin' each other and before you know it we're makin' love again. But by then Axel was sitting up and smiling. He told us that he had been given a plan."

"What plan?"

"He didn't say," Dream Dog said, shaking his head and smiling. "But he was happy and we all went to sleep. We slept for twenty-four hours and when we woke up Axel was all calm and sure. That was when he started doin' all'a that travelin' and stuff."

"How long ago was that?" I asked.

"A year maybe. A little more."

"Around the time his father died?" I asked.

"Now that you say it . . . yeah. His father died two weeks before — that's why we did acid."

"And where is this Polly or Molly?"

"Her? I dunno, man. She was goin' from door to door sellin' brownies. Axel an' me were ready to trip and we asked her if she wanted to join in. Axel told her that if she did he'd buy all'a her brownies."

"But I thought you said that you were at this other place. Asham?"

"Ashram," Dream Dog said. "That's the prayer temple that Axel built out behind the trees in his backyard. That's his holy place."

"Where do you live?" I asked Dream Dog.

"On this block mainly."

"Which house?"

"There's about five or six let me crash now and then. You know it depends on how they're feelin' and if I got some money to throw in for the soup."

"If I need to find you is there somebody around here that might know how to get in touch?" I asked.

"Sadie down in the purple place at the end of the block. They call her place the Roller Derby 'cause of the street and because so many people crash there. She knows where I am usually. Yeah, Sadie."

Dream Dog's gaze wandered down the street, fastening upon a young woman wearing a red wraparound dress and a crimson scarf. She was barefoot.

"Hey, Ruby!" Dream Dog called. "Wait up."

The girl smiled and waved.

"One more thing," I said before he could sprint away.

"What's that, Dupree?"

"Do you know where Axel's San Francisco office is?"

"The People's Legal Aid Center. Just go on down to Haight-Ashbury and ask anyone."

I handed Dream Dog a twenty-dollar bill and proffered my hand. He smiled and pulled me into a fragrant hug. Then he ran off to join the red-clad Ruby.

The idea of karma was still buzzing around my head. I was thinking that maybe if I was nice to Dream Dog, someone somewhere would be kind to my little girl.

I WALKED AROUND the block after Dream Dog was gone. I didn't want him or anybody else to see me investigate the ashram, so I came in through one of the neighbors' driveways and into the backyard of Axel Bowers.

It was a garden house set behind two weeping willows. You might not have seen it even looking straight at it because the walls and doors were painted green like the leaves and lawn.

The door was unlocked.

Axel's holy place was a single room with bare and unfinished pine floors and a niche in one of the walls where there sat a large brass elephant that had six arms. Its beard sprouted many half-burned sticks of incense. Their sweet odor filled the room but there was a stink under that.

A five-foot-square bamboo mat marked the exact center of the floor but beyond that there was no other furniture.

All of the smells, both good and bad, seemed to emanate from the brass elephant. It was five feet high and the same in width. At its feet lay a traveling trunk with the decals of many nations glued to it.

Somebody had already snapped off the padlock, and so all I had to do was throw the trunk open. Because of the foul odor that cowered underneath the sweet incense I thought that I'd find a body in the trunk. It was too small for a man but maybe, I thought, there would be some animal sacrificed in the holy ashram.

Failing an animal corpse, I thought I might find some other fine art like the pieces that graced the house.

The last thing I expected was a trove of Nazi memorabilia.

And not just the run-of-the-mill pictures of Adolf Hitler and Nazi flags. There was a dagger that had a garnet-encrusted swastika on its hilt, and the leather-bound copy of *Mein Kampf* was signed by Hitler himself. The contents of the trunk were all jumbled, which added to the theory that someone had already searched it. Bobby Lee said that he'd sent people to look for Philomena — maybe this was their work.

There was a pair of leather motorcycle gloves in the trunk. I accepted this providence and donned the gloves. I'd made sure to touch as few surfaces as possible in the house but gloves were even better.

A box for a deck of cards held instead a stack of pocket photographs of a man I did not recognize posing with Mussolini and Hitler, Göring and Hess. The man had an ugly-looking scar around his left eye. That orb looked out in stunned blindness. For a moment I remembered the boy I killed in Germany after he had slaughtered the white Americans who'd made fun of me. I also remembered the concentration camp we'd liberated and the starved, skeletal bodies of the few survivors.

The putrid odor was worse inside the trunk but there was no evidence of even a dead rat. There were a Nazi captain's uniform and various weapons, including a well-oiled Luger with three clips of ammo. There was also, hidden inside a package that looked like it contained soap, a thick stack of homemade pornographic postcards. They were photographs of the same heavyset man who had posed with the Nazi leaders. Now he was in various sexual positions with young women and girls. He had a very large erection and all of the pictures were of him penetrating women from in front or behind. One photo centered on a teenage girl's face — she was screaming in pain as he lowered on her from overhead.

I took the Luger and the clips of ammo, then I tried to move the trunk but I could see that it was anchored to the floor somehow. I got down on my knees and sniffed around the base of the trunk — the smell was definitely coming from underneath.

After looking around the base I decided to pull away the carpet that surrounded the trunk. There I saw a brass latch. I lifted this and the trunk flipped backward, revealing the corpse of a man crushed into an almost perfect rectangle — the size of the space beneath the trunk.

The man's head was facing upward, framed by his forearms.

It was the face of the young man hugging his mother — Axel Bowers.

12

I had seen my share of dead bodies. Many of them had died under violent circumstances. But I had never seen anything like Axel Bowers. His killer treated the body like just another thing that needed to be hidden, not like a human being at all. The bones were broken and his forehead was crushed by the trunk coming down on it.

The smell was overwhelming. Soon the neighbors would begin to detect it. I wondered if the person who had searched the trunk had found Axel. Not necessarily; if they'd been there a few days before, there might not have been a smell yet, so they'd have had no reason to suspect there was a secret compartment.

It was a gruesome sight. But even then, in the presence of such awful violence and evil intent, I thought about Feather lying in her bed. I felt like running from there as fast as I could.

But instead I forced myself to wait and think about how even this horror might help her.

The knife was worth nothing and I didn't think that I had the kind of contacts to sell Hitler's signature. For that matter the signature might have been a fake.

I considered taking a couple of the Klee paintings from the house, but again I didn't know where to sell them. And if I got caught trying to fence stolen paintings I could end up in jail before getting the money I needed.

For a while I thought about burning down the ashram. I wanted to get rid of the evidence of the murder so that I wouldn't be implicated by Dream Dog or some other hippie on the block.

I even went so far as to get a can of gasoline from the garage. I also took tapered candles from the house to use as a kind of slow-burning fuse. But then I decided that fire would call attention to the murder instead of away from it. And what if the flames spread and killed someone in a nearby house?

The stench made my eyes tear and my gorge rise. I had wiped off the places I had touched in the ashram and the house. Dream Dog would think twice before giving information about breaking into Axel's place. Besides, he didn't know my name.

At some point I realized that I was finding it hard to leave. There was something in me that wanted to help Axel find some peace. The humiliation of his interment made me uncomfortable. Maybe it was the memory of the German boy I killed or the fragility of my adopted daughter's life. Maybe it was something deeper that had been instilled in me when I was a child among the superstitious country people of Louisiana.

Finally I decided that the only thing I could do for Axel was to make him a promise.

"I can't give you a proper burial, Mr. Bowers," I said. "But I swear that if I find out who did this to you I will do my best to make sure that they pay for their crime. Rest easy and go with the faith you lived with."

Those words spoken, I lowered the trunk and stole away from the white man's home, luckier to be a poor black man in America than Axel Bowers had been with his white skin and all his wealth.

I DROVE DOWN Telegraph into Oakland and the black part of town. There I found a motel called Sleepy Time Inn. It was set on a hillside, with the small stucco rooms stacked like box stairs for some giant leading up toward the sky.

Melba, the night clerk, gave me the top room for eighteen dollars in cash. They didn't take credit cards at Sleepy Time. When I looked at the cash I remembered that enameled pin in Bonnie's purse. For a moment I couldn't hear what Melba was saying. I could see her mouth moving. She was a short woman with skin that was actually black. But the rest of her features were more Caucasian than Negroid. Thin lips and round eyes, hair that had been straightened and a Roman nose.

". . . parties in the rooms," she was saying.

"What?"

"We don't want any carousing or parties in the rooms," she repeated. "You can have a guest but these rooms are residential. We don't want any loud crowds."

"Only noise I make is snoring," I said.

She smiled, indicating that she believed me. That simple gesture almost brought me to tears.

THE TELEVISION had a coin slot attached to it. It cost a quarter per hour to watch. If Feather was there with me she'd be begging for quarters to see her shows and to get grape soda from the machine down below. I put in a coin and switched channels until I came across *Gigantor*, her favorite afternoon cartoon. Letting the cartoon play, it felt a little like she was there with me.

That calmed me down enough to think about the mess I'd fallen into.

The man Robert E. Lee was looking for had been murdered. The initials on the empty briefcase in his room might have belonged to him or to somebody related to him. But then again, maybe he'd switched briefcases after removing the papers from the one Lee said he'd stolen.

At any other time I would have taken the fifteen hundred and gone home to Bonnie. But there was no more going home for me, and even if there was, Feather needed nearer to thirty-five thousand than fifteen hundred.

I couldn't call Lee. He might pull me off the case if he knew Axel was dead. And there was still Cinnamon — Philomena — to find. Maybe she knew where the papers were. I had to have those papers, because ten thousand dollars was a hard nut to crack.

I read one of the letters I'd taken from Axel's bureau. It was typewritten under the business heading of Haffernon, Schmidt, Tourneau and Bowers — a legal firm in San Francisco.

```
Dear Axel:
  I have read your letter of February 12 and
I must say that I find it intriguing. As far
as I know, your father had no business deal-
ings in Cairo during the period you indicated
and this firm certainly has not. Of course,
I'm not aware of all your father's personal
business dealings. Each of the partners had
```

his own portfolio from before the formation
of our investment group. But I must say that
your fears seem far-fetched, and even if they
weren't, Arthur is dead. How can an inquiry
of this sort have any productive outcome?
Only your family, it seems, will have a price
to pay.

At any rate, I have no information to bring
to bear on the matter of the briefcase you
got from his safe-deposit box. Call me if you
have any further questions, and please consider your actions before rushing into anything.

Yours truly,
Leonard Haffernon, Esq.

Something happened with Axel's father, something that could
still cause grief for the son and maybe others. Maybe Haffernon
knew something about it. Maybe he killed Axel because of it.

Lee had told me that Axel had stolen a briefcase, but this letter indicated that he received it legally. It could have been another case . . .

The handwritten letter was a different temperature. There
was no heading.

Really, Axel. I can see no reason for you to follow this
line of questioning. Your father is dead. Anyone that
had anything to do with this matter is either dead or
so old that it doesn't make any difference. You cannot
judge them. You don't know how it was back then. Think
of your law offices in San Francisco. Think of the good
you have done, will be able to do. Don't throw it all

away over something that's done and gone. Think of your own generation. I'm begging you. Please do not bring these ugly matters to light.

N.

Whoever N was, he or she had something to hide. And that something was about to be exposed to the world by Axel Bowers.

If I had had a good feeling about Bobby Lee I would have taken the letters and reconnaissance to him. But we didn't like each other and I couldn't be sure that he wouldn't take what I gave him and cut me out of my bonus. My second choice was to tell Saul but he would have been torn in allegiance between me and the Civil War buff. No. I had to go this one alone for a while longer.

Later that evening I was asking the operator to make a collect call to a Webster exchange in West Los Angeles.

"Hello?" Bonnie said into my ear.

"Collect call to anyone from Easy," the operator said quickly as if she feared that I might slip a message past her and hang up.

"I'll accept, operator. Easy?"

I tried to speak but couldn't manage to raise the volume in my lungs.

"Easy, is that you?"

"Yeah," I said, just a whisper.

"What's wrong?"

"Tired," I said. "Just tired. How's Feather?"

"She sat up for a while and watched *Gigantor* this afternoon," Bonnie said hopefully, her voice full of love. "She's been trying to stay awake until you called."

I had to exert extraordinary self-control not to put my fist through the wall.

"Did you get the job?" she asked.

"Yeah, yeah. I got it all right. There's a few snags but I think I can work 'em if I try."

"I'm so happy," she said. It sounded as if she really meant it. "When you went out to meet with Raymond I was afraid that you'd do something you'd regret."

I laughed. I was filled with regrets.

"What's wrong, Easy?"

I couldn't tell her. My whole life I'd walked softly around difficulties when I knew my best defense was to keep quiet. I needed Bonnie to save my little girl. Nothing I felt could get in the way of that. I had to maintain a civil bearing. I had to keep her on my side.

"I'm just tired, baby," I said. "This case is gonna be a ballbreaker. Nobody I can trust out here."

"You can trust me, Easy."

"I know, baby," I lied. "I know. Is Feather still awake?"

"You bet," Bonnie said.

I had installed a long cord on the telephone so that the receiver could reach into Feather's room. I heard the shushing sounds of Bonnie moving through the rooms and then her voice gently talking to Feather.

"Daddy?" she whispered into the line.

"Hi, babygirl. How you doin'?"

"Fine. When you comin' home, Daddy?"

"Tomorrow sometime, honey. Probably just before you go to sleep."

"I dreamed that I was lookin' for you, Daddy, but you was gone and so was Juice. I was all alone in a tiny little house and there wasn't a TV or phone or nothing."

"That was just a dream, baby. Just a dream. You got a big house and lots of people who love you. Love you." I had to say the words twice.

"I know," she said. "But the dream scared me and I thought that you might really be gone."

"I'm right here, honey. I'm comin' home tomorrow. You can count on that."

The phone made a weightless noise and Bonnie was on the line again.

"She's tired, Easy. Almost asleep now that she's talked to you."

"I better be goin'," I said.

"Did you want to talk about the job?" Bonnie asked.

"I'm beat. I better get to bed," I said.

Just before I took the receiver from my ear I heard Bonnie say, "Oh."

13

The Haight, as it came to be called, was teeming with hippie life. But this wasn't like Derby. Most of the people on that Berkeley block still had one foot in real life at a job or the university. But the majority of the people down along Haight had completely dropped out. There was more dirt here, but that's not what made things different. Here you could distinguish different kinds of hippies. There were the clean-cut ones who washed their hair and ironed their hippie frocks. There were the dirty bearded ones on Harley-Davidson motorcycles. There were the drug users, the angry ones. There were the young (very young) runaways who had come here to blend in behind the free love philosophy. Bright colors and all that hair is what I remember mainly.

A young man wearing only a loincloth stood in the middle of a busy intersection holding up a sign that read END THE WAR. Nobody paid much attention to him. Cars drove around him.

"Hey, mister, you got some spare change?" a lovely young raven-haired girl asked me. She wore a purple dress that barely made it to her thighs.

"Sorry," I said. "I'm strapped."

"That's cool," she replied and walked on.

Psychedelic posters for concerts were plastered to walls. Here and there brave knots of tourists walked through, marveling at the counterculture they'd discovered.

I was reminded of a day when a mortar shell in the ammunition hut of our base camp in northern Italy exploded for no apparent reason. No one was killed but a shock ran through the whole company. All of a sudden whatever we had been doing or thinking, wherever we had been going, was forgotten. One man started laughing uncontrollably, another went to the mess tent and wrote a letter to his mother. I kept noticing things that I'd never seen before. For instance, the hand-painted sign above the infirmary read HOSPItAL, all in capital letters except for the *t*. That one character was in lower case. I had seen that sign a thousand times but only after the explosion did I really look at it.

The Haight was another kind of explosion, a stunning surge of intuition that broke down all the ways you thought life had to be. In other circumstances I might have stayed around for a while and talked to the people, trying to figure out how they got there. But I didn't have the time to wander and explore.

I'd gotten the address of the People's Legal Aid Center from the information operator. It had been a storefront at one time where a family named Gnocci sold fresh vegetables. There wasn't even a door, just a heavy canvas curtain that the grocer raised when he was open for business.

The store was open and three desks sat there in the recess. Two professional women and one man talked to their clients.

The man, who was white with short hair, wore a dark suit with a white shirt and a slate-blue tie. He was talking to a fat hippie mama who had a babe in arms and a small boy and girl clutching the hem of her Indian printed dress.

"They're evicting me," the woman was saying in a white Texan drawl I knew and feared. "What they expect me to do with these kids? Live in the street?"

"What is the landlord's name, Miss Braxton?" the street lawyer asked.

"Shit," she said and the little girl giggled.

At that moment the boy decided to run across the sidewalk, headed for the street.

"Aldous!" the hippie mama yelled, reaching out unsuccessfully for the boy.

I bent down on reflex, scooping the child up in my arms as I had done hundreds of times with Feather when she was smaller, and with Jesus before that.

"Thank you, mister. Thank you," the mother was saying. She had lifted her bulk from the lawyer's folding chair and was now taking the grinning boy from my arms. I could see in his face that he wasn't what other Texans would call a white child.

The woman smiled at me and patted my forearm.

"Thank you," she said again.

Her looking into my eyes with such deep gratitude was to be the defining moment in my hippie experience. Her gaze held no fear or condescension, even though her accent meant that she had to have been raised among a people who held themselves apart from mine. She didn't want to give me a tip but only to touch me.

I knew that if I had been twenty years younger, I would have been a hippie too.

"May I help you?" a woman's voice asked.

She was of medium height with a more or less normal frame, but somewhere in the mix there must have been a Teutonic Valkyrie because she had the figure of a Norse fertility goddess. Her eyes were a deep ocean blue and though her face was not particularly attractive there was something otherworldly about it. As far as clothes were concerned she was conservatively dressed in a cranberry dress that went down below her knees and wore a cream-colored woolen jacket over that. There was a silver strand around her neck from which hung a largish pearl with a dark nacre hue. Her glasses were framed in white.

All in all she was a Poindexter built like Jayne Mansfield.

"Hi. My name is Ezekiel P. Rawlins." I held out a hand.

A big grin came across her stern face but somehow the mirth didn't make it to her eyes. She shook my hand.

"How can I help you?"

"I'm a private detective from down in L.A.," I said. "I've been hired to find a woman named Philomena Cargill . . . by her family."

"Cinnamon," the woman said without hesitation. "Axel's friend."

"That's Axel Bowers?"

"Yes. He's my partner here."

She looked around the storefront. I did too.

"Not a very lucrative business," I speculated.

The woman laughed. It was a real laugh.

"That depends on what you see as profit, Mr. Rawlins. Axel and I are committed to helping the poor people of this society get a fair shake from the legal system."

"You're both lawyers?"

"Yes," she said. "I got my degree from UCLA and Axel got his across the Bay in Berkeley. I worked for the state for a while but

I didn't feel very good about that. When Axel asked me to join him I jumped at the chance."

"What's your name?" I asked.

"Oh. Excuse my manners. My name is Cynthia Aubec."

"French?"

"I was born in Canada," she said. "Montreal."

"Have you seen your partner lately?" I asked.

"Come on in," she replied.

She turned to go through another canvas flap, this one standing as a door to the back room of the defunct grocery.

There were two desks at opposite ends of the long room we entered. It was gloomy in there, and the floors had sawdust on them as if it were still a vegetable stand.

"We keep sawdust on the floor because the garage next door sometimes uses too much water and it seeps under the wall on our floor," she said, noticing my inspection.

"I see."

"Have a seat."

She switched on a desk lamp and I was gone from the hippie world of Haight Street. I wasn't in modern America at all. Cynthia Aubec, who was French Canadian but had no accent, lived earlier in the century, walking on sawdust and working for the poor.

"I haven't seen Axel for over a week," she said, looking directly into my gaze.

"Where is he?"

"He said that he was going to Algeria but I can never be sure."

"Algeria? I met a guy who told me that Axel was all over the world. Egypt, Paris, Berlin . . . Now you tell me he's in Algeria. There's got to be some money somewhere."

"Axel's family supports this office. They're quite wealthy. Actually his parents are dead. Now I guess it's Axel's money that runs our firm. But it was his father who gave us our start." She was still looking at me. In this light she was more Mansfield than Poindexter.

"Do you know when he might be back?"

"No. Why? I thought you were looking for Cinnamon."

"Well . . . the way I hear it Philomena and Axel had a thing going on. Actually that's why I'm here."

"I don't understand," she said with a smile that was far away from Axel and Philomena.

"Philomena's parents are racists," I explained, "not like you and me. They don't think that blacks and whites should be mixing. Well . . . they told Philomena that she was out of the family because of the relationship she had with your partner, but now that she hasn't called in over two months they're having second thoughts. She won't talk to them and so they hired me to come make their case."

"And you're really a private detective?" she asked, cocking one eyebrow.

I took out my wallet and handed her the license. I hadn't shown it to Lee out of spite. She glanced at it but I could see that she stopped to read the name and identify the photo.

"Why don't you just go to Cinnamon's apartment?" Cynthia suggested.

"I was told that she was living with Axel on Derby. I went there but no one was around."

"I have an address for her," Cynthia told me. Then she hesitated. "You aren't lying to me are you?"

"What would I have to lie about?"

"I wouldn't know." Her smile was suggestive but her eyes had not yet decided upon the nature of the proposal.

"No ma'am," I said. "I just need to find Philomena and tell her that her parents are willing to accept her as she is."

Cynthia took out a sheet of paper and scrawled an address in very large characters, taking up the whole page.

"This is her address," she said, handing me the leaf. "I live in Daly City. Do you know the Bay Area, Mr. Rawlins?"

"Not very well."

"I'll put my number on the back. Maybe if you're free for dinner I could show you around. I mean — as long as you're in town."

Yes sir. Twenty years younger and I'd have bushy hair down to my knees.

14

Philomena's apartment was on Avery Street, at Post, in the Fillmore District, on the fourth floor of an old brick building that had been christened The Opal Shrine. A sign above the front door told me that there were apartments available and that I could inquire at apartment 1a. There was no elevator so I climbed to the fourth floor to knock at the door of apartment 4e, the number given me by Cynthia Aubec.

There was no answer so I went back down to the first floor and tried the super's door.

He was a coffee-brown man with hair that might have been dyed cotton. He was smiling when he opened the door, a cloud of marijuana smoke attending him.

"Yes sir?" he said with a sly grin. "What can I do for you?"

"Apartment four-e."

"Fo'ty fi'e a mont', gas an' 'lectric not included. Got to clean it out yo' own self an' it's a extra ten for dogs. You can have a cat for free." He smiled again and I couldn't help but like him.

"I think I used to know a girl lived there. Cindy, Cinnamon . . . somethin'."

"Cinnamon," he said, still grinning like a coyote. "That girl had a butt on her. An' from what I hear she knew how to use it too."

"She move?"

"Gone's more like it," he said. "First'a the mont' came and the rent wasn't in my box. She ain't come back. I'ont know where she is."

"You call the cops?"

"Are you crazy? Cops? The on'y reason you call a cop is if you white or already behind bars."

I did like him.

"Can I see it?" I asked.

He reached over to his left, next to the door, and produced a brass key tethered to a multicolored flat string.

I took the key and grinned in thanks. He grinned *you're welcome*. The door closed and I was on my way back upstairs.

PHILOMENA CARGILL had left the apartment fully furnished, though I was sure that the super had emptied it of all loose change, jewelry, and other valuables. Most of the possessions I was interested in were still there. She had a bookcase filled with books and papers and a pile of *Wall Street Journal*s on the floor next to the two-burner stove. There was a small diary tacked up on the wall next to the phone and a stack of bills and some other mail on the kitchen table.

I pulled a chair up to the table and looked out of the window onto Post Street. San Francisco was much more of a city than

L.A. was back in '66. It had tall buildings and people who walked when they could and who talked to each other.

There was a ceramic bear on the table. He was half filled with crystallized honey. There was a teacup that had been left out. In it were the dried dregs of jasmine tea — nothing like the flavor left on Axel's dressing table.

There were also two dog-eared books out, *The Wealth of Nations* and *Das Kapital*. On the first page of Marx's opus she had written, *Marx seems to be at odds with himself over the effect that capitalism has on human nature. On the one hand he says that it is the dialectical force of history that forms the economic system, but on the other he seems to feel that certain human beings (capitalists) are evil by nature. But if we are pressed forward by empirical forces, then aren't we all innocent? Or at least equally guilty?* I was impressed by her argument. I had had similar thoughts when reading about the Mr. Moneybags capitalist in Marx's major work.

She had a big pine bed and all her plates, saucers, and cups were made from red glass. The floor was clean and her clothes, at least a lot of them, still hung in the closet. That bothered me. It was as if she just didn't come home one day rather than moved out.

The trash can was empty.

The bathroom cabinet was filled with condoms and the same lubricant used by Bowers.

He'd died instantly, between lighting a cigarette and the first drag. She had seemingly disappeared in the same way.

I decided to search the entire apartment from top to bottom. The super, I figured, was downstairs with his joint. I didn't have to worry about him worrying about me.

The more I explored the more I feared for the bright young woman's safety. I found a drawer filled with makeup and soaps.

She had a dozen panties and four bras in her underwear drawer. There were sewing kits and cheap fountain pens, sanitary napkins and sunglasses — all left behind.

Luckily there was no brass elephant grinning at me from the closet, no trunk filled with pornography and the accoutrements of war.

After about an hour I was convinced that Philomena Cargill was dead. It was only then that I began to sift through her mail. There were bills from various clothing stores and utilities, a bank statement that said she had two hundred ninety-six dollars and forty-two cents to her name. And there was a homemade postcard with the photograph of a smiling black woman on it. I knew the woman — Lena Macalister. She was standing in front of the long-closed Rose of Texas, a restaurant that had had some vogue in L.A. in the forties and fifties.

Dear Phil,

Your life sounds so exciting. New man. New job. And maybe a little something that every woman who's really a woman wants. My hopes and prayers are with you darling. God knows the both of us could use a break.

Tommy had to leave. He was good from about nine at night to daybreak. But when the sun came up all he could do was sleep. And you know I don't need no man resting on my rent. Don't worry about me though. You just keep on doing what you're doing.

Love,
L

It was certainly a friendly card. That gave me an idea. I went through Philomena's phone bill picking out telephone numbers with 213 area codes. I found three. The first number had been disconnected.

The second was answered by a woman.

"Westerly Nursing Home," she said. "How may we be of service?"

"Hi," I said, stalling for inspiration. "I'm calling on behalf of Philomena Cargill. She had a sudden case of appendicitis —"

"Oh that's terrible," the operator said.

"Yes. Yes, but we got it in time. I'm a PN here and the doctor told me to call because Miss Cargill was supposed to visit her aunt at Westerly but of course now you see . . ."

"Of course. What did you say was her aunt's name?"

"I just know her name," I said. "Philomena Cargill."

"There's no Cargill here, Mr. . . ."

"Avery," I said.

"Well, Mr. Avery, there's no Cargill, and I'm unaware of any Philomena Cargill who comes to visit. You know we have a very select clientele."

"Maybe it was her husband's relative," I conjectured. "Mr. Axel Bowers."

"No. No. No Bowers either. Are you sure you have the right place?"

"I thought so," I said. "But I'll go back to the doctor. Thank you very much for your help."

"YEEEEES?" the male voice of the last number crooned.

"Philomena please," I said in a clipped, sure tone.

"Who's this?" the voice asked, no longer playful.

"Miller," I said. "Miller Jones. I'm an employee of Bowers up here and he wanted me to get in touch with Cinnamon. He gave me this number."

"I don't know you," the voice said. "And even if I did, I haven't seen Philomena in months. She's in Berkeley."

"She was," I said. "To whom am I speaking?"

The click of the phone in my ear made me grimace. I should have taken another tack. Maybe claimed to have found some lost article from her apartment.

I sat in the college student's kitchen chair and stared at the street. This was an ugly job and it was likely to get uglier. But that was okay. I was feeling ugly, ugly as a sore on a dead man's forehead.

I left the apartment, taking the two books she'd been reading and Lena's postcard. I took them out to my rented Ford and then went back to return the key. I knocked, knocked again, called out for the super, and then gave up. He was either unconscious, otherwise engaged, or out. I slipped the key under the door wrapped in a two-dollar bill.

15

Haffernon, Schmidt, Tourneau and Bowers occupied the penthouse of a modern office building on California Street. There was a special elevator car dedicated solely to their floors.

"May I help you?" a white-haired matron, who had no such intention, asked me. Her nameplate read THERESA PONTE.

She was very white. There was a ring with a large garnet stone on her right hand. The gem looked like a knot of blood that had congealed upon her finger. A cup of coffee steamed next to her telephone. She was wearing a gray jacket over a yellow blouse, seated behind a magnificent mahogany desk. Behind her was a mountain of fog that was perpetually descending upon but rarely managing to reach the city.

"Leonard Haffernon," I said.

"Are you delivering?"

I was wearing the same jacket and pants that I'd had on for two days. But I'd made use of the iron in my motel room and I didn't smell. I wore a tie and I'd even dragged a razor over my chin. I held no packages or envelopes.

"No ma'am," I said patiently. "I have business with him."

"Business?"

"Yes. Business."

She moved her head in a birdlike manner, indicating that she needed more of an explanation.

"May I see him?" I asked.

"What is your business?"

From a door to my left emerged a large strawberry blond man. His chest was bulky with muscles under a tan jacket. Maybe one of those sinews was a gun. I had Axel's Luger in my belt. I thought of reaching for it and then I thought of Feather.

A moment of silence accompanied all that thinking.

"Tell him that I've come about Axel Bowers," I said. "My name is Easy Rawlins and I'm looking for someone named Cargill."

"Cargill who?" the receptionist asked.

"This is not the moment at which you should test your authority, Theresa," I said.

The combination of vocabulary, grammar, and intimacy disconcerted the woman.

"There a problem?" the Aryan asked.

"Not with me," I said to him while looking at her.

She picked up the phone, pressed a button, waited a beat, and then said, "Let me speak to him." Another beat and she said, "A man called Rawlins is here about Axel and someone named Cargill." She listened then looked up at me and said, "Please have a seat."

The big boy came to stand next to my chair.

My heart was thundering. My mind was at an intersection of many possible paths. I wanted to ask that woman what she was thinking when she asked me if I was a delivery boy when obviously I was not. Was she trying to be rude or did my skin color rob her of reason? I wanted to ask the bodyguard why he felt it necessary to stand over me as if I were a prisoner or a criminal when I hadn't done anything but ask to see his boss. I wanted to yell and pull out my gun and start shooting.

But all I did was sit there staring up at the white ceiling.

I thought about that coat of paint upon the plaster. It meant that at one time a man in a white jumpsuit had stood on a ladder in the middle of that room running a roller or maybe waving a brush above his head. That was another room but the same, at another time when there was no tension but only labor. That man probably had children at home, I decided. His hard work turned into food and clothing for them.

That white ceiling made me happy. After a moment I forgot about my bodyguard and the woman who couldn't see the man standing in front of her but only the man she had been trained to see.

"Mr. Rawlins?" a man said.

He was tall, slender, and very erect. The dark blue suit he wore would have made the down payment on my car. His scarlet tie was a thing of beauty and the gray at his temples would remind anyone of their father — even me.

"Mr. Haffernon?" I rose.

The bodyguard stiffened.

"That will be all, Robert," Haffernon said, not even deigning to look at his serf.

Robert turned away without complaint and disappeared behind the door that had spawned him.

"Follow me," Haffernon said.

He led me back past the elevator and through a double door. Here we entered into a wide hallway. The floors were bright ash and the doors along the way were too. These doors opened into anterooms where men and women assistants talked and typed and wrote. Beyond each assistant was a closed door behind which, I imagined, lawyers talked and typed and wrote.

At the end of the hall were large glass doors that we went through.

Haffernon had three female assistants. One, a buxom forty-year-old with horn-rimmed glasses and a flouncy full-length dress, came up to him reading from a clipboard.

"The Clarks had to reschedule for Friday, sir. He's had an emergency dental problem. He says that he'll need to rest after that."

"Fine," Haffernon said. "Call my wife and tell her that I will be coming to the opera after all."

"Yes sir," the woman said. "Mr. Phillipo decided to leave the country. His company will settle."

"Good, Dina. I can't be interrupted for anything except family."

"Yes sir."

She opened a door behind the three desks and Haffernon stepped in. In passing I caught the assistant's eye and gave her a quick nod. She smiled at me and let her head drift to the side, letting me know that the counterculture had infiltrated every pore of the city.

HAFFERNON HAD A BIG DESK under a picture window but he took me into a corner where he had a rose-colored couch with a matching stuffed chair. He took the chair and waved me onto the sofa.

"What is your business with me, Mr. Rawlins?" he asked.

I hesitated, relishing the fact that I had this man by the short hairs. I knew this because he had told Dina not to bother him for anything but the blood of blood. When powerful white men like that make time for you there's something serious going on.

"What problem did Axel Bowers come to you with?" I asked.

"Who are you, Mr. Rawlins?"

"Private detective from down in L.A.," I said, feeling somehow like a fraud but knowing I was not.

"And what do Axel's . . . problems, as you call them, have to do with your client?"

"I don't know," I said. "I'm looking for Axel and your name popped up. Have you seen Mr. Bowers lately?"

"Who are you working for?"

"Confidential," I said with the apology in my face.

"You walk in here, ask me about the son of one of my best friends and business associates, and refuse to tell me who wants to know?"

"I'm looking for a woman named Philomena Cargill," I said. "She's a black woman, lover of your friend's son. He's gone. She's gone. It came to my attention that you and he were in negotiations about something that had to do with his father. I figured that if he was off looking into that problem that you might know where he was. He, in turn, might know about Philomena."

Haffernon sat back in his chair and clasped his hands. His stare was a spectacle to behold. He had cornflower-blue eyes and black brows that arced like descending birds of prey.

This was a white man whom other white men feared. He was wealthy and powerful. He was used to getting his way. Maybe if I hadn't been fighting for my daughter's life I would have felt the weight of that stare. But as it was I felt safe from any threat he could make. My greatest fear flowed in a little girl's veins.

"You have no idea who you're messing with," he said, believing the threatening gaze had worked.

"Do you know Philomena?" I asked.

"What information do you have about me and Axel?"

"All I know is that a hippie I met said that Axel has been spending time in Cairo. That same man said that Axel had asked you about his father and Egypt."

His right eye twitched. I was sure that there were Supreme Court justices who couldn't have had that effect on Leonard Haffernon. I lost control of myself and smirked.

"Who do you work for, Mr. Rawlins?" he asked again.

"Are you a collector, Mr. Haffernon?"

"What?"

"That hippie told me that Axel collected Nazi memorabilia. Daggers, photographs. Do you collect anything like that?"

Haffernon stood then.

"Please leave."

I stood also. "Sure."

I sauntered toward the door not sure of why I was being so tough on this powerful white man. I had baited him out of instinct. I wondered if I was being a fool.

OUTSIDE HIS OFFICE I asked Dina for a pencil and paper.

I wrote down my name and the phone of my motel and handed it to her. She looked up at me in wonder, a small smile on her lips.

"I wish it was for you," I said. "But give it to your boss. When he calms down he might want to give me a call."

16

I ate a very late lunch at a stand-up fried clam booth on Fisherman's Wharf. It was beautiful there. The smell of the ocean and the fish market reminded me of Galveston when I was a boy. At any other time in my life those few scraps of fried flour over chewy clam flesh would have been soothing. But I didn't want to feel good until I knew that Feather was going to be okay. She and Jesus were all I had left.

I went to a pay phone and made the collect call.

Benny answered and accepted.

"Hi, Mr. Rawlins," she said, a little breathless.

"Where's Bonnie, Benita?"

"She went out shoppin' for a wheelchair to take Feather with. Me an' Juice just hangin' out here an' makin' sure Feather okay. She sleep. You want me to wake her up?"

"No, honey. Let her sleep."

"You wanna talk to Juice?"

"You know, Benita, I really like you," I said.

"I like you too, Mr. Rawlins."

"And I know how messed up you were when Mouse did you like he did."

She didn't say anything to that.

"And I care very deeply about my children . . ." I let the words trail off.

For a few moments there was silence on the line. And then in a whisper Benita Flag said, "I love 'im, Mr. Rawlins. I do. He's just a boy, I know, but he better than any man I ever met. He sweet an' he know how to treat me. I didn't mean to do nuthin' wrong."

"That's okay, girl," I said. "I know what it is to fall."

"So you not mad?"

"Let him down easy if you have to," I said. "That's all I can ask."

"Okay."

"And tell Feather I had to stay another day but that I will bring her back a big present because I had to be late."

We said our good-byes and I went to my car.

ON THE WAY BACK to the motel I picked up a couple of newspapers to keep my mind occupied.

Vietnam was half of the newspaper. The army had ordered the evacuation of the Vietnamese city of Hue, where they were on the edge of revolt. Da Nang was threatening revolution and the Buddhists were demonstrating against Ky in Saigon.

Jimmy Hoffa was on the truck manufacturers for the unions and some poor schnook in Detroit had been arrested for bank robbery when the tellers mistook his car for the robber's getaway car. He was a white guy on crutches.

I found that I couldn't concentrate on the stories so I put the paper down. I could feel the fear about Feather rising in my chest.

In order to distract myself I tried to focus on Lee's case. The man he wanted to talk to was dead. The papers the dead man had were gone — I had no idea where to. Cinnamon Cargill was probably dead also. Or maybe she was the killer. Maybe they were tripping together and he died, by accident, and she pressed him into the space below the brass elephant.

I had the telephone numbers of an old folks' home for rich people and a secretive man whose voice was effeminate, and I had a postcard.

All in all that was a lot, but there was nothing I could do about it until the morning. That is unless Haffernon called. Haffernon knew about the trouble Axel was in. He might even have known about the young man's death.

I took out the Nazi Luger I'd stolen from the dead man's treasure chest and placed it on the night table next to the bed.

Then I sat back thinking about the few good years that I'd had with Bonnie and the kids. We had family picnics and long tearful nights helping the kids through the pain of growing up. But all of that was done. A specter had come over us and the life we'd known was gone.

I tried to think about other things, other times. I tried to feel fear over the payroll robbery that Mouse wanted me to join in on. But all I could think about was the loss in my heart.

At eleven o'clock I picked up the phone and dialed a number.

"Hello?" she said.

"Hi."

"Mr. Rawlins? Is that you?"

"You're a lawyer, right, Miss Aubec?"

"You know I am. You were at my office this morning."

"I know that's what you said."

"I am a lawyer," she said. There was no sleep in her voice or annoyance at my late-night call.

"How does the law look on a man who commits a crime when he's under great strain?"

"That depends," she said.

"On what?"

"Well . . . what is the crime?"

"A bad one," I said. "Armed robbery or maybe murder."

"Murder would be simpler," she said. "You can murder someone in the heat of the moment, but a robbery is quite another thing. Unless the property you stole just fell into your lap the law would look upon it as a premeditated crime."

"Let's say that it's a man who's about to lose everything, that if he didn't rob that bank someone he loved might die."

"The courts are not all that sympathetic when it comes to crimes against property," Cynthia said. "But you might have a case."

"In what situation?"

"Well," she said. "Your level of legal representation means a lot. A court-appointed attorney won't do very much for you."

I already knew about the courts and their leanings toward the rich, but her honesty still was a comfort.

"Then of course there's race," she said.

"Black man's not gonna get an even break, huh?"

"No. Not really."

"I didn't think so," I said. And yet somehow hearing it said out loud made me feel better. "How does a young white girl like you know all this stuff?"

"I've sent my share of innocent men to prison," she said. "I worked in the prosecutor's office before going into business with Axel."

"I guess you got to be a sinner to know a sin when you see it."

"Why don't you come over," she suggested.

"I wouldn't be very good company."

"I don't care," she said. "You sound lonely. I'm here alone, wide awake."

"You know a man named Haffernon?" I asked then.

"He was Axel's father's business partner. The families have been friends since the eighteen hundreds."

"Was?"

"Axel's father died eighteen months ago."

"What do you think of Haffernon?"

"Leonard? He was born with a silver spoon up his ass. Always wears a suit, even when he's at the beach, and the only time he ever laughs is when he's with old school friends from Yale. I can't stand him."

"What did Axel think of him?"

"Did?"

"Yeah," I said coolly even though I could feel the sweat spread over my forehead. "Before today, right?"

"Axel has a thing about his family," Cynthia said, her voice clear and trusting still. "He thinks that they're all like enlightened royalty. They *did* put money into our little law office."

"But Haffernon's not family," I said. "He didn't put any money into your office did he?"

"No."

"No what?"

"He didn't give us any money. He doesn't have much sympathy for poor people. He's not related to Axel either — by blood anyway. But the families are so close that Axel treats him like an uncle."

"I see." Calm was returning to my breath and the sweat had subsided.

"So?" Cynthia Aubec asked.

"So what?"

"Are you coming over?"

I felt the question as if it were a fist in my gut.

"Really, Cynthia, I don't think it's a good idea for me tonight."

"I understand. I'm not your type, right?"

"Honey, you're *the* type. A figure like you got on you belongs in the art museum and up on the movie screen. It's not that I don't want to come, it's just a bad time for me."

"So who is this man who might commit a crime under pressure?" she asked, switching tack as easily as Jesus would the single sail of his homemade boat.

"Friend'a mine. A guy who's got a lot on his mind."

"Maybe he needs a vacation," Cynthia suggested. "Time away with a girl. Maybe on a beach."

"Yeah. In a few months that would be great."

"I'll be here."

"You don't even know my friend," I said.

"Would I like him?"

"How would I know what you'd like?"

"From talking to me do you think I'd like him?"

That got me to laugh.

"What's so funny?" Cynthia asked.

"You."

"Come over."

I began to think that it might be a good idea. It was late and there was nothing to hold me back.

There came a knock at the door. A loud knock.

"What's that?" Cynthia asked.

"Somebody at the door," I said, reaching for the German automatic.

"Who?"

"I gotta call you back, Cindy," I said, making the contraction on her name naturally.

"I live on Elm Street in Daly City," she said and then she told me the numbers. "Come over anytime tonight."

There was another knock.

"I'll call," I said and then I hung up.

"Who is it?" I shouted at the door.

"The Fuller Brush man," a sensual voice replied.

I opened the door and there stood Maya Adamant wrapped in a fake white fur coat.

"Come on in," I said.

I had made all the connections before the door was closed.

"So the Nazis brought you out of Mr. Lee's den."

She moved to the bed, then turned to regard me. The way she sat down could not have been learned in finishing school.

"Haffernon called Lee," she said. "He was very upset and now Lee is too. I was out on a date when he called my answering service and they called the club. You're supposed to be in Los Angeles looking for Miss Cargill."

I perched on the edge of the loungelike orange chair that came with my room. I couldn't help leering. Maya's coat opened a bit, exposing her short skirt and long legs. My talk with Cynthia had prepared me to appreciate a sight like that.

"There was no reason for me to think that Philomena had left the Bay Area," I said. "And even if she did she needn't have gone down south. There's Portland and Seattle. Hell, she could be in Mexico City."

"We didn't ask you about Mexico City."

"If you know where she is why do you need me?" I asked.

I forced my eyes up to hers. She smiled, appreciating my will power with a little pout.

"What is this about Nazi memorabilia?" she asked.

"I met a guy who told me that Axel collected the stuff. I just figured that Haffernon might know about it."

"So you've guessed that Leonard Haffernon is our client?"

"I don't guess, Miss Adamant. I just ask questions and go where they lead me."

"Who have you been talking to?" Her nostrils flared.

"Hippies."

She sighed and shifted on the bed. "Have you found Philomena?"

"Not yet," I said. "She left her apartment in an awful hurry though. I doubt she took a change of underwear."

"It would have been nice to meet you under other circumstances, Mr. Rawlins."

"You're right about that."

She stood up and smiled at my gaze.

"Are you ready to go back to L.A.?"

"First thing in the morning."

"Good."

She walked out the door. I watched her move on the stairs. It was a pleasurable sight.

There was a car waiting for her on the street. She got into the passenger's side. I wondered who her companion was as the dark sedan glided off.

I WENT TO BED consciously not calling Bonnie or Cynthia or Maya. I pulled up the covers to my chin and stared at the window until the dawn light illuminated the dirty glass.

17

That morning I headed out toward the San Francisco airport. Just at the mouth of the freeway on-ramp, with the entire sky at their backs, two young hippies stood with their thumbs out. I pulled to the side of the road and cranked down the window.

"Hey man," a sixteen- or seventeen-year-old red-bearded youth said with a grin. "Where you headed?"

"Airport."

"Could you take us that far?"

"Sure," I said. "Hop in."

The boy got in the front seat and the girl, younger than he was, a very blond slip of a thing, got in the back with their backpacks.

She was the reason I had stopped. She wasn't that much older than Feather. Just a child and here she was on the road with her man. I couldn't pass them by.

When I drove up the on-ramp a blue Chevy honked at me and then sped past. I didn't think that I'd cut him off so I figured he was making a statement about drivers who picked up hitch-hikers.

"Thanks, man," the hippie boy said. "We been out there for an hour an' all the straights just passed us by."

"Where you headed?" I asked.

"Shasta," the girl said. She leaned up against the seat between me and her boyfriend. I could see her grinning into my eyes through the rearview mirror.

"That's where you live?"

"We heard about this commune up there," the boy said. He smelled of patchouli oil and sweat.

"What's that?"

"What's what?" he asked.

"Commune. What's that?"

"You never heard of a commune, man?" the boy asked.

"My name's Easy," I said. "Easy Rawlins."

"Cool," the girl crooned.

I suppose she meant my name.

"Eric," the boy said.

"Like the Viking," I said. "You got the red hair for it."

He took this as a compliment.

"I'm Star," the girl said. "An' a commune is where everybody lives and works together without anybody owning shit or tellin' anybody else how to live."

"Kinda like the kibbutz or the Russian farms," I said.

"Hey man," Eric said, "don't put that shit on us."

"I'm not puttin' anything on you," I replied. "I'm just trying to understand what you're saying by comparing it with other places that sound like your commune."

"There's never been anything like us, man," Eric said, filled with the glory of his own dreams. "We're not gonna live like you people did. We're gettin' away from that nine-to-five bullshit. People don't have to own everything. The wild lands are free."

"Yeah," Star said. Her tone was filled with Eric's love for himself. "At Cresta everybody gets their own tepee and a share in what everybody else has."

"Cresta is the name for your commune?"

"That's right," Eric said with such certainty that I almost laughed.

"Why don't you come with us?" Star asked from the backseat.

I looked up and into her eyes through the rearview mirror. There was a yearning there but I couldn't tell if it was hers or mine. Her simple offer shocked me. I could have kept on driving north with those children, to their hippie farm in the middle of nowhere. I knew how to raise a garden and build a fire. I knew how to be poor and in love.

"Watch it!" Eric shouted.

I had drifted into the left lane. A car's horn blared. I jerked my rented car back just in time. When I looked up into the mirror, Star was still there looking into my eyes.

"That was close, man," Eric said. Now his voice also contained the pride of saving us. I was once an arrogant boy like him.

"I can't," I said into the mirror.

"Why not?" she asked.

"How old are you?"

"Fifteen . . . almost."

"I got a daughter just a few years younger than you. She's real sick. Real sick. I got to get her to a doctor in Switzerland or she'll die. So no woods for me quite yet."

"Where is your daughter?" Star asked.

"Los Angeles."

"Maybe it's the smog killin' her," Eric said. "Maybe if you got her out of there she'd be okay."

Eric would never know how close he'd come to getting his nose broken in a moving car. It was only Star's steady gaze that saved him.

"I had a friend once," I said. "Him and me were something like you guys. We used to ride the rails down in Texas and Louisiana."

"Ride the rails?" Eric said.

"Jumping into empty boxcars, trains," I said.

"Like hitchin'," Eric said.

"Yeah. One night in Galveston we went out on a tear —"

"What's that?" Star asked.

"A drinking binge. Anyway the next day I woke up and Hollister was nowhere to be seen. He was completely gone. I waited a day or two but then I had to move on before the local authorities arrested me for vagrancy and put me on the chain gang."

I could see that Eric was now seeing me in a new light. But I didn't care about that young fool.

"What happened to your friend?" Star asked.

"Twenty years later I was driving down in Compton and I saw him walking down the street. He'd gotten fat and his hair was thinning but it was Hollister all right."

"Did you ask him what happened?" Eric asked.

"He'd met a girl after I'd passed out that night. They spent the night together and the next couple'a days. They drank the whole time. One day Holly woke up and realized that at some point they'd gotten married — he didn't even remember saying I do."

"Whoa," Eric said in a low tone.

"Did they stay together?" Star wanted to know.

"I went back with Hollister to his house and met her there. They had four kids. He was a plumber for the county and she baked pies for a restaurant down the street. You know what she told me?"

"What?" both children asked at once.

"That on the evening she'd met Holly I had picked her up at the local juke joint. We'd hit it off pretty good but I drank too much and passed out. When Holly came into the lean-to where we were stayin', Sherry, that was his wife's name, asked him if he would walk her home. That was when they got together."

"He took your woman?" Eric said indignantly.

"Not mine, brother," I said. "That lean-to was our own private little commune. What was mine was me, and Sherry had her own thing to give."

Eric frowned at that, and I believed that I was the first shadow on his bright notions of communal life. That made me smile.

I let them out at the foot of the off-ramp I had to take to get to the airport.

While Eric was wrestling the backpacks out of the backseat Star put her skinny arms around my neck and kissed me on the lips.

"Thanks," she said. "You're really great."

I gave her ten dollars and told her to stay safe.

"God's looking after me," she said.

Eric handed her a backpack then and they crossed the road.

18

After leaving my Hertz car at their airport lot I went to the ticket counter. The flight from San Francisco to Los Angeles on Western Airlines was $24.95.

They took my credit card with no problem.

While waiting for my flight I called home and got Jesus. I gave him the flight number and told him to be there to pick me up.

He didn't ask any questions. Jesus would have crossed the Pacific for me and never asked why.

In a small airport store — where they sold candy bars, newspapers, and cigarettes — I bought a large brown teddy bear for $6.95.

I sat in the bulkhead aisle seat next to a young white woman who wore a rainbow-print dress that came to about midthigh. She was a beauty but I wasn't thinking about her.

I buckled my seat belt and unfolded the morning paper.

Ky had given in to Buddhist pressure and agreed to have free elections in South Vietnam. The bastion of democracy, the United States, however, said publicly that it still backed the dictator.

A couple who were going to lose a baby they were trying to adopt had attempted suicide. They didn't die but their baby did.

I put that paper away.

The captain told us to fasten our seat belts and the stewardess showed us how it was done. The engine on the big 707 began to roar and whine.

"Hello," the young woman said.

"Hi." I gave her just a glance.

"My name is Candice." She held out a hand.

It would have been impolite for me to ignore her gesture of friendship.

"Easy Rawlins."

"Do you fly often, Mr. Rawlins?"

"Every now and then. My girlfriend's a stewardess for Air France."

"I don't. This is only my second flight and I'm scared to death."

She wouldn't let go of my hand. I squeezed and said, "We'll make it through this one together."

We held hands through the takeoff and for five minutes into the ascent. Every now and then she increased the pressure. I matched the force of her grip. By the time we were at full altitude she had calmed down.

"Thank you," she said.

"No problem."

I picked up the paper again but the words scrambled away from my line of vision. I was thinking about Dream Dog and karma, then about Axel Bowers and the humiliating treatment he'd received after his death. I thought about that white girl who just needed somebody to hold on to regardless of his color.

Maybe the hippies were right, I thought. Maybe we should all go outside in our underwear and protest the way of the world.

THE YOUNG WOMAN and I didn't speak another word to each other. There was no need to.

When I got out of the gate in L.A., Jesus was there waiting for me.

"Hi, Dad," he said and shook my hand.

He'd driven my car to the airport and I let him drive going back home. He took La Cienega where I would have taken the freeway but that was okay by me.

"Feather had fever again this morning," he said. "Bonnie gave her Mama Jo's medicine and it came down."

"Good," I said, trying to hide my fear.

"Is she gonna die, Dad?"

"Why you say that?"

"Bonnie told Benny why she had to stay and look after Feather and Benny told me. Is she gonna die?"

There never was a brother and sister closer than Jesus and Feather. I had taken him out of a bad situation when he was an infant, and when I brought Feather into our home he took to her like a mother hen.

"I don't know," I said. "Maybe."

"But if Bonnie takes her to Switzerland they might save her?"

"Yeah. They saved other people with infections like hers."

"Do you want me to go with them?"

"No. The doctors can help. What I need is the money to pay those doctors."

"I could sell my boat."

That boat was everything to Jesus.

"No, son. I think I got a line on a moneymaker. It's gonna be okay."

I had planned to talk to him about Benita and the difference in their ages. But when he offered to give his boat up for Feather I couldn't imagine what there was I had to tell him.

BONNIE HAD PACKED a large traveling suitcase for Feather. It seemed as if she'd taken every toy, doll, dress, and book that Feather owned. When I got there they were ready to go to the airport.

There was a bright chrome and red canvas wheelchair in the living room.

Bonnie came out and kissed me, and even though I tried to put some tenderness into the caress she leaned away and gave me an odd stare.

"What's wrong?"

"If I was to tell you the things I'd seen in the last two days you wouldn't be asking me that," I said truthfully.

Bonnie nodded, still frowning.

"Could you put the suitcase into the trunk?" she asked. "The wheelchair folds up and can go on top."

I knew that they had to get to the airport soon and so I got to work. Jesus helped me figure out that the wheelchair had to go in the backseat.

When I got back in the house Feather was screaming. I ran into her room to find her struggling with Bonnie.

"I want you to carry me, Daddy," she pleaded.

"It's okay," I said and I took her up in my arms.

*　*　*

BONNIE DROVE, Feather slept on my lap, and I stared out the window, wondering how long it would take to drive down to Palestine, Texas. I knew that my work for Lee would be a dead end. Axel was dead. Philomena was probably dead. The papers were long gone. I had gotten a Luger and fifteen hundred dollars in the deal. I could use the German pistol to press against Rayford's willing neck.

FEATHER WOKE UP when we pulled into the employees' lot at the airport. She was happy to have a wheelchair and she raced ahead of us at the special employee entrance to TWA. They had to go to San Francisco first and then transfer to the polar flight to Paris. I saw them to the special entrance for the crew.

A woman I recognized met us there — Giselle Martin.

"Aunt Giselle," Feather cried.

Giselle was a friend of Bonnie's. She was tall and thin, a brunette with a delicate porcelain beauty that you'd miss if you didn't take time with it. They worked together for Air France. She was there to help with Feather.

"Allo, ma chérie," the French flight attendant said to my little girl. "These big strong men are going to carry you up into the plane."

Two brawny white men were coming toward us from a doorway to the terminal building.

"I want Daddy to take me," Feather said.

"It is the rules, ma chérie," Giselle said.

"That's okay, honey," I said to Feather. "They'll carry you up and then I'll come buckle you in."

"You promise?"

"I swear."

The workmen took hold of the chair from the front and back.

Feather grabbed on to the armrests, looking scared. I was scared too. I watched them go all the way up the ramp.

I was about to follow when Bonnie touched my arm and asked, "What's wrong, Easy?"

I had planned for that moment. I thought that if we found ourselves alone and Bonnie wondered at my behavior, I'd tell her all the grisly details of Axel Bowers's death. I turned to her, but when she looked into my eyes, as so many women had in the past few days, I couldn't bring myself to lie.

"I read a lot, you know," I said.

"I know that." Her dark skin and almond eyes were the most beautiful I had ever seen. Two days ago I had wanted to marry her.

"I read the papers and all about anything I have an interest in. I read about a group of African dignitaries getting the Senegalese award of service that was symbolized by a bronze pin with a little design enameled on it — a bird in red and white . . ."

There was no panic on Bonnie's face. The fact that I knew that she had recently received such an important gift from a suitor only served to sadden her.

"He was the only one who could get Feather into that hospital, Easy . . ."

"So there's nothing between you?"

Bonnie opened her mouth but it was her turn not to lie.

"Thank him for me . . . when you see him," I said.

I walked past her and up into the plane.

"WILL YOU COME and see me in the Alps, Daddy?" Feather asked as I buckled her seat belt.

The plane was still empty.

"I'll try. But you know Bonnie'll be there to look after you. And before you know it you'll be all better and back home again."

"But you'll try and come?"

"I will, honey."

I walked past Bonnie as she came up the aisle.

Neither of us spoke.

What was there to say?

19

From the terminal building I could make out the white bow in Feather's hair through a porthole in the plane. And even though she looked out now and then she never saw me waving. Her skin had been warm when I buckled her in but her eyes weren't feverish. Bonnie had Mama Jo's last ball of medicine, I'd made sure of that. Bonnie wouldn't let Feather die no matter who her heart belonged to.

The passengers filed on. Final boarding was announced. The jet taxied away and finally, after a long delay, it nosed its way above the amber layer of smog that covered the city.

I stayed at the window watching as a dozen jets lined up and took off.

"Mister?"

She was past sixty with blue-gray hair and a big red coat made from cotton — the Southern California answer to the eastern overcoat. There was concern on her lined white face.

"Yes?" My voice cracked.

"Are you all right?"

That's when I realized that tears were running from my eyes. I tried to speak but my throat closed. I nodded and touched the woman's shoulder. Then I staggered away amid the stares of dozens of travelers.

I DIDN'T TURN the ignition key right away.

"Snap out of it, Easy," a voice, only partly my own, said. "You know once a man break down the wreck ain't far off. You don't have no time to wallow. You don't have it like some rich boy can feel sorry for hisself."

I drove on surface streets with no destination in mind. Even the next day I couldn't have recalled the route I'd taken. But my instinct was to head in the direction of my office.

I was on Avalon, crossing Manchester, when I heard two horns. I looked up just as my car slammed into a white Chrysler. The next thing I did was to check out the traffic light — it was against me. I had been distracted and a fool for the past few days, but something told me to take that German pistol out of my pocket and hide it under my seat before I did anything else.

I jumped out of my car and ran to the boatlike Chrysler.

There was a middle-aged black couple in the front seat. The man, who wore a brown suit, was clutching his arm and the woman, who was easily twice the man's size, was bleeding freely from a cut over her left eye.

"Nate," she was saying. "Nate, are you okay?"

The man held his left arm between the elbow and shoulder.

I opened the door.

"Let's get you outta there, man," I said.

"Thank you," he mouthed, his face twisted with the pain.

When I got him set up against the hood of his car I went around to the passenger's side. It was then that I heard the first siren, a distant cry.

"Is my husband okay?" the woman asked.

She and Nate both had very dark skin and large facial features. Her mouth was wide and so were her nostrils. The blood was coming down but she didn't seem to notice.

"Just a hurt arm," I said. "He's standing up on the other side."

I took off my shirt and tore it in half, then I pressed the material against her wound.

"Why you pushin' on my head?"

"You're bleeding."

"I am?" she said, the growing panic crowding her words.

When she looked down at her hands her eyes, nostrils, and mouth all grew to extraordinary proportions.

She screamed.

"Alicia!" Nate called. He was shambling around the front of the car.

A lanky woman came up to steady him.

There were people all around but most of them stayed back.

Three sirens wailed not far away.

"It's okay, ma'am," I was saying. "I stopped the bleeding now."

"Am I bleedin'?" she asked. "Am I bleedin'?"

"No," I said. "I stopped it with this bandage."

"All right now, back away!" a voice said.

Two white men dressed all in white except for their shoes ran up.

"Two, Joseph," one man said. "A stretch for each."

"Got it," the other man said.

The nearest ambulance attendant took the torn shirt from my hands and began speaking to the woman.

"What's your name, lady?" he asked.

"Alicia Roman."

"I need you to lie down, Alicia, so that I can get you into the ambulance and stop this cut from bleeding."

There was authority in the white man's voice. Alicia allowed him to lower her onto the asphalt. The other attendant, Joseph, came up with a stretcher. This he put down beside her.

The lanky woman was helping Nate to the back of the ambulance. She was plain looking and high brown, like a polished pecan. There was no expression on her face. She was just doing her part.

I looked down at my hands. Alicia's blood had trailed over my palms and down my forearms. The blood had splattered onto my T-shirt too.

"Are you hurt?" a man asked me.

It was a policeman who came up from the crowd. I saw three other policemen directing traffic and keeping pedestrians out of the street.

"No," I said. "This is her blood."

"Were you in their car?" The cop was blond but he had what white people call swarthy skin. The racial blend hadn't worked too well on him. I remember thinking that the top of his head was in Sweden but his face reflected the Maghreb.

"No," I said. "I ran into them."

"They ran the light?"

"No. I did."

A surprised look came into his face.

"Come over here," he said, leading me to the curb.

He made me touch my nose then walk a straight line, turn around, and come back again.

"You seem sober," he told me.

The ambulance was taking off.

"Are they gonna be okay?" I asked.

"I don't know. Put your hands behind your back."

THEY TOOK AWAY my belt, which was a good thing. I was so miserable in that cell that I might have done myself in. Jesus wasn't home. Neither was Raymond or Jackson, Etta or Saul Lynx. If I stayed in jail until the trial Feather might be kicked out of the clinic and die. I wondered if Joguye Cham, Bonnie's African prince, would help my little girl. I'd be the best man at their wedding if he did that for me.

I finally got Theodore Steinman at his shoe shop down the street from my house. I told him to keep calling EttaMae.

"I'll come down and get you, Ezekiel," Steinman said.

"Wait for Etta," I told him. "She does this shit with Mouse at least once every few months."

"CIGARETTE?" my cellmate asked.

I didn't know if he was offering or wanting one but I didn't reply. I hadn't uttered more than three sentences since the arrest. The police were surprisingly gentle with me. No slaps or insults. They even called me mister and corrected me with respect when I turned the wrong way or didn't understand their commands.

The officer who arrested me, Patrolman Briggs, even dropped by the cell to inform me that Nate and Alicia Roman were doing just fine and were both expected to be released from the hospital that day.

"Here you go," my cellmate said.

He was holding out a hand-rolled cigarette. I took it and he lit it. The smoke in my lungs brought my mind back into the cell.

My benefactor was a white man about ten years my junior, thirty-five or -six. He had stringy black hair that came down to his armpits and sparse facial hair. His shirt was made from various bright-colored scraps. His eyes were different colors too.

"Reefer Bob," he said.

"Easy Rawlins."

"What they got you for, Easy?"

"I ran into two people in their car. Ran a red light. You?"

"They found me with a burlap sack in a field of marijuana up in the hills."

"Really? In the middle of the day?"

"It was midnight. I guess I should'a kept the flashlight off."

I chuckled and then felt a tidal wave of hysterical laughter in my chest. I took a deep draw on the cigarette to stem the surge.

"Yeah," Reefer Bob was saying. "I was stupid but they can't keep me."

"Why not?"

"Because the bag was empty. My lawyer'll tell 'em that I was just looking for my way outta the woods, that I'm a naturalist and was looking for mushrooms."

He grinned and I thought about Dream Dog.

"Good for you," I said.

"You wanna get high, Easy?"

"No thanks."

"I got some reefer in a couple'a these cigarettes here."

"You know, Bob," I said. "The cops put spies in these cells. And they'd love nothing more than to catch you with contraband in here."

"You a spy, Easy?" he asked.

"No. A spy would never let you know."

"You blowin' my mind, man," he said. "You blowin' my mind."

He crawled into the lower bunk in our eight-by-six cell. I laid on my stomach in the upper bed and stared out of the criss-crossed bars of steel. I thought back to midday, when I'd buckled Feather into her seat.

Axel Bowers was far off in my mind.

I felt that somehow I'd been defeated by my own lack of heart.

GUARDS CAME DOWN the hallway at midnight exactly. The jail was dark but they had flashlights to show them the way. When they came into the cell Reefer Bob yelled, "He killed Axel. He told me when he thought I wasn't listening. He killed him and then stuffed him up in a elephant's ass."

They told me to get up and I obeyed. They asked me if I needed handcuffs and I shook my head.

We walked down the long aisle toward a faraway light.

When we reached the room I realized that this was the day of my execution. They strapped me into the gas chamber chair. On the wall there was the stopwatch that Jesus used to have to time his races when he was in high school.

I had one minute left to live when they closed the door to the chamber.

A hornet was buzzing at the portal of the door. It flew right at my eyes. I shook my head around trying to get the stinger away from my face. When it finally flew off I looked back at the stop-watch: I only had three seconds left to live.

20

Rawlins!" The guard's shout jarred me awake.
I'd dozed off for only a few moments.

"Yo!" I hopped down to the concrete floor.

Bob was huddled into a ball in the back corner of his bunk. I wondered if he really thought I was a spy. If so he'd flush the dope into our corroded tin toilet. I might have saved him three years of hard time.

ETTAMAE HARRIS was in the transit room when they got me there.

She was a big woman but no larger that day than she had been back when we were coming up in the late thirties in Fifth Ward, Houston, Texas. Back then she was everything I ever wanted in a woman except for the fact that she was Mouse's wife.

She hugged me and kissed my forehead while I was buckling my belt.

Etta didn't utter more than three words in the jailhouse. She didn't talk around cops. That was an old habit that never died with her. In her eyes the police were the enemy.

She wasn't wrong.

Out in front of the precinct building LaMarque Alexander, Raymond and Etta's boy, sat behind the wheel of his father's red El Dorado. He was a willowy boy with his father's eyes. But where Mouse had supremely confident bravado in his mien his son was petulant and somewhat petty. Even though he was pushing twenty he was still just a kid.

By the time Raymond was his son's age he had already killed three men — that I knew of.

I tumbled into the backseat. Etta climbed in the front and turned around to regard me.

"Your office?" she asked.

"Yeah."

It was only a few blocks from the precinct. LaMarque pulled away from the curb.

"How's college, LaMarque?" I asked the taciturn boy.

"Okay."

"What you studyin'?"

"Nuthin'."

"He's learnin' about electronics and computers, Easy," Etta said.

"If he wants to know about computers he should talk to Jackson Blue. Jackson knows everything about computers."

"You hear that, LaMarque?"

"Yeah."

When he pulled up in front of my office building at Eighty-sixth and Central, Etta said, "Wait here till I come back down."

"But I was goin' down to Craig's, Mom," he complained.

EttaMae didn't even answer him. She just grunted and opened her door. I jumped out and helped her. Then together we walked up the stairs to the fourth floor.

I ushered her into my office and held my client's chair for her.

Only when we were both settled did Etta feel it was time to talk.

"How's your baby doin'?" she asked.

"Bonnie took her to Europe. They got doctors over there worked with these kinds of blood diseases."

Etta heard more in my tone and squinted at me. For my part I felt like I was floating on a tidal wave of panic. I stayed very still while the world seemed to move around me.

Etta stared for half a minute or so and then she broke out with a smile. The smile turned into a grin.

"What you smirkin' 'bout?" I asked.

"You," she said with emphasis.

"Ain't nuthin' funny 'bout me."

"Oh yes there is."

"How do you see that?"

"Easy Rawlins," she said, "if you wandered into a minefield you'd make it through whole. You could sleep with a girl named Typhoid an' wake up with just sniffles. If you fell out a windah you could be sure that there'd be a bush down on the ground t' break yo' fall. Now it might be a thorn bush but what's a few scratches up next to death?"

I had to laugh. Seeing myself through Etta's eyes gave me hope out there in the void. I guess I was lucky compared to all those I'd known who'd died of disease, gunshot wounds, lynching, and alcohol poisoning. Maybe I did have a lucky star. Dim — but lucky still and all.

"How's that boy Peter?" I asked.

Peter Rhone was a white man whom I'd saved from the LAPD when they needed to pin a murder on somebody his color. His only crime was that he loved a black woman. That love had killed her. And when it was all over Peter had a breakdown and Etta took him in.

"He bettah," she said, the trace of a grin still on her lips. "I got him livin' out on the back porch. He do the shoppin' an' any odd jobs I might need."

"An' Mouse doesn't mind?"

"Naw. The first day I brought him home he called Raymond Mr. Alexander. You know Ray always been a sucker for a white boy with manners."

We both laughed.

Etta reached into her purse and pulled out the Luger that had been under the seat of my Ford. She put it on the desk.

"Primo got your car out the pound. He left his Pontiac parked out back." She brought out a silver key and placed it next to the pistol. "He said that he'll have your Ford ready in two weeks."

I had friends in the world. For a moment there I had more than an inkling that things would turn out okay.

Etta stood up.

"Oh yeah," she said. "Here."

She reached into her purse and came out with a roll of twenty-dollar bills.

"Raymond told me to give you this."

I took the money even though I knew he'd see it as a down payment on the heist he wanted me to join him in.

* * *

THE '56 PONTIAC PRIMO left for me was aqua-colored with red flames painted down the passenger's side and across the hood. It wasn't the kind of car I could shadow with but at least it had wheels.

Sitting upright in the passenger's seat was the teddy bear I'd bought in San Francisco. It had been forgotten in our rush to the airport. Primo must have found it along with the pistol.

When I got home there was a note from Benny on the kitchen table. She and Jesus were going to Catalina Island for two days. They were going to camp on the beach but there was a number for the harbormaster of the dock where they were staying. I could call him if there was an emergency.

I showered and shaved, shined my shoes, and made a pan of scrambled eggs and diced andouille sausages. After eating and a good scrubbing I felt ready to try to find any trail that Cinnamon Cargill might have left. I dressed in black slacks and a peach-colored Hawaiian shirt and sat down to the phone.

"HELLO?" She answered the phone after three rings.

"Alva?" I said.

"Oh." There was a brief pause.

I knew what her hesitation meant. I had saved her son from being killed in a police ambush a few years before. At that time she had been married to John, one of my oldest and closest friends.

In order to save Brawly I'd had to shoot him in the leg. The doctors said that he'd have that limp for the rest of his life.

"Hello, Mr. Rawlins." I'd given up getting her to call me Easy.

"I need to speak to Lena Macalister. She's a friend of yours isn't she?"

More silence on the line. And then: "I don't usually give out my friends' numbers without their permission, Mr. Rawlins."

"I need her address, Alva. This is serious."

We both knew that she couldn't refuse me. Her boy had survived to shuffle in the sun because of me.

She hemmed and hawed a few minutes more but then came
across with the address.

"Thanks," I said when she finally relented. "Say hi to Brawly
for me."

She hung up the phone in my ear.

I was going toward my East L.A. hot rod when the next-door
neighbor, Nathaniel Pulley, hailed me.

"Mr. Rawlins."

He was a short white man with a potbelly and no muscle
whatsoever. His blond hair had kept its color but was thinning
just the same. Nathaniel was the assistant manager of the Bank
of Palms in Santa Monica. It was a small position at a minuscule
financial institution but Pulley saw himself as a lion of finance.
He was a liberal and in his largesse he treated me as an equal.
I'm sure he bragged to his wife and children about how wonderful he was to consider a janitor among his friends.

"Afternoon, Nathaniel," I said.

"There was a guy here asking for you a few hours ago. He was
scary looking."

"Black guy?"

"No. White. He wore a jacket made out of snakeskin I think.
And his eyes . . . I don't know. They looked mean."

"What did he say?"

"Just if I knew when you were coming back. I asked him if he
had a message. He didn't even answer. Just walked off like I
wasn't even there."

Pulley was afraid of a car backfiring. He once told me that
he couldn't watch westerns because the violence gave him

nightmares. Whoever scared him might have been an insurance agent or a door-to-door salesman.

I was taken by his words, though, *Like I wasn't even there*. Pulley was a new neighbor. He'd only been in that house for a year or so. I'd been there more than six years — settled by L.A. standards. But I was still a nomad because everybody around me was always moving in or moving out. Even if I stayed in the same place my neighborhood was always changing.

"Thanks," I said. "I'll look out for him."

We shook hands and I drove off, thinking that nothing in the southland ever stayed the same.

21

My first destination was the Safeway down on Pico. I got ground round, pork chops, calf's liver, broccoli, cauliflower, a head of lettuce, two bottles of milk, and stewed tomatoes in cans. Then I stopped at the liquor store and bought a fifth of Johnnie Walker Black.

After shopping I drove back down to South L.A.

Lena Macalister lived in a dirty pink tenement house three blocks off Hooper. I climbed the stairs and knocked on her door.

"Who is it?" a sweet voice laced with Houston asked.

"Easy Rawlins, Lena."

A chain rattled, three locks snapped back. The door came open and the broad-faced restaurateur smiled her welcome as I had seen her do many times at the Texas Rose.

"Come in. Come in."

She was leaning on a gnarled cane and her glasses had lenses with two different thicknesses. But there was still something stately about her presence.

The house smelled of vitamins.

"Sit. Sit."

The carpet was blue and red with a floral pattern woven in. The furniture belonged in a better neighborhood and a larger room. On the wall hung oil paintings of her West Indian parents, her deceased Tennessee husband, and her son, also dead. The low coffee table was well oiled and everything was drenched in sunlight from the window.

When I set the groceries down on the table I realized that I'd forgotten the scotch in the backseat of my car.

"What's this?" she asked, pointing at the bag.

"Your name came up recently and I realized that I had to ask you a couple'a questions. So I thought, as long as I was comin', you might need some things."

"Aren't you sweet."

She backed up to the stuffed chair, made sure of where she was standing, and let herself fall.

"Let's put them away later," she said with a deep sigh. "You know it takes a lot outta me these days just to answer the door."

"You sick?"

"If you call getting old sick, then I sure am that." She smiled anyway and I let the subject drop.

"How long has it been since you closed the Rose?"

"Eight years," she said, smiling. "Those were some days. Hubert and Brendon were both alive and working in the kitchen. We had every important black person in the country, in the world, coming to us for dinner."

She spoke as if I were a reporter or a biographer coming to get down her life story.

"Yeah," I said. "That was somethin' else."

Lena smiled and sighed. "The Lord only lets you have breath for a short time. You got to take it in while you can."

I nodded, thinking about Feather and then about Jesus out on some beach with Benita.

"Alva called. Why are you coming to see me, Mr. Rawlins?"

While inhaling I considered lying. I held the breath for a beat and then let it go.

"I think Philomena Cargill is in trouble. Some people hired me to find her up in Frisco, and even though I didn't, what I did find makes me think that she might need some help."

"Why are these people looking for Cindy?" Lena asked.

"Her boss walked off with something that didn't belong to him. At least that's what they told me. He disappeared and then, a little while later, she did too."

"And why are you coming to me?"

"I found a postcard from you in Philomena's apartment."

"You broke into her place?"

"No. As a matter of fact that's one of the reasons I'm worried about her. They had her place up for rent. She'd left everything behind."

I let these words sink in. Lena lifted her gaze above the glasses as if to get a better view of my heart. I have no idea what her nearly blind eyes saw.

"I don't know where she is, Easy," Lena said. "The last I heard she was in San Francisco working for a man named Bowers."

"Are her parents here?"

"When her father died her mother moved to Chicago to live with a sister."

"Brothers? Sisters?"

"Her brothers are both in the service, Vietnam. Her sister married a Chinese man and they moved to Jamaica."

There was something Lena wasn't telling me.

"What's she like — Cinnamon?"

"Reach over in that drawer in the end table," she said, waving in that general direction.

The drawer was filled with papers, ballpoint pens, and pencils.

"Under all that," she said. "It's a frame."

The small gilded frame held a three-by-five photo of a pretty young woman in a graduation cap and gown. She was smiling like I would have liked my daughter to do on her graduation day. The photograph was black-and-white but you could almost see the reddish hue to her skin through the shading. There was a certainty in her eyes. She knew what she was seeing.

"She's the kind of woman that men hate because she's not afraid to be out there in a man's world. Broke all'a the records at Jordan High School. Made it to the top of her class at University of California at Berkeley. Ready to fly, that child is . . ."

"She honest?"

"Let me tell you something, young man," Lena said. "The reason I know her is that she worked in my restaurant in the last two years. She was just a girl but sharp and true. She loved to work and learn. I wished my own son had her wits. After the restaurant closed she came to see me every week to learn from what I knew. She was no crook."

"Did she have any close friends down here?"

"I didn't know her friends. She saw boys but they were never serious. The young men around here don't value a woman with brains and talent."

"Do you know how I can find her?" I asked, giving up subtlety.

"No."

Maybe I thought she was lying because all I could see was the opaque reflective surface of her glasses.

"If you hear from her will you tell her that I'm looking for the documents Bowers took?"

"What documents?"

"All I know is that he took some papers that have red seals on them. But I'm not worried about them as much as I'm worried about Miss Cargill's safety."

Lena nodded. If she did know where Philomena was she'd be sure to give her the message. I wrote down my home and office numbers. And then I helped Lena put away the groceries.

Her refrigerator was empty except for two hard-boiled eggs.

"With my legs the way they are it's hard for me to get out shopping very much," she said, apologizing for her meager fare.

I nodded and smiled.

"I come down to my office at least twice a week, Lena. I can always make a supermarket run for you."

She patted my forearm and said, "Bless you."

There are all kinds of freedom in America — free speech, the right to bear arms — but when the years have piled up so high on their back that they can't stand up straight anymore, many Americans find out they also have the freedom to starve.

AT A PHONE BOOTH down the street from Lena's house I looked up a number and then made a call.

"Hello?" a man answered.

"Billy?"

"Hey, Easy. She ain't here."

"You know when she'll be in?"

"She at work, man."

"On Saturday?"

"They pay her to sit down in her office when the band comes in for practice. She opens up the music building at nine and then closes it at three. Not bad for time and a half."

"Okay," I said. "I'll go over and see her there."

"Bye, Easy. Take care."

Jordan High School had a sprawling campus. There were over three thousand students enrolled. I came in through the athletic gate and made my way toward the boiler room. That's where Helen McCoy made her private office. She was the building supervisor of the school, a position two grades above the one I'd just left.

Helen was short and redheaded, smart as they come, and tougher than most men. I had seen her kill a man in Third Ward one night. He'd slapped her face and then balled up a fist. When she pressed five inches of a Texas jackknife into his chest he sat down on the floor — dying as he did so.

"Hi, Easy," she said with a smile.

She was sitting at a long table next to the boiler, writing on a small white card. There was a large stack of blank cards on her left and a smaller stack on the right. The right-side cards had already been written on.

"Party?" I asked.

"My daughter Vanessa's gettin' married. These the invitations. You gettin' one."

I sat down and waited.

When Helen finished writing the card she sat back and smiled, indicating that I had her attention.

"Philomena 'Cinnamon' Cargill," I said. "I hear she was a student here some years ago."

"Li'l young," Helen suggested.

"It's my other job," I said. "I'm lookin' for her for somebody."

"Grapevine says you quit the board."

"Sabbatical."

"Don't shit me, Easy. You quit."

I didn't argue.

"Smart girl, that Philomena," Helen said. "Lettered in track and archery. Gave the big speech at her graduation. She was wild too."

"Wild how?"

"She wasn't shy of boys, that one. One time I found her in the boys' locker room after hours with Maurice Johnson. Her drawers was down and her hands was busy." Helen grinned. She'd been wild herself.

"I was told that her father died and her mother left for Chicago," I said. "You know anybody else she might be in touch with?"

"She had a school friend named Raphael Reed. He was funny, if you know what I mean, so he never got jealous of her runnin' around."

"That all?"

"All I can think of."

"You think you could go down and pull Reed's records for me?"

Helen considered my request.

"We known each other a long time haven't we, Easy?"

"Sure have."

"You the one got me this job."

"And you moved up past me in grade in two years."

"I don't have no job on the side to distract me," she said.

I nodded, submitting to her logic.

"You know I ain't s'posed t' give the public information on students or faculty."

"I know that."

She laughed then. "I guess we all do things we ain't s'posed to do sometimes."

"Can't help it," I agreed.

"Wait here," she said, patting the table with her knife hand. "I'll be back in a few minutes."

22

I told Raphael's mother — a small, dark woman with big, brown, hopeful eyes — that I was Philomena Cargill's uncle and that I needed to talk to her son about a pie-baking business that my niece and I were starting up in Oakland. All I hoped for was a phone number, but Althea was so happy about the chance for a job for her son that she gave me his address too.

This brought me to a three-story wooden apartment building on Santa Barbara Boulevard. It was a wide building that had begun to sag in the middle. Maybe that's why the landlord painted it bright turquoise, to make it seem young and sprightly.

I walked up the sighing stairs to 2a. The door was painted with black and turquoise zebra stripes and the letters RR RR were carved into the center.

The young man who answered my knock wore only black jeans. His body was slender and strong. His hair was long (but not hippie long) and straightened — then curled. He wasn't very tall, and the sneer on his lips was almost comical.

"Yeeees?" he asked in such a way that he seemed to be suggesting something obscene.

I knew right then that this was the young man who'd hung up on me, the one I'd called from Philomena's apartment.

"Raphael Reed?"

"And who are you?"

"Easy Rawlins," I said.

"What can I do for you, Easy Rawlins?" he asked while appraising my stature and style.

"I think that a friend of yours may have been the victim of foul play."

"What friend?"

"Cinnamon."

It was all in the young man's eyes. Suddenly the brash flirtation and sneering façade disappeared. Now there was a man standing before me, a man who was ready to take serious action depending on what I said next.

"Come in."

It was a studio apartment. A Murphy bed had been pulled down from the wall. It was unmade and jumbled with dirty clothes and dishes. A black-and-white portable TV with bent-up rabbit-ear antennas sat on a maple chair at the foot of the bed. There was no sofa, but three big chairs, upholstered with green carpeting, were set in a circle facing each other at the center of the room.

The room smelled strongly of perfumes and body odors. This scent of sex and sensuality was off-putting on a Saturday afternoon.

"Come on out, Roget," Raphael said.

A door opened and another young man, nearly a carbon copy of the first, emerged. They were the same height and had the same hairstyle. Roget also wore black jeans, no shirt, and a sneer. But where Raphael had the dark skin of his mother, Roget was the color of light brown sugar and had freckles on his nose and shoulders.

"Sit," Raphael said to me.

We all went to the chairs in a circle. I liked the configuration but it still felt odd somehow.

"What about Philomena?" Raphael asked.

"Her boss disappeared," I said. "A man named Adams hired me to find him. He also told me that Philomena had disappeared a couple of days later. I went to her apartment and found that she'd moved out without even taking her clothes."

Raphael glanced at his friend, but Roget was inspecting his nails.

"So what?"

"You're her friend," I said. "Aren't you worried?"

"Who says I'm her friend?"

"At Jordan you two shared notes on boys."

"What the hell do you mean by that?" he asked.

I realized that I had gone too far, that no matter how much it seemed that these young men were homosexuals, I was not allowed to talk about it.

"Just that she had a lot of boyfriends," I said.

Roget made a catty little grunt. It was the closest he came to speaking.

"Well," Raphael said, "I haven't even spoken to her since the day she graduated."

"Valedictorian wasn't she?"

"She sure was," Raphael said with some pride in his tone.

"Is Roget here a friend'a hers?"

"What?"

"She did call here didn't she?" I asked.

"You the niggah called the other day," Raphael said. "I thought I knew your voice."

"Look, man. I'm not tryin' to mess with you or your friends. I don't care about anything but finding Bowers for the man hired me. I think that Philomena is in trouble, because why else would she leave her place without taking her clothes and personal things? If you know where she is tell her that I'm looking for her."

"I don't know where she is."

"Take my number. If she calls give it to her."

"I don't need your number."

I wondered if my daughter could die because of this petulant boy. The thought made me want to slap him. But I held my temper.

"You're makin' a mistake," I said. "Your friend could get hurt — bad."

Raphael's lips formed a snarl and his head reared back, snakelike — but he didn't say a word.

I got up and walked out, glad that I'd left my new stolen Luger at home.

23

I drove home carefully, making sure to check every traffic light — twice.

Once in my house I gave in to a kind of weariness. It's not that I was tired, but there was nothing I could do. I'd done all I could about Philomena Cargill. And even though I'd chummed the waters for her I doubted that she was alive to take the bait.

Bonnie was off, probably with Joguye Cham, her prince.

And Feather would die unless I made thirty-five thousand dollars quickly. She might die anyway. She might already be dead.

I hadn't had a drink in many years.

Liquor took a toll on me. But Johnnie Walker was still in the backseat of the car and I went to my front door more than once, intent on retrieving him.

And why not take up the bottle again? There was no one to disapprove. Oblivion called to me. I could navigate the tidal wave of my life on a full tank; I'd be a black Ulysses singing with the stars.

It was early evening when I went out the front door and to my borrowed car. I looked in the window at the slender brown bag on the backseat. I wanted to open the door but I couldn't. Because even though there was no trace of Feather she still was there. Looking at the backseat I thought about her riding in the backseat of my Ford. She was laughing, leaning up against the seat as the young hippie Star had done, telling me and Jesus about her wild adventures on the playground and in the classroom. Sometimes she made up stories about her and Billy Chipkin crossing Olympic and going up to the County Art Museum. There, she'd say, they had seen pictures of naked ladies and kings.

I remembered her sitting by my side in the front seat reading *Little Women*, snarling whenever I interrupted her with questions about what she wanted for dinner or when she was going to pick up her room.

Dozens of memories came between me and that door handle. I got dizzy and sat down on the lawn. I put my head in my hands and pressed all ten fingers hard against my scalp.

"Go back in the house," the voice that was me and not me said. "Go back an' do it until she's in her room dreamin' again. Then, when she safe, you can have that bottle all night long."

The phone rang at that moment. It was a weak jingle, almost not there. I struggled to my feet, staggering as if Feather were already healed and I was drunk on the celebration. My pants were wet from the grass.

The weak bleating of the phone grew loud when I opened the door.

"Hello."

"So what's it gonna be, Ease?" Mouse asked.

It made me laugh.

"I got to move on this, brother," he continued. "Opportunity don't wait around."

"I'll call you in the mornin', Ray," I said.

"What time?"

"After I wake up."

"This is serious, man," he told me.

Those words from his lips had been the prelude to many a man's death but I didn't care.

"Tomorrow," I said. "In the mornin'." And then I hung up.

I turned on the radio. There was a jazz station from USC that was playing twenty-four hours of John Coltrane. I liked the new jazz but my heart was still with Fats Waller and Duke Ellington — that big band sound.

I turned on the TV. Some detective show was on. I don't know what it was about, just a lot of shouting and cars screeching, a shot now and then, and a woman who screamed when she got scared.

I'd been rereading *Native Son* by Richard Wright lately so I hefted it off the shelf and opened to a dog-eared page. The words scrambled and the radio hummed. Every now and then I'd look up to see that a new show was on the boob tube. By midnight every light in the house was burning. I'd switched them on one at a time as I got up now and then to check out various parts of the house.

I was reading about a group of boys masturbating in a movie theater when the phone rang again. For a moment I resisted answering. If Mouse had gotten mad I didn't know if I could placate him. If it was Bonnie telling me that Feather was dead I didn't know that I could survive.

"Hello."

"Mr. Rawlins?" It was Maya Adamant.

"How'd you get my home number?"

"Saul Lynx gave it to me."

"What do you want, Miss Adamant?"

"There has been a resolution to the Bowers case," she said.

"You found the briefcase?"

"All I can tell you is that we have reached a determination about the disposition of the papers and of Mr. Bowers."

"You don't even want me to report on what I've found?" I asked.

This caused a momentary pause in my dismissal.

"What information?" she asked.

"I found Axel," I said.

"Really?"

"Yes, really. He came down to L.A. to get away from Haffernon. Also to be nearer to Miss Cargill."

"She's down there? You've seen her?"

"Sure have," I lied.

Another silence. In that time I tried to figure Maya's response to my talking to Cinnamon. Her surprise might have been a clue that she knew Philomena was dead. Then again . . . maybe she'd been given contradictory information . . .

"What did Bowers say?" she asked.

"Am I fired, Miss Adamant?"

"You've been paid fifteen hundred dollars."

"Against ten thousand," I added.

"Does that mean you are withholding intelligence from Mr. Lee?"

"I'm not talking to Mr. Lee."

"I carry his authority."

"I spent a summer unloading cargo ships down in Galveston back in the thirties," I said. "Smelled like tar and fish, and you know I was only fifteen — with a sensitive nose. My back hurt carryin' them cartons of clothes and fine china and whatever else the man said I should carry for thirty-five cents a day. I had his authority but I was just a day laborer still and all."

"What did Axel say?"

"Am I fired?"

"No," she said after a very long pause.

"Let Lee call me back and say that."

"Robert E. Lee is not a man to fool with, Mr. Rawlins."

"I like it when you call me mister," I said. "It shows that you respect me. So listen up — if I'm fired then I'm through. If Lee wants me to be a consultant based on what I know then let him call me himself."

"You're making a big mistake, Easy."

"Mistake was made before I was even born, honey. I came into it cryin' and I'll go out hollerin' too."

She hung up without another word. I couldn't blame her. But neither could I walk away without trying to make my daughter's money.

I SAUTÉED chopped garlic, minced fresh jalapeño, green pepper, and a diced shallot in ghee that I'd rendered myself. I added some ground beef and, after the meat had browned, I put in some cooked rice from a pot in the refrigerator. That was my meal for the night.

I fell asleep on the loveseat with every light in the house on, the television flashing, and John Coltrane bleating about his favorite things.

24

I moved the trunk in front of the big brass elephant. Underneath was the crushed, cubical body of Axel Bowers. I watched him, worrying once again about the degradation of his carcass. I told him that I was sorry and he moved his head in a little semicircle as if trying to work out a kink in his neck. With his hands he lifted his head, raising it up from the hole. It took him a long while to crawl out of the makeshift grave — and longer still to straighten out all of the bloody, cracked, and shattered limbs. He looked to me like a butterfly just out of the cocoon, unfolding its wet wings.

All of that work he did without noticing me. Pulling on his left arm, turning his foot around until the ankle snapped into place, pressing his temples until his forehead was once more round and hard.

He was putting his fingers back into alignment when he happened to look up and notice me.

"I'm going to need a new hip," he said.

"What?"

"The hip bones don't reform like other bones," he said. "They need to be replaced or I won't be able to walk very far."

"Where you got to go?" I asked.

"There's a Nazi hiding in Egypt. He's going to assassinate the president."

"The president was assassinated three years ago," I said.

"There's a new president," Axel assured me. "And if this one goes we'll be in deep shit."

The phone rang.

"You going to get that?" Axel asked.

"I should stay with you."

"Don't worry, I can't go anywhere. I'm stuck right here on my broken hips."

The phone rang.

I wandered back through the house. In the kitchen Dizzy Gillespie had taken Coltrane's place. He was standing in front of the sink with his cheeks puffed out like a bullfrog's, blowing on that trumpet. The front door was open and *The Mummy* was playing outside. The movie was now somehow like a play being enacted in the street. On the sidewalks all the way up to the corners, extras and actors with small roles were smoking cigarettes and talking, waiting to come onstage to do their parts.

Egypt, I thought and the phone rang.

I came back in the house but the phone wasn't on its little table. Above, on the bookshelf, Bigger Thomas was strangling a woman who was laughing at him.

"You can't kill me," she said. "I'm better than you are. I'm still alive."

The phone rang again.

I returned to the brass elephant to tell Axel something but he was back in his hole, crushed and debased.

"My hips were my downfall," he said.

"You can make it," I told him. "Lots of people live in wheelchairs."

"I will not be a cripple."

The phone rang and he disappeared.

I opened my eyes. *The Mummy,* with Boris Karloff, was playing on TV. Coltrane had not been replaced, and every light in the house was still on.

I wondered about the coincidence of a movie about a corpse rising from the dead in Egypt and Axel's trips to that country.

The phone rang.

"Somebody must really wanna talk," I said to myself, thinking that the phone must have rung nearly a dozen times.

I went to the podium and picked up the receiver.

"Hello."

"Why are you looking for me?" a woman's voice asked.

"Philomena? Is that you?"

"I asked you a question."

My lips felt numb. Coltrane hit a discordant note.

"I thought you were dead," I said. "You didn't even take any underwear as far as I could tell. What woman leaves without a change of underwear?"

"I am alive," she said. "So you can stop looking for me."

"I'm not lookin' for you, honey. It's your boyfriend Axel an' them papers he stole."

"Axel's gone."

"Dead?"

"Who said anything about dead? He's gone. Left the country."

"Just up and left his house without tellin' anybody? Not even Dream Dog?"

"Who are you working for, Mr. Rawlins?"

"Call me Easy."

"Who are you working for?"

"I don't know."

"What do you mean you don't know?"

"A man I know came to me with fifteen hundred dollars and said that another man, up in Frisco, was willing to pay that and more for locating Axel Bowers. That man said he was working for somebody else but he didn't tell me who. After I looked around I found out that you and Axel were friends, that you disappeared too. So here I am with you on the phone, just a breath away."

"You weren't that far wrong about me, Easy," the woman called Cinnamon said.

"What exactly was I right about?"

"I think there is a man trying to kill me. A man who wants the papers that Axel has."

"What's this man's name?" I asked, made brave by the anonymity of the phone lines.

"I don't know his name. He's a white man with dead eyes."

"He wear a snakeskin jacket?" I asked on a hunch.

"Yes."

"Where are you?"

"Hiding," she said. "Safe."

"I'll come to you and we'll try and work this thing out."

"No. I don't want your help. What I want is for you to stop looking for me."

"Nothing would make me happier than to let this drop, but

I'm in it now. All the way in it," I said, thinking about Axel's hip bones. "So either we get together or I talk to the man pays my salary."

"He's probably the one trying to have me killed."

"You don't know that."

"Axel told me. He said that people would kill for those papers. Then that man . . . he . . ."

"He what?"

She hung up the phone.

I held on to the receiver for a full minute at least. Sitting there I thought again about my dream, about the corpse trying to resuscitate himself. Philomena had described a killer who had been at my doorstep. All of a sudden the prospect of robbing an armored car delivery didn't seem so dangerous.

I had a good laugh then. There I was all alone in the night with killers and thieves milling outside in the darkness.

I rooted my .38 out of the closet and made sure that it was loaded. The Luger was a fine gun but I had no idea how old its ammo was. I went around the house turning off lights.

In bed I was overcome by a feeling of giddiness. I felt as if I had just missed a fatal accident by a few inches. In a little while Bonnie's infidelity and Feather's dire illness would return to disturb my rest, but right then I was at peace in my bed, all alone and safe.

Then the phone rang.

I had to answer it. It might be Bonnie. It might be my little girl wanting me to tell her that things would be fine. It could be Mouse or Saul or Maya Adamant. But I knew that it wasn't any of them.

"Hello."

"I'm at the Pixie Inn on Slauson," she said. "But I'm very tired. Can you come in the morning?"

"What's the room number?"

"Six."

"What size dress you wear?" I asked.

"Two," she said. "Why?"

"I'll see you at seven."

I hung up and wondered at the mathematics of my mind. Why had I agreed to go to her when I'd just been thankful for a peaceful heist?

"'Cause you the son of a fool and the father of nothing," the voice that had abandoned me for so many years said.

25

I couldn't sleep anymore that night.

At four I got up and started cooking. First I fried three strips of bacon. I cracked two eggs and dropped them into the bacon fat, then I covered one slice of whole wheat bread with yellow mustard and another one with mayonnaise. I grated orange cheddar on the eggs after I flipped them, put the lid on the frying pan, and turned off the gas flame. I made a strong brew of coffee, which I poured into a two-quart thermos. Then I made the eggs and bacon into a sandwich that I wrapped in wax paper.

Riding down Slauson at five-fifteen with the brown paper bag next to me and Johnnie Walker in the backseat, I tried to come up with some kind of plan. I considered Maya and Lee, dead Axel and scared Cinnamon — and the man in the snakeskin jacket. There was no sense to it; no goal to work toward except making enough money to pay for Feather's hospital bill.

I parked across the street from the motel. It was of a modern design, three stories high, with doors that opened to unenclosed platforms. Number 6 was on the ground floor. Its door opened onto the parking lot. I supposed that Philomena wanted to be able to jump out the back window if need be.

I sat in my car wondering what I should ask the girl.

What should I tell her? Should it be truth?

When my Timex read six-eighteen the door of number 6 opened. A tall woman wearing dark slacks and a long white T-shirt came out. Even from that distance I could see that she was braless and barefoot. Her skin had a reddish hue and her hair was long and straightened.

She walked to the soda machine near the motel office, put in her coins, and then bent down to get the soda that fell out. The streets were so quiet that I heard the jumbling glass.

She walked back to the door, looked around, then went inside.

A minute later I was walking toward her door.

I listened for a moment. There was no sound. I knocked. Still no sound. I knocked again. Then I heard a shushing sound like the slide of a window.

"It's me, Philomena," I said loudly. "Easy Rawlins."

It only took her half a minute to come to the door and open it.

Five nine with chiseled features and big, dramatic eyes, that was Philomena Cargill. Her skin was indeed cinnamon red. Lena's photograph of her had faithfully recorded the face but it hadn't given even a hint of her beauty.

I held out the paper bag.

"What's this?"

"An egg sandwich an' coffee," I said.

While she didn't actually grab the bag she did take it with eager hands.

She went to one of the two single beds and sat with the sack on her lap. After closing the door I put the cloth bag I'd brought on the bed across from her and sat next to it.

There were three lamps in the room. They were all on but the light was dim at best.

Philomena tore open the sandwich and took a big bite out of it.

"I'm a vegetarian usually," she said with her mouth full, "but this bacon is good."

While she ate I poured her a plastic cup full of coffee.

"I put milk in it," I said as she took the cup from me.

"I don't care if you put vinegar in it. I need this. I left my house with only forty dollars in my purse. It's all gone now."

She didn't speak again until the cup was drained and the sandwich was gone.

"What's in the other bag?" she asked. I believe she was hoping for another sandwich.

"Two dresses, some panties, and tennis shoes."

She came to sit on the other side of the bag, taking out the clothes and examining them with an expert feminine eye.

"The dress is perfect," she said. "And the shoes'll do. Where'd you get these?"

"My son's girlfriend left them. She's a skinny thing too."

When Cinnamon smiled at me I understood the danger she represented. She was more than pretty or lovely or even beautiful. There was something regal about her. I almost felt like bowing to show her how much I appreciated the largesse of her smile.

"They say that Hitler was a vegetarian too," I said and the smile shriveled on her lips.

"So what?"

"Why don't you tell me, Philomena?"

After regarding me for a moment she said, "Why should I trust you?"

"Because I'm on your side," I said. "I don't want any harm coming to you and I'll work to see that no one else hurts you either."

"I don't know any of that."

"Sure you do," I said. "You talked to Lena about me. She gave you my number. She told you that I've traded tough favors down around here for nearly twenty years."

"She also said that she's heard that people you've helped have wound up hurt and even dead sometimes."

"That might be, but any girl bein' followed by a snakeskin killer got to expect some danger," I countered. "I'd be a fool if I told you everything'll work out fine and you'd be a fool to believe it. But if you all mixed up with murder then you need somebody like me. It don't matter that you got a business degree from UC Berkeley and a boyfriend got Paul Klee paintings hangin' on his walls. If somethin' goes wrong you the first one they gonna look at. An' if a white killer wanna kill somebody a black woman will be the first on his list. 'Cause you know the cops will ask if you had a boyfriend they could pin it on, an' if you don't they'll call you a whore and close the book."

Philomena listened very carefully to my speech. Her royal visage made me feel like some kind of minister to the crown.

"What do want from me?" she asked.

"What papers did Axel steal?"

"He didn't steal anything. He found those papers in a safe-deposit box his father had. He kept them with memorabilia he had from Germany. When Mr. Bowers died, he left the key to Axel."

"If that's so then why did Haffernon tell the man who hired me that Axel stole the papers from him?"

"Who hired you?"

I told her about Robert Lee and his Amazon assistant. She had never heard of either one.

"Haffernon and Mr. Bowers and another man were partners before the war. They worked in chemicals," Philomena said.

"Who was their partner?"

"A man named Tourneau, Rega Tourneau. They did some bad things, illegal things during the war."

"What kind of things?"

"Treason."

"No." I was still a good American back in those days. It was almost impossible for me to believe that American businessmen would betray the country that had made them rich.

"The papers are Swiss bearer bonds issued in 1943 for work done by the Karnak Chemical Company in Cairo," Philomena said. "And even though the bonds themselves are only endorsed by the banks there's a letter from top Nazi officials that details the expectations that the Nazis had of Karnak."

"Whoa. And Axel wanted to cash the bonds?"

"No. He didn't know what he wanted exactly, but he knew that something should be done to make amends for his father's sins."

"But Haffernon doesn't want to pay the price," I said. "What about this Tourneau guy?"

"I don't know about him. Axel just said that he's out of it."

"Dead?"

"I don't know."

"What did his father's company do for the Nazis?" I asked.

"They developed special kinds of explosives that the Germans used for construction in a few of their slave labor camps."

"And what do you get outta all'a this?" I asked.

"Me? I was just helping him."

"No. I don't hardly know you at all, girl, but I do know that you look out for number one. What's Axel gonna do for you?"

Cinnamon let her left shoulder rise, ceding a point that was hardly worth the effort.

"He had friends in business. He was going to set me in a job somewhere. But he would have done that even if I hadn't tried to help."

I was suddenly aware of a slight dizziness.

"But it didn't hurt," I said. "You could work all you wanted."

"What?" she asked.

I realized that the last part of what I said didn't make sense.

I blinked, finding it hard to open my eyes again.

I shook my head but the cobwebs went nowhere.

"Philomena."

"Yes?"

"Would you mind if I just laid out here a minute? I haven't got much sleep lookin' for you and I'm tired. Real tired."

Her smile was a thing to behold.

"Maybe I could rest too," she said. "I've been so scared alone in this room."

"Let's get a short nap and then we can finish talkin' in a while." I lay back on the bed as I spoke.

She said something. It seemed like a really long sentence but I couldn't make out the words. I closed my eyes.

"Uh-huh," I said out of courtesy and then I was asleep.

26

In the dream I was kissing Bonnie. She whispered something
sweet and kissed my forehead, then my lips. I tried to hold
myself back, to tell her how angry I was. But every time her lips
touched mine my mouth opened and her tongue washed away
all my angry words.

"I need you," she told me and I had to strain to hold back the
tears.

She pressed her body against mine. I held her so tight that
she pulled away for a moment, but then she was kissing me
again.

"Thank God," I whispered. "Thank God."

I reached down into her panties and she moaned.

But when I felt her cold hand on my erection I realized that it
wasn't Bonnie. It wasn't Bonnie because it wasn't a dream and
Bonnie was in Switzerland.

Who was in my bed? Nobody. Another deeply felt kiss. I was in a motel room . . . with Cinnamon Cargill.

I raised up, pushing her away as I did so. Her T-shirt was up to her midriff. My erection was standing straighter than it had in some while. She reached out and stroked it lightly with two fingers. The groan came from my lips against my will.

I stood up, pushed the urgent cock back behind the zipper.

Cinnamon sat up and smiled.

"I was scared," she explained. "I just lay down next to you and went to sleep."

What could I say?

"I guess you must have kissed me in your sleep," she said. "It was nice."

"Yeah." I wondered if it was me who cast the first kiss. "I'm sorry about that."

"Nothing to be sorry about. It's natural. I have protection."

Even her sexy nonchalance was imperial.

"Where'd you get that?" I asked her. "You left with nothing."

"I always have a backup in my wallet," she said, sounding decidedly like a man.

"Let's go get some breakfast," I said.

A shadow of disappointment darkened her features for a moment and then she pulled on her pants, which she'd dropped on the floor next to my bed.

I WANTED BREAKFAST even though it was two in the afternoon. Philomena and I had slept for almost eight hours before we started making out.

Brenda's Burgers had everything I needed: an all-day breakfast menu and a booth at the back of her tiny diner where you could talk without being overheard. It was a small restaurant with pitted floors and mismatched furniture. The cook and waiter was a dark-skinned mustachioed man with mistrustful eyes.

I ordered fried ham and buttermilk biscuits. Philomena wanted a steak with collard greens, mashed potatoes, and salad.

"I thought you were vegetarian?" I asked.

"Need to keep up my strength," she replied.

I was a little off because the erection hadn't gone all the way down. My heart was thrumming and every time she smiled I wanted to suggest going back to her room and finishing off what we had started.

"What's wrong?" she asked me.

"Nuthin'. Why you ask?"

"You seem kind of nervous."

"This is just the way I am," I said.

"Okay."

"Tell me about the man in the snakeskin jacket," I said, watching the cook eye us from behind the kitchen window.

"He came to Axel's house one day last week. I was in the hallway that led to the bedroom but I could see them through a crack in the double doors."

"They didn't know you were there?"

"Axel knew but the other guy didn't. He told Axel that he needed the papers his father left. Axel told him that they'd been given to a third party who would make them public upon his death."

Watching her, listening to her story made me sweat. Maybe it was the heat from the kitchen but I didn't think so. Neither did I feel my temperature came from anything having to do with sex.

"Did he threaten Axel?"

"Yes. He said, 'A man can get hurt if he doesn't know when to fold.'"

"He's right about that," I said, wanting to stave off the details of Axel's murder.

"He was a frightening man. Axel was scared but he stood up to him."

"What happened then?"

"The man left."

"He didn't . . . hurt Axel?"

"No. But he put the fear of God into him. He told me to get out of there, not even to go home. He gave me the money he had in his pocket and said to go down to L.A. until he figured out what to do."

"Why you?" I asked. "He wasn't after you."

"Axel and I were close." There was a brazen look on Cinnamon's face, as if she were daring me to question her choice of lovers.

"So you have the papers," I said.

She didn't deny it.

"Those papers can get you killed," I said.

"I've been trying to call Axel for days," she said, agreeing with me in her tone. "I called his cousin but Harmon hadn't heard from him and there's no answer at his house."

"How about his office?"

"He never tells them anything."

"How many people know where you are now?" I asked.

"No one."

"What about Lena?"

"I call her every other day or so but I don't tell her where I am."

"And Raphael?"

That was the first time I'd surprised her.

"How did you . . . ?"

"I'm a real live detective, honey. Finding out things is what I do."

"No. I mean I've talked to Rafe but I didn't tell him where I was staying."

"Have you seen anybody you know or have they seen you?"

"I don't think so."

"Are you willing to trade those papers for your life?" I asked.

"Axel made me promise to turn them in if anything happened," she said.

"Axel's dead," I said.

"You don't know that."

"Yes I do and you know it too," I told her. "This is big money here. You learn more outta this than five PhDs at Harvard could ever tell ya. Axel messed with some big men's money and now he's dead. If you wanna live you had better think straight."

"I . . . I have to think about this. I should at least try to find Axel once more."

I didn't want to implicate myself in the particulars of Axel's demise. So I reached into my pocket and peeled off five of Mouse's twenties. I palmed the wad and handed it to her under the table. At first she thought I was trying to hold her hand. She clutched at my fingers and then felt the bills.

"What's this?"

"Money. Pay for your room and some food. But don't go out much. Try to hide your face if you do. You got my office number too?"

She nodded.

"I'll call you tonight or at the latest tomorrow morning. You got to decide though, honey."

She nodded. "You want to come back to the room with me?"

"I'll walk you but then I got to get goin'. Got to get a bead on how we get you outta this jam."

Her shoulder heaved again, saying that a roll in the hay would have been nice but okay.

I knew she was just afraid to be alone.

I MADE IT to my office a little bit before four.

There were three messages on the machine. The first was from Feather.

"Hi, Daddy. Me an' Bonnie got here after a loooong time on three airplanes. Now I'm in a house on a lake but tomorrow they're gonna take me to the clinic. I met the doctor and he was real nice but he talks funny. I miss you, Daddy, and I wish you would come and see me soon. . . . Oh yeah, an' Bonnie says that she misses you too."

I turned off the machine for a while after that. In my mind every phrase she used turned over and over. Bonnie saying that she missed me, the doctor's accent. She sounded happy, not like a dying girl at all.

I was so distracted by these thoughts that I didn't hear him open the door. I looked up on instinct and he was standing there, not six feet from where I sat head in hands.

He was a white man, slender and tall, wearing dark green slacks and a jacket of tan and brown scales. His hat was also dark green, with a small brim. His skin was olive-colored and his pale eyes seemed to have no color at all.

"Ezekiel Rawlins?"

"Who're you?"

"Are you Ezekiel Rawlins?"

"Who the fuck are you?"

There was a moment there for us to fight. He was peeved at me not answering his question. I was mad at myself for not hearing him open the door. Or maybe I hadn't closed it behind me. Either way I was an idiot.

But then Snakeskin smiled.

"Joe Cicero," he said. "I'm a private operative too."

"Detective?"

"Not exactly." His smile had no humor in it.

"What do you want?"

"Are you Ezekiel Rawlins?"

"Yeah. Why?"

"I'm looking for a girl."

"Try down on Avalon near Florence. There's a cathouse behind the Laundromat."

"Philomena Cargill."

"Never heard of her."

"Oh yeah. You have. You talked to her and now I need to do the same thing."

I remembered the first day I opened the office two years earlier. I'd had a little party to celebrate the opening. All of my friends, the ones who were still alive, had come. Mouse was there drinking and eating onion dip that Bonnie'd made. He waited until everyone else had gone before handing me a paper bag that held a pistol, some chicken wire, and a few U-shaped tacks.

"Let's put this suckah in," he said.

"In what?"

"Under the desk, fool. You know you cain't be workin' wit' these niggahs down here without havin' a edge. Shit, some mothahfuckah come in here all mad or vengeful an' there you are without a pot to piss in. No, brothah, we gotta put this here gun undah yo' desk so that when the shit hit the fan at least you got a even chance."

I slid my hand around the smooth butt of the .25 caliber gift.

"I don't know no Cargill," I said. "Who says that I do?"

Cicero made an easy move with his hand and I came out with my gun. I pointed it at his head just in case he was wearing something bulletproof on his chassis.

The threat just made him smile.

"Nervous aren't you, son?" he said. "Well . . . you should be."

"Who said I know this woman?"

"You have twenty-four hours, Mr. Rawlins," he replied. "Twenty-four or things will get bad."

"Do you see this gun?" I asked him.

He grinned and said, "Family man like you has to think about his liabilities. Me, I'm just a soldier. Knock one down and two take his place. But you — you have Feather and Jesus and whats-hername, Bonnie, yeah Bonnie, to think about."

With that he turned and walked out the door.

I'd met men with eyes like his before — killers, every one of them. I knew that his threats were serious. I would have shot him if I could have gotten away with it. But my floor had five other tenants and not one of them would have lied to save my ass.

Two minutes after Joe Cicero walked out the door I went to the hall to make sure that he was gone. I checked both stairwells and then made sure to lock my own door behind me.

27

The second phone message was from Mouse.

"I called it off, Easy," he said in a subdued voice. "I figure you don't want it bad enough an' I already got a business t' run. Call me when you get a chance."

The last message was from Maya Adamant.

"Mr. Rawlins, Mr. Lee is willing to come to an agreement about your information. And where he cannot see paying you the full amount, he's willing to compromise. Call me at my home number."

Instead I called the harbormaster at the Catalina marina and left a message for my son. Then the international operator connected me with a number Bonnie had left.

"Hello?" a man said. His voice was very sophisticated and European.

"Bonnie Shay," I uttered in the same muted tones that Mouse had used.

"Miss Shay is not in at the moment. Is there a message?"

I almost hung up the phone. If I were a younger man I would have.

"Could you write this down please?" I asked Joguye Cham.

"Hold a minute," he said. Then, after a moment, he said, "Go on."

"Tell her that there's a problem at the house. It could be dangerous. Tell her not to go there before calling EttaMae. And say that this has nothing to do with our talk before she left. It's business and it's serious."

"I have it," he said and then he read it back to me. He got every word. His voice had taken on an element of concern.

I disconnected the line and took a deep breath. That was all the energy I could expend on Bonnie and Joguye. I didn't have time to act the fool.

I dialed another number.

"Saul Lynx investigations," a woman's voice answered.

It was Saul's business line in his home.

"Doreen?"

"Hi, Easy. How're you?"

"If blessings were pennies I wouldn't even be able to buy one stick of gum."

Doreen had a beautiful laugh. I could imagine her soft brown features raising into that smile of hers.

"Saul's in San Diego, Easy," she said, and then, more seriously, "He told me about Feather. How is she?"

"We got her into a clinic in Switzerland. All we can do now is hope."

"And pray," she reminded me.

"I need you to give Saul a message, Doreen. It's very important."

"What is it?"

"You got a pencil and paper?"

"Right here."

"Tell him that the Bowers case has gone sour, rancid, that I had a visit from Adamant and a man came here that, uh . . . Just tell Saul that I need to talk to him soon."

"I'll tell him when he calls, Easy. I hope everything's okay."

"Me too."

I pressed the button down with my thumb and the phone rang under my hand. Actually it vibrated first and then rang. I remember because it got me thinking about the mechanism of my phone.

"Yeah?"

"Dad, what's wrong?" Jesus asked. "Is Feather okay?"

"She's fine," I said, glad to be giving at least one piece of good news. "But I need you to leave Catalina right now and go down to that place you dock near San Diego."

"Okay. But why?"

"I crossed a bad guy and he knows where we live. Bonnie and Feather are safe in Europe but I don't know if he got into the house and read Benny's note. So go to San Diego and don't come home until I tell you to. And don't tell anybody, anybody, where you're going."

"Do you need help, Dad?"

"No. I just need time. And you stayin' down there will give it to me."

"I'll call EttaMae if I need to talk to you?"

"You know the drill."

I ERASED ALL THE MESSAGES and then disconnected the answering machine so that Cicero wouldn't be able to break in and listen to my news. I left the building by a little-used side entrance and walked around the block to get to my car. I drove straight from there over to Cox Bar.

Ginny told me that Mouse hadn't been around yet that day and so he'd probably be there soon. I took a seat in the darkest corner nursing a Pepsi.

The denizens of Cox Bar drifted in and out. Grave men and now and then a wretched woman or two. They came in quietly, drank, then left again. They hunched over tables murmuring empty secrets and recalling times that were not at all what they remembered.

At other occasions I had felt superior to them. I'd had a job, a house in West L.A., a beautiful girlfriend who loved me, two wonderful children, and an office. But now I was one step away from losing all of that. All of it. At least most of the people at Cox Bar had a bed to sleep in and someone to hold them.

After an hour I gave up waiting and drove off in my souped-up Pontiac.

ETTAMAE AND MOUSE had a nice little house in Compton. The yard sloped upward toward the porch, where they had a padded bench and a redwood table. In the evenings they sat outside eating ham hocks and greeting their neighbors.

Etta's sepia hue and large frame, her lovely face and iron-willed gaze, would always be my standard for beauty. She came to the screen door when I knocked. She smiled in such a way that I knew Mouse wasn't home. That's because she knew, and I did too, that if there had been no Raymond Alexander we would have been married with a half-dozen grown kids. I had always been her second choice.

When I was a young man that was my sorrow.

"Hi, Easy."

"Etta."

"Come on in."

The entrance to their small house was also the dining room. There were stacks of paper on the table and clothes hung on the backs of chairs.

"'Scuse the mess, honey. I'm jes' doin' my spring cleanin'."

"Where's Mouse, Etta?"

"I don't know."

"When you expect him?"

"No time soon."

"He left for Texas?"

"I don't know where he went . . . after I kicked his butt out."

I wasn't ready for that. Every once in a while Etta would kick Mouse out of the house. I had never figured out why. It wasn't for anything he'd done or even anything that she suspected. It was almost as if spring cleaning included getting rid of a man.

The problem was I needed Raymond, and with him being gone from the house he could be anywhere.

"Hello, Mr. Rawlins," a man said from the inner door to the dining room.

The white man was tall, and even though he was in his mid-thirties his face belonged on a boy nearer to twenty. Blue eyes, blond hair, and the fairest of fair skin — that was Peter Rhone, a man I'd cleared of murder charges after the riots that decimated Watts. He'd met Etta at a funeral I gave for the young black woman, Nola Payne, who had been his lover. Gruff EttaMae was so moved by the pain this white man felt over the loss of a black woman that she offered to take him in.

His wife had left him. He had no one else.

He wore jeans and a T-shirt and the saddest face a man can have.

"Hey, Pete. How's it goin'?"

He sighed and shook his head.

"I'm trying to get on my feet," he said. "I'll probably go back to school to learn auto mechanics or something like that."

"I got a friend livin' in a house I own on One-sixteen," I said. "Primo. He's a mechanic. If I ask him I'm sure he'll show you the ropes."

Rhone had been a salesman brokering advertising deals with companies that didn't have offices in Los Angeles. But he had a new life now, or at least the old life was over and he was waiting on Etta's porch for the new one to kick in.

"Don't take my boy away from me so quick, Easy," Etta said. "You know he earns his keep just workin' round the house here."

Peter flashed a smile. I could see that he liked being kept on the back porch by EttaMae.

"You know where I can find Mouse?" I asked.

"No," Etta said.

Peter shook his head.

"Well okay then," I said. "I got to find him, so if he calls tell him that. And if Bonnie or Jesus call just tell 'em to stay away until I say they can come back."

"What's goin' on, Easy?" Etta asked, suddenly suspicious.

"I just need a little help on somethin'."

"Be careful now," she said. "I kicked him out but that don't mean I want him in a casket."

"Etta, how you expect somebody like me to be a threat to him?" I asked even though I had once nearly gotten her man killed.

"You the most dangerous man in any room you in, Easy," she said.

I didn't argue with her assessment because I suspected that she might be right.

28

There was a place called Hennie's on Alameda. It took up the third floor of a building that occupied an entire block. That building once housed a furniture store before the riots depleted its stock. Hennie's wasn't a bar or a restaurant; it wasn't a club or private fraternity either — but it was any one of those things and more at different times of the week. It had a kitchen in the back and round folding tables in the hall. One evening Hennie's would host a recital for some church diva from a local choir; later that same night there might be a high-stakes poker game for gangsters in from St. Louis. There had been retirement parties for aldermen and numbers runners there. It was an all-purpose room for a select few.

You never went to Hennie's unless you'd been invited. At least I never did. For some people the door was always open. Mouse was one of them.

Marcel John stood at the downstairs alley door that led up to Hennie's. Marcel was a big man with a heavyweight's physique and an old woman's face. He had a countenance of sad kindliness but I knew that he'd killed half a dozen men for money before coming to work for Hennie. He wore an old-fashioned brown woolen suit with a gold watch chain in evidence. A purple flower drooped in his lapel.

"Marcel," I said in greeting.

He raised his head in a half-inch salutation, watching me with those watery grandmother eyes.

"Lookin' for Mouse," I said.

I'd said those words so many times in my forty-six years that they might have been an incantation.

"Not here."

"He needs to be found."

Marcel's wide nostrils flared even further as he tried to get the scent of my purpose. He took in a deep breath and then nodded. I walked past him into the narrow stairway that went upward without a turn, to the third-floor entrance on the other side of the building.

When I neared the top the ebony wood door swung open and Bob the Baptist came out to meet me.

Bob the Baptist's skin was toasted gold. His features were neither Caucasian nor Negroid. Maybe his grandmother had been an Eskimo or a Hindu deity. Bob was always grinning. And I knew that if he hadn't gotten the signal from Marcel he would have been ready to shoot me in the forehead.

"Easy," Bob said. "What's your business, brother?"

"Lookin' for Mouse."

"Not here." Bob, who was wearing loose white trousers and a blue box-cut shirt, twisted his perfect lips to add, *Oh well, see you later.*

"He needs finding," I said, knowing that even the self-important employees of Hennie's wouldn't want to cross Raymond Alexander.

He had to let me in but he didn't have to like it.

"You armed?" he asked, the godlike grin wan on his lips.

"Yes I am," I said.

He sniffed, considering if I was a threat, decided I was not, and moved aside.

Hennie's was mostly one big room that took up nearly the entire floor. It was empty that day. As I walked from Bob's post to the other side my footfalls echoed, announcing my approach.

Hennie was sitting at a small round table against the far wall. There was a brandy snifter in front of him, also the *Los Angeles Examiner,* opened to the sports page. He had a half-smoked cigar smoldering in a cut crystal ashtray.

He was a dapper soul, wearing a dark blue suit, an off-white satin shirt, and a red tie held down by a pearl tack. The shirt was so bright that it seemed to flare from his breast. His hair was close-cropped and his skin was black as an undertaker's shoes.

"I'm readin' the paper," he said, not inviting me to sit. He didn't even look up to meet my eye.

"You see Mouse in there?" I took out my pack of Parliaments and produced a cigarette, which I proceeded to light.

"Raymond didn't leave me any messages for you, Easy Rawlins."

"The message is for him," I said.

He finally looked up.

"What is it?" Hennie's eyes had no sparkle to them whatsoever, giving the impression that he had seen such bad times that all of his hope had died.

"It's for Mouse," I said.

Hennie stared at me for a few seconds and then called out, "Melba!"

"Yes, Daddy," a high-toned woman's voice called back.

She came into a doorway about ten feet away.

"Bring me the phone."

"Yes, Daddy."

Melba belonged with that crew. Her skin was the color of a reddish-brown plantain. Her breasts were small but her butt was quite large. She balanced precariously on high heels that were on their way to becoming stilts. The black dress was midthigh and she walked with a circular movement which made even that pedestrian activity seem like dancing.

She brought a black phone on an extremely long cord. If she'd wanted to she could have dragged it all the way to Bob the Baptist's chair.

She offered the phone to Hennie.

He declined, saying, "Dial Raymond."

She did so, though she seemed to have some difficulty maintaining her balance and dialing at the same time.

The moments lagged by.

"Mr. Alexander?" she asked in her child's voice. "Hold on, I got Daddy on the line."

She handed the receiver to Hennie. He took it while staring at my forehead.

"Raymond? . . . I got Easy Rawlins here sayin' that you need findin'. . . . Uh-huh . . . uh-huh. . . . You got that thing covered for Julius? . . . All right then. Talk to you."

He handed the receiver back to Melba and she sashayed away.

"You know the funeral parlor down on Denker?" Hennie asked me.

"Powell's?"

"Yeah. There's a red house next door that got a garage behind it. Raymond's in the apartment above that."

"Thank you," I said taking in a deep draft of smoke.

"And don't come here no more if I don't ask ya," he added.

"So you sayin' that if I'm lookin' for Raymond don't ask you?" I asked innocently.

And Hennie winced. I liked that. I liked it a lot.

I DROVE from Hennie's to Powell's funeral parlor. I marched down the driveway to the garage next door. But there I stopped. The door was ajar and those stairs were daring me to come on. It was twilight and the world around me was slowly blending into gray. Going to Mouse over this problem would, I knew, create problems of its own. With no exaggeration Mouse was one of the most dangerous individuals on the face of the earth.

And so I stopped to consider.

But I didn't have a choice.

Still, I took the stairs one at a time.

The apartment door was also partly open. That was a bad sign.

I heard women's voices inside. They were laughing and cooing.

"Raymond?" I said.

"Come on in, Easy."

The sitting room was the size of a tourist-class cabin on an ocean liner. The only place to sit comfortably was a plush red couch. Mouse had the middle cushion and two large, shapely women took up the sides.

"Well, well, well. There you are at last. Where you been?"

"Gettin' into trouble," I said.

Mouse grinned.

"This is Georgette," he said, waving a hand at the woman on his right. "Georgette, this Easy Rawlins."

She stood up and stuck out her hand.

"Hi, Easy. Pleased to meet you."

She was tall for a woman, five eight or so, the color of tree bark. She hadn't made twenty-five, which was why the weight she carried seemed to defy the pull of gravity. For all her size her waist was slender, but that wasn't her most arresting feature. Georgette gave off the most amazing odor. It was like the smell of a whole acre of tomato plants — earthy and pungent. I took the hand and raised it to my lips so that I could get my nose up next to her skin.

She giggled and I remembered that I was single.

"And this here is Pinky," Mouse said.

Pinky's body was similar to her friend's but she was lighter skinned. She didn't stand up but only waved her hand and gave me a half smile.

I hunkered down on the coffee table that sat before the couch.

"How you all doin'?" I asked.

"We ready to party tonight — right, girls?" Mouse said.

They both laughed. Pinky leaned over and gave Raymond a deep soul kiss. Georgette smiled at me and moved her butt around on the cushion.

"What you up to, Easy?" Mouse asked.

He planned to have a party with just him and the two women. At any other time I would have given some excuse and beaten a hasty retreat. But I didn't have the time to waste. And I knew that I had to explain to Mouse why I didn't go on the heist with him before I could ask for help.

"I need to talk to you, Ray," I said, expecting him to tell me I had to wait till tomorrow.

"Okay," he said. "Girls, we should have some good liquor for this party. Why'ont you two go to Victory Liquors over on Santa Barbara and get us some champagne?"

He reached into his pocket and came out with two hundred-dollar bills.

"Why we gotta go way ovah there?" Pinky complained. "There's a package sto' right down the street."

"C'mon, Pinky," Georgette said as she rose again. "These men gotta do some business before we party."

When she walked past me Georgette held her hand out — palm upward. I kissed that palm as if it were my mother's hand reaching out to me from long ago. She shuddered. I did too.

Mouse had killed men for lesser offenses but I was in the frame of mind where danger was a foregone conclusion.

After the women were gone I turned to Raymond.

He was smiling at me.

"You dog," he said.

29

S orry 'bout the job, Ray."

   I moved over to the couch. He slid to the side to give me room.

"That's okay, Ease. I knew it wasn't your thing. But you wanted money an' that Chicago syndicate's been my cash cow."

"Did I cause you a problem with them?"

"They ain't gonna fuck wit' me," Mouse said with a sneer.

He sat back and blew a cloud of smoke at the ceiling. He wore a burgundy satin shirt and yellow trousers.

"What's wrong then?" I asked.

"What you mean?"

"I don't know. Why you send those girls off?"

"I was tired anyway. You wanna get outta here?"

"What about Pinky and Georgette?"

"I'ont know. Shit . . . all they wanna do is laugh an' drink up my liquor."

"An' you wanna talk?"

"I ain't got nuthin' t' laugh about."

Living my life I've come to realize that everybody has different jobs to do. There's your wage job, your responsibility to your children, your sexual urges, and then there are the special duties that every man and woman takes on. Some people are artists or have political interests, some are obsessed with collecting seashells or pictures of movie stars. One of my special duties was to keep Raymond Alexander from falling into a dark humor. Because whenever he lost interest in having a good time someone, somewhere, was likely to die. And even though I had pressing business of my own, I asked a question.

"What's goin' on, Ray?"

"You have dreams, Easy?"

I laughed partly because of the dreams I did have and partly to put him at ease.

"Sure I do. Matter'a fact dreams been kickin' my butt this last week."

"Yeah? Me too." He shook his head and reached for a fifth of scotch that sat at the side of the red sofa.

"What kinda dreams?"

"I was glass," he said after taking a deep draft.

He looked up at me. I would have thought that wide-eyed vulnerability was fear in another man's face.

"Glass?"

"Yeah. People would walk past me an' look back because they saw sumpin' but they didn't know what it was. An' then, then I bumped inta this wall an' my arm broke off."

"Broke off?" I said as a parishioner might repeat a minister's phrase — for emphasis.

"Yeah. Broke right off. I tried to catch it but my other hand was glass too an' slippery. The broke arm fell to the ground an' shattered in a million pieces. An' the people was just walkin' by not even seein' me."

"Damn," I said.

I was amazed not by the content but by the sophistication of Mouse's dream. I had always thought of the diminutive killer as a brute who was free from complex thoughts or imagination. Here we'd known each other since our teens and I was just now seeing a whole other side of him.

"Yeah," Mouse warbled. "I took a step an' my foot broke off. I fell to the ground an' broke all to pieces. An' the people jes' walked on me breakin' me down inta sand."

"That's sumpin' else, man," I said just to keep him in the conversation.

"That ain't all," he declared. "Then, when I was crushed inta dust the wind come an' all I am is dust blowin' in the air. I'm everywhere. I see everything. You'n Etta's married an' LaMarque is callin' you Daddy. People is wearin' my jewelry an' drivin' my car. An' I'm still there but cain't nobody see me or hear me. Ain't nobody care."

In a moment of sudden intuition I realized then the logic behind Etta's periodic banishment of Mouse. She knew how much he needed her, but he was unaware, and so she'd send him away to have these dreams and then, when he came back again, he'd be pleasant and appreciative of her worth — never knowing exactly why.

"You know, Easy," he said. "I been wit' two women every night since I walked out on Etta. An' I can still go all night long. Got them girls callin' in languages they didn't know they could talk. But even if I sleep on a bed full'a women I still have them dreams."

"Maybe you should give Etta another chance," I suggested. "I know she misses you."

"She do?" he asked me with all of the innocence of the child he never was.

"Yes sir," I said. "I saw her just today."

"Well," Mouse said then. "Maybe I'll make her wait a couple'a days an' then give her a break."

I doubted if Mouse connected the dream with Etta even though she came into the conversation so easily. But I could see that he was getting better by the moment. The prospect of a homecoming lifted his dark mood.

For a while he regaled me with stories of his sexual prowess. I didn't mind. Mouse knew how to tell a story and I had to wait to ask for my favor.

Half an hour later the door downstairs banged against the wall and the loud women started their raucous climb up the stairs.

"I better be goin', Ray," I said. "But I need your help in the mornin'."

I stood up.

"Stay, Easy," he said. "Georgette likes you an' Pinky gets all jealous when she got to share. Stay, brothah. An' then in the mornin' we take care'a this trouble you in."

Before I could say no the women came in the door.

"Hi, Ray," Pinky said. She had two champagne bottles under each arm. "We got a bottle for everybody."

Georgette lit up when she saw that I was still there. She perched on the table in front of me and put her hands on my knees.

Raymond smiled and I shook my head.

"I got to be goin'," I said.

BUT THE EVENING wore on and I was still there. I had nowhere to go. Mouse popped three corks and the ladies laughed. He was a great storyteller. And I rarely heard him tell the same story twice.

After midnight Pinky started kissing Ray in earnest. Georgette and I were on the couch with them, sitting very close. We were talking to each other, whispering really, when Georgette looked over and gave a little gasp.

I turned and saw that Pinky had worked Ray's erection out of his pants and was pulling on it vigorously. He was leaning back with closed eyes and a big smile on his lips.

"Let's go in the other room and give 'em some privacy," Georgette whispered in my ear.

The bedroom was small too, only large enough to accommodate a king-size bed and a single stack of maple drawers.

I closed the door and when I turned to face Georgette she kissed me. It was as passionate an embrace as I had ever known. Our tongues were speaking to each other. Hers telling me that I had her full attention and everything within her power to give. And mine telling her that I was desperately in need of someone to give me life and hope.

I put my hand under her coral blouse and laid the hot palm at the base of her neck. She groaned and so did Pinky in the next room.

Georgette reached for the lamp and turned it off.

"Turn it back on," I said.

She did.

I sat on the bed and stood her between my knees. Then I

started on the buttons of her blouse. She stood still, breathing lightly as I drew the silky top down and dropped it to the floor. She moved then, attempting to sit next to me, but I grabbed onto her forearms, making it clear that she was to stay where she was. I moved close to get my arms around to unhook the black bra she wore.

Her nipples were long, hard things. I licked them very lightly and she held my head, moving it the way she wanted my tongue to move.

The black miniskirt was tight around her butt, and taking it off while kissing her hard nipples I pulled the pink panties down too. Her pubic hair was broad and dense. I buried my face in it to get the full scent of that field of tomatoes. If I had any notion of stopping, it evaporated then.

Georgette was a large woman. And even though she was slim of waist her belly protruded a bit. Her navel was a deep hole, dark against even her dark skin. Tentatively I poked my tongue inside.

She gasped and jumped back, holding both hands in front of her stomach.

"Come back here," I said.

Georgette shook her head with a pleading look on her face.

Pinky started yelping in the next room.

"Come back here," I said again.

"It's too sensitive," she said.

I held out a hand and she allowed me to draw her near. I positioned her between my knees again and moved slowly toward the belly button.

This time I stuck my tongue all the way in so I could feel the rough skin at the bottom. I moved the tip of my tongue around and she shuddered, holding my head for support.

After a few seconds she cried, "Stop!"

I moved my head back and looked up into her eyes.

"This is like food to me, Georgette," I said. "Do you understand? Food for me."

She replied by pressing my face against her stomach. My tongue lanced out again and she screamed.

After another minute she moved my face back.

"Can I lay down now, baby?" she asked.

I moved to the side and she got down on her back.

We did things that night that I had never done with any woman. She did things to me that even now make me tremble with fervor and humiliation.

We fell asleep in each other's arms, still kissing, still rubbing.

But when I jolted awake, I found myself alone.

I stumbled to the toilet and then back into the living room. Mouse was laid out naked on the couch with his hands crossed over his chest like a dead king on display for the public to mourn. Pinky was gone.

30

Sensing me, Mouse roused from his slumber. He opened his eyes and frowned. Then he sat up and moved his head in a circle. His neck bones cracked loudly.

"Mornin', Easy."

"Ray."

"The girls gone?"

"I guess so."

"Good. Now we can take care'a business an' not have to mess with them."

He stood up and stomped into the bedroom toward the toilet.

I sat down and fell asleep in that position.

The flush of the toilet jolted me awake.

When Raymond came back in he'd put on black slacks and a black T-shirt — his work clothes.

"Place ain't got no kitchen," he said. "If you want coffee we gotta go to Jelly's down the street."

"What time they open?" I asked.

"What time you got?"

"Twenty past five."

"Let's go."

WE WALKED the few blocks down Denker. The sun was a crimson promise behind the San Bernardino Mountains.

"What you got, Easy?" Mouse asked when we were halfway to the doughnut shop.

"Man up in Frisco hired me to find a black girl named Cinnamon. I went to her boyfriend's house and found him dead —"

"Damn," Mouse said. "Dead?"

"Yeah. Then I came back down to L.A. I found the girl but she told me about a dude in a snakeskin jacket she thinks killed him. That day a man in a snakeskin jacket come around askin' at my house for me."

"He find Bonnie an' the kids?"

"She and Feather are in Switzerland and Jesus is out on his boat." I decided not to mention that Ray's ex-girlfriend was with my son.

"Good."

"So the guy shows up at my office. Says his name is Joe Cicero. He's a stone killer, I could see it in his eyes. He threatened my family."

"You fight him?"

"I took out the gun you gave me and he left."

"Why'idn't you shoot him?"

"There was other people around. I didn't think they'd lie for me."

Mouse shrugged at my excuse, neither agreeing nor disagreeing with the logic I offered. We'd arrived at the doughnut place. He pushed the glass door open and I followed him in.

Jelly's seating arrangement was a long counter in front of which stood a dozen stools anchored in a concrete shelf. Behind the counter were eight long slanted shelves lit by fluorescent lights. These shelves were crowded with every kind of doughnut.

A brown woman stood at the edge of the counter smoking a cigarette and staring off into space.

"Millie," Mouse said in greeting.

"Mr. Alexander," she replied.

"Coffee for me an' my friend." He took a seat nearest the door and I sat next to him. "What you eatin', Ease?"

"I'll take lemon filled."

"Two lemon an' two buttermilk," Mouse said to Millie.

She was already pouring our coffees into large paper cups.

I needed the caffeine. The way I figured it Georgette and I hadn't gotten to sleep until past three.

Our doughnuts came. We fired up cigarettes and drank coffee. Millie refilled our cups and then moved to the far end of the counter. I could tell that she was used to giving my friend his privacy.

"Thanks for talkin' to me last night, Easy," Mouse said.

"Sure." I wasn't used to gratitude from him.

"How you spell that guy's name?"

"The Roman is C-I-C-E-R-O but he didn't spell it for me."

"I'ma use a pay phone in back to ask around," he said. "Sit tight."

"Early to be callin' people isn't it?"

"Early for a man workin' for somebody else. But a self-employed man gotta get up when the cock crow." With that he walked toward the back of the shop and through a green doorway.

I sat there smoking and thinking about Joe Cicero. It didn't really make sense that he worked for Lee, because why would Lee fire me and then put a man on my tail? But there seemed to be a divide between Lee and his assistant. Maybe she had put Cicero on me. But again, why not just let me work for Lee and bring them what information I got? She was my only contact with the man.

A cool breeze blew on my back. I turned to see an older black man come in. His clothes were rumpled as if he had slept in them and he gave off an odor of dust as he went past. He sat two seats down from me and gestured to Millie (who never smiled) and murmured his order.

I put out my cigarette and thought about Haffernon. Maybe he hired Cicero. That could be. He was a powerful man. Then there was Philomena. But she had said that she was afraid of the snakeskin killer. That made me grin. The day I started believing what people told me would probably be the day I died.

The man next to me said something to the waitress. *Nice day,* I think.

And didn't Philomena say something about a cousin? And of course there was Saul. Maybe he knew more than he was letting on. Maybe he stumbled across something and was trying to get around me. No. Not Saul. At least not yet.

"They havin' a festival down Watts," I overheard the man saying to Millie. She didn't answer or maybe she whispered a reply or nodded.

Of course anyone who was involved in the business deal in Egypt might have hired Cicero. Anyone interested in those bearer bonds.

"So you too lofty to talk to me, huh?" the man was saying to Millie.

His anger caught my attention and so I glanced in his direction. Millie was at the far end of the counter and the rumpled man was staring at me.

"Excuse me?" I said.

"You too lofty to speak?" he asked.

"I didn't know you were talkin' to me, man," I said. "I thought you were speaking to the woman."

"Yeah," he said, not really replying, "I gots all kindsa time at sea with men from every station. Just 'cause my clothes is old don't mean I'm dirt."

"I didn't mean to say that . . . I was just thinkin'."

"In the merchant marines I seen it all," he said. "War, mutiny, an' so much money you choke a fuckin' elephant wit' it. I got chirren all over the world. In Guinea and New Zealand. I got a wife in Norway so china white an' beautiful she'd make you cry."

My mind was primed to wonder. I just moved it over to think about this man and all of his children and all of his women.

"Easy Rawlins," I said. I held out my hand.

"Briny Thomas." He took my hand and held on to it while peering into my eyes. "But you know the most important thing I ever learned in all my travels?"

"What's that?"

"The only law that matters is yo' own troof. You stick to what you think is right and when the day is done you will be satisfied."

Mouse was coming out from the green doorway.

I pulled my hand away from Briny.

Raymond stopped between us.

"Move on down the row, man," he said to the merchant marine. "Go on."

The old man had a good sense of character. He didn't even think twice, just picked up his coffee and moved four seats down.

"You should'a kilt that mothahfuckah, Easy. You should'a kilt him."

"Cicero?"

"My people tell me he's a bad man — a very bad man. Called him a assassin. Did work for the government, they said, an' then went out on his own."

Mouse had been frowning while telling me about Cicero but then, suddenly, he smiled.

"This gonna be goooood. Man like that let you know what you made of."

"Flesh and blood," I said.

"That ain't good enough, brother. You need some iron an' gunpowder an' maybe a little luck to get ya past a mothahfuckah like this here."

Raymond was happy. The challenge of Joe Cicero made him feel alive. And I have to say that I wasn't too worried either. It's not that I took a government-trained assassin lightly. But I had other work to do and my survival wasn't the most important thing on the list. If I died saving Feather then it was a good trade. So I smiled along with my friend.

Over his shoulder I saw Briny lift his coffee in a toast.

This gesture also gave me confidence.

31

After six cups of coffee, four doughnuts apiece, and half a pack of cigarettes, we made our way back to Mouse's pied-à-terre. He took the bedroom this time and I stretched out on the couch. That was a little shy of seven.

I didn't get up again until almost eleven.

It was a great sleep. To begin with there was no light in the cabinlike living room, and the couch was both soft and firm, filled as it was with foam rubber. No one knew where I was and I had Mouse to ride with me when I finally had to go out in the world. I had to believe that Feather's doctors would keep her alive and Bonnie didn't enter my thoughts at all. It's not that I was over her, but there's only so much turmoil that a heart can keep focused on.

Bonnie was a problem that had to come later.

While I was getting dressed I heard the toilet flush. Mouse

slept more lightly than a pride of lions. He once told me that he could hear a leaf thinking about falling from a tree.

He came out wearing a blue dress shirt under a herringbone jacket. His slacks were black. I went through to the restroom. There I shaved and washed the stink from my body with a washrag because Mouse's hideaway didn't have a shower or a tub.

At the door, on the way out, he asked me, "You armed?"

"I got a thirty-eight in my pocket, a Luger in my belt, and that twenty-five you gave me in the band of my sock."

He gave me an approving nod and led the way down the stairs.

IN 1966, L.A.'s downtown was mostly brick and mortar, plaster and stone. There were a few new towers of steel and glass but mostly squat red and brown buildings made up the business community.

I needed to gather some financial information and the best way to do that, I knew, was at the foot of the cowardly genius — Jackson Blue.

Jackson had left his job at Tyler after going out on a maintenance call to Proxy Nine Insurance Group, a consortium of international bank insurers. Jackson had come in to fix their computer's card reader and then (almost as an afterthought, to hear him tell it) he revamped the way they conducted their daily business. Their president, Federico Bignardi, was so impressed that he offered to double Jackson's salary and put him in charge of their new data processing department.

I drove down to about a block from Jackson's office and went to a phone booth. I was looking up the number in the white pages while Mouse leaned up against the door.

"Easy," he said in warning.

I looked up in time to see the police car rolling up to the curb.

I had found Jackson's company's number but I only had one coin. I didn't drop the dime, reasoning that I might have to make the call later on, from jail.

The other reason I held back was because I had to pay very close attention to events as they unfolded. There was always the potential for gunplay when you mixed Raymond Alexander and the police in the same bowl. He saw them as his enemy. They saw him as their enemy. And neither side would hesitate to take the other one down.

As the two six-foot white cops (who might have been brothers) stalked up to us, each with a hand on the butt of his pistol, I couldn't help but think about the cold war going on inside the borders of the United States. The police were on one side and Raymond and his breed were on the other.

I came out of the phone booth with my hands in clear sight. Raymond grinned.

"Good morning," one of the white men said. To my eyes only his mustache distinguished him from his partner.

"Officer," Mouse allowed.

"What are you doing here?"

"Calling a Mr. Blue," I said.

"Mr. Blue?" the policeman countered.

"He's a friend'a ours," I replied to his partial question. "He's a computer expert but we're here to ask him about bearer bonds."

"Bonds?" the cop with the hairless lip said.

"Yeah," Mouse said. "Bonds."

The way he said the word made me think of chains, not monetary instruments.

"And what do you need to know about bonds for?" one of the cops, I can't remember which one, asked.

My job was to make those cops feel that Raymond and I had a legitimate reason to be there at that phone booth on that street corner. Most Americans wouldn't understand why two well-dressed men would have to explain why they were standing on a public street. But most Americans cannot comprehend the scrutiny that black people have been under since the days we were dragged here in bondage. Those two cops felt fully authorized to stop us with no reason and no warrant. They felt that they could question us and search us and cart us off to jail if there was the slightest flaw in how we explained our business.

Even with all the urgency I felt at that moment I had a small space to hate what those policemen represented in my life.

But I could hate as much as I wanted: I still didn't have the luxury to defy their authority.

"I'm a private detective, Officer," I said. "Working for a man named Saul Lynx. He's got an office on La Brea."

"Detective?" No Mustache said. He was a king of the one-word question.

I took the license from my shirt pocket. Seeing this state-issue authorization so disconcerted them that they went back to their car to natter on their two-way radio.

"Bonds?" Mouse asked.

"Yeah. The man I told you about had gotten some Swiss bonds. Maybe it was Nazi money. I don't know."

"How much money?" he asked.

Why hadn't I asked that question of Cinnamon? The only answer that came to me was Cinnamon's kiss.

The cops came back and handed me my license.

"Checks out," one of them said.

"So may we continue?" I asked.

"Who are you investigating?"

"It's a private investigation. I can't talk about it."

And even though I don't remember which cop I was talking to, I do remember his eyes. There was hatred in them. Real hate. It's a continual revelation when you come to understand that the only thing you can expect in return for your own dignity is hatred in the eyes of others.

"BLUE," Jackson answered when the Proxy Nine operator transferred my call.

"I'm down here with Mouse, Jackson," I said. "We need to talk."

I could feel his hesitation in the silence on the line. That was often the way with poor people who had finally crawled out of hardship and privation. The only thing one of your old friends could do would be to pull you back down or bleed you dry. If it was anybody but me he would have made up some excuse. But Jackson was too deeply indebted to me for even his ungrateful nature to turn a deaf ear to my call.

"McGuire's Steak House down on Grant," he said in clipped words. "Meet you there at one-fifteen."

It was twelve fifty-five. Raymond and I walked to McGuire's at a leisurely pace. He was in a good mood, looking forward to getting back with Etta.

"You don't mind that white boy stayin' there while you gone?" I asked near the time of our meeting.

"Naw, man. I look at him like he the pet Etta never had. You know — a white dog."

There was something very ugly in the words and the way he said them. But ugly was the life we lived.

* * *

THE MAÎTRE D' frowned when we entered the second-floor restaurant but he changed his attitude when I mentioned Jackson Blue.

"Oh, Mr. Blue," he said in a slight French accent. "Yes, he is waiting for you."

With a snap of his fingers he caught the attention of a lovely young white woman wearing a black miniskirt and T-shirt top.

"These are Mr. Blue's guests," he said and she smiled at us like we were distant cousins that she was meeting for the first time.

The door she led us to opened on a private dining room dominated by a round table that could seat eight people comfortably.

Jackson stood up nervously when we walked in. He wore an elegant gray suit and sported the prescriptionless glasses that he claimed made him seem less threatening to white folks.

I didn't see how anyone could be intimidated by Jackson in the first place. He was short and thin with almost jet skin. His mouth was always ready to grin and he'd jump at the sound of a door slamming. But from the moment he put on those glasses white people all over L.A. started offering him jobs. I often thought that when he donned those frames he became another mild-mannered person. But what did I know?

"Jackson," Mouse hailed.

Jackson forced a grin and shook the killer's hand.

"Mouse, Easy, how you boys doin'?"

"Hungry as a mothahfuckah," Mouse said.

"I ordered already," Jackson told him. "Porterhouse steaks and Beaujolais wine."

"All right, boy. Shit, that bank treatin' you fine."

"Insurance company," Jackson corrected.

"They insure banks, right?" Mouse asked.

"Yeah. So, Easy, what's up?"

"Can I sit down first, Jackson?"

"Oh yeah, yeah, yeah, yeah. Sit, sit, sit."

The room was round too, with pastoral paintings on the wall. Real oil paintings and a vase with silk roses on a podium next to the door.

"How's life treatin' you, Jackson?"

"All right, I guess."

"Seems better than that. This is a fine place and they know your name at the door."

"Yeah . . . I guess."

I realized then that Jackson had been holding in tension. His face let go and there were traces of grief around his eyes and mouth.

"What's wrong, man?" I asked.

"Nuthin'."

"Is it Jewelle?"

"Naw, she fine. She managin' a motel down in Malibu."

"So what is it?"

"Nuthin'."

"Come on, Jackson," Mouse said then. "Easy an' me got serious business, so get on wit' it here. You look like the doctor just give you six months."

For a moment I thought the bespectacled genius was going to break down and cry.

"Well," he said, "if you have to know, it's a computer tape."

"You messed it up or somethin'?"

"Naw. I mean it's messed up all right. It's the TXT tape they drop on my desk ev'ry mornin' at three twenty-five."

"What's a TXT tape?" I asked.

"Transaction transmissions from all around the world . . . financial transactions."

"What about it?"

"Proxy got a hunnert banks for clients in the United States alone an' twice that in European banks. They transfer stock investments for special customers for less than a broker do."

"So what?" I asked.

"It's anywhere from three hunnert thousand to four million dollars in transactions every day."

That got a long whistle from Mouse.

Jackson began to sweat.

"Yeah," Jackson said. "Every time I look at that thing my heart starts to thunderin'. It's like if some fine-assed girl took off her clothes and jump in yo' bed an' then say, 'I know you won't take advantage'a me, now will you?'"

Mouse laughed. I did too.

"Listen, Jackson," I said. "I need to know about Swiss bearer bonds."

"What kind?"

I told him all that I learned from Cinnamon.

"Yeah," he said in a way that I knew he was still thinking about that tape. "Yeah, if you bring me one I should be able to work up a pedigree. The people I work with use bonds like that all the time. I got access to everything they do. If a bearer bond got a special origin I could prob'ly sniff it out."

Our steaks came soon after that. Mouse ate like two men. Jackson didn't even touch his food. After the meal was over Jackson took the check. I had known him nearly thirty years and that was the first time he ever willingly paid for a meal.

We made small talk for a while. Mouse caught Jackson up on what our mutual friends were doing. Who was up, who was dead. After forty-five minutes or so Jackson looked at his watch and said that he had to get back to work.

At the door Mouse took him by the arm.

"You like that little girl Jewelle?" he asked.

"Love her," Jackson said.

"How 'bout yo' car an' clothes an' this here job?"

"Great. I never been so happy. Shit, I do stuff most people don't even know that they don't know about."

"Then why you so hot and bothered over a few dollars on a tape? Fuck that tape, man. That money ain't gonna suck yo' dick. Shit, if you happy then keep on doin' what you doin' an' don't let the niggah in you run riot."

Raymond's words transformed Jackson as he heard them. He gave a little nod and the hopelessness in his eyes faded a little.

"Yeah, you right," he said. "You right."

"Damn straight," Mouse said. "We ain't dogs, man. We ain't have to sniff after them. Shit. You an' me an' Easy here do things our mamas an' papas never even dreamed they could do."

I appreciated being included in the group but I realized that Mouse and Jackson were living on a higher plane. One was a master criminal and the other just a genius, but both of them saw the world beyond a paycheck and the rent. They were beyond the workaday world. I wondered at what moment they had left me behind.

32

I dropped Mouse off at his apartment on Denker. He told me that he was going to look into Cicero, his habits and friends.

"If you lucky, Ease," he told me, "the mothahfuckah be dead by the time you see me again."

Most other times I would have tried to calm Mouse down. But I had looked into Joe Cicero's eyes deeply enough to know, all other things being equal, that he was the killer and I was the prey.

SAUL LYNX AND DOREEN lived on Vista Loma in View Park at that time. Their kids had a yard to play in and colored neighbors who, on the whole, didn't mind the interracial marriage.

Doreen came to the door with a toddler crying in her arms.

"Hi, Easy," she said.

We had a pretty good relationship. I respected her husband and didn't have any problem with their union.

"Saul call yet, honey?"

"No. I mean . . . he called once but George answered it and he didn't call me. I was hanging clothes on the line out back."

I could see my disappointment register on her face.

"I'm sure that he'll call soon though," she said. "He calls every evening about six."

It was just past three.

"Do you mind if I come back at about five-thirty or so? I really have to talk to Saul."

"Sure, Easy. Can I help you?"

"I don't think so, honey."

"How's it going with Feather?"

"I'll catch you in a couple'a hours," I said. I didn't have the heart to talk about Feather one more time.

WHEN CINNAMON DIDN'T ANSWER my knock I figured that either she was dead or out eating. If she'd been killed, there wouldn't be anything to learn from her body. If she'd had the bonds they'd be gone, and so the only thing I could gain by breaking in would be another possible murder charge. So I decided to sit at a bus stop bench across the street and wait until she returned or it was time for me to go talk to Saul.

While waiting I thought about my plan of action. Survival was the priority. I had to believe that Joe Cicero wanted to kill Cinnamon and anyone else that got in his way. Therefore he had to go — one way or another. The police wouldn't help me. I had no evidence against him. Axel Bowers was dead but I couldn't prove who had killed him. All I could do would be to tell the cops where his body was hidden — and that would point a finger at me.

Money was the next thing on my mind. I needed to pay for Feather. It was then that I remembered Maya Adamant's last call.

There was a phone booth down the street from the Pixie Inn. I called my old friend the long-distance operator and asked for another collect call.

"Lee investigations," Maya answered.

"I have a collect call for anyone from Easy Rawlins. Do you accept the charges?"

"Yes, operator," she said a little nervously.

"How much?" I asked.

"You were supposed to call me yesterday — at my house."

"I'm callin' you now." I wondered if Bobby Lee had his phones bugged too. Maya was probably thinking the same.

"Where are you?"

"Down the street from the apartment where Cinnamon Cargill is staying."

"What's that address?"

"How much?" I asked again.

"Three thousand dollars for the addresses of Cargill and Bowers."

"It's the same address," I said.

"Okay."

I couldn't tell if she knew about Bowers's death so I decided to try another approach.

"Tell me about Joe Cicero," I said.

"What about him?" she asked at about half the volume of her regular voice.

"Did you put him on me?"

"I don't know what you're talking about, Mr. Rawlins. I know the name and the reputation of the man Joe Cicero but I have never had any dealings with him."

"No? Then what was Joe Cicero doin' at my office askin' about Cinnamon Cargill?"

"I have no idea. But you'd be smart to look out for a man like that. He's a killer, Mr. Rawlins. The best thing you could do would be to give Mr. Lee the information he wants, take the money, and then leave town for a while."

I had to smile. Usually when I was working I was the one who did the manipulating of people's fears. But here Maya was trying to maneuver me.

"Thirty thousand dollars," I said.

"What?"

"Thirty grand and I give you everything you want. But it gots to be thirty and it gots to be today. Tomorrow it goes up to thirty-five."

"A dead man has no use for money, Ezekiel."

"You'd be surprised, Maya."

"Why would you think that Mr. Lee would be willing to pay such an outrageous figure?"

"First, I don't think Mr. Lee knows a thing about this conversation. Second, I don't know the exact amount on those bearer bonds —"

"What bearer bonds?"

"Don't try an' mess wit' me, girl. I know about the bonds because I've talked to Philomena. So like I was sayin' . . . I don't know exactly how much they're worth but I'm willing to wager that even after the thirty grand you and Joe Cicero will have enough left over to make me look like a bum."

"I have no business with Cicero," she said.

"But you know about the bonds."

"Call me this evening on my home phone," she said. "Call me then and we'll talk."

* * *

TWENTY MINUTES LATER Cinnamon walked up to her motel door. She was carrying a brown supermarket bag. It made me
like her more to see that she was conserving her money, buying
groceries instead of restaurant meals.

"Miss Cargill," I called from across the street.

She turned and waved to me as if I were an old friend.

She used her key on the lock and walked in, leaving the door
open for me. She was taking a box of chocolate-covered doughnuts from the bag when I came in.

"Have you heard anything about Axel?" were the first words
she said.

"Not yet. I had a visit from your friend in the snakeskin jacket
though."

There was fear in her eyes, no mistaking that. But that didn't
make her innocent, just sensible.

"What did he say?"

"He wanted to know where you were."

"And what did you tell him?"

"I pointed a gun at his eyeball and all he did was shrug. It's a
bad man who's not even afraid of a gun in his face."

"Did you shoot him?" she whispered.

"Somebody else asked me that," I replied. "I sure hope that
you're not like him."

"Did you shoot him?"

"No."

The fear crept over her face like night over a broad plain.

"What are you gonna do, Philomena?"

"What do you mean?"

"Nobody is interested in you. It's those bonds they want, and
that letter."

"I promised Axel that I'd hold them for him."

"Have you been calling him?" I asked.

"Yes. But he's nowhere to be found."

"Does he know how to get in touch with you?"

"Yes. Yes, he has Lena's number."

"What does that tell you, Philomena?" I asked, knowing that her boyfriend was long dead.

"But how can I be sure?"

"Those bonds are like a bull's-eye on you, girl," I said. "You need to use them to deal yourself out of danger."

I didn't feel guilty that getting those bonds might also net me thirty thousand dollars. I was trying to save Philomena's life too. You couldn't put a price tag on that.

"I don't know," she said sadly, hanging her head. She sat down on the bed. "I promised Axel to make sure the world knew about those bonds if he failed."

"What for?"

"Because they were wrong to do that work. Axel felt that it was a blight on him to live knowing that his father dealt with the Nazis."

"But his father's dead and he is too, probably. What good will it do you to join them?"

She clasped her hands together and began rocking back and forth.

Something about this motion made me think about her San Francisco apartment. That reminded me of something else.

"Who do you know in the Westerly Nursing Home?"

She looked up at me. There was no knowledge behind her eyes. She shook her head and stopped rocking.

"You called there from your home phone."

"I didn't. Maybe Axel did. He stayed over sometimes. If he used my phone he'd pay for it later."

I stared into those lovely eyes a moment longer.

"I don't know anyone in a nursing home," she said.

Whether she did or didn't, I couldn't tell. I moved on.

"Listen," I said. "Think about how much those bonds will be worth to you dead. Think it over. Talk with whoever you trust. I'm gonna write a number down on this paper here on the desk."

"What is it?"

"It's the phone number and address of a friend of mine — Primo. He lives in a house down on One-sixteen. Call him, go to him if you're scared. I'll be back later on tonight. But remember, if you want to get on with your life you got to work this thing out."

33

I got to Saul's at a quarter to six. Doreen and I sat in the living room surrounded by their three kids. Their eight-year-old daughter, Miriam, was listening to a pink transistor radio that hung from her neck on a string necklace, also pink. She had brown hair that drooped down in ringlets and green eyes, a gift from her father. George, the five-year-old, had the TV on and he was jumping around on a threadbare patch of carpet, acting out some swashbuckling derring-do. Simon, the toddler, was wandering back and forth between his sister and brother, making sounds that wouldn't be understood for another six months or so.

"So how long will Feather have to be in the clinic?" Doreen asked.

"Might be as long as six months."

"Six months?" Miriam cried. "I could go visit her if she's lonely."

"It's in Switzerland," I explained to the good girl.

"We could go to 'itzerland," George said, bravely swinging his imaginary sword.

"It's way far away in the Valley," Miriam told her brother.

"I know that," George said. "We could still go."

"Can we go, Mom?" Miriam asked Doreen.

"We'll see."

It was then that the phone rang.

"Daddy!" George yelled.

"No, George," Doreen said but the boy leaped for the phone on the coffee table.

Doreen put out her hand and George bounced backward, falling on his backside. As Doreen was saying hello, George began to howl. I saw her mouth Saul's name but I couldn't hear what she was saying because Simon was crying too and Miriam was shouting for them both to be quiet.

Doreen gestured toward the kitchen. I knew they had an extension in there and so I went on through, closing the door behind me.

"Hello!" I yelled. "I got it, Doreen!"

When she hung up the sound of the crying subsided somewhat.

"Easy," Saul said. "What's wrong?"

"I got a visit from a guy yesterday," I said. "He knew that I was working on the Lee case. He told me to give him what I knew or he'd kill me and my family too."

"What was this guy's name?"

"Cicero."

"Joe Cicero?"

"You know him?"

"Don't go home, Easy. Don't go to your office or your job. Call this number." He gave me an area code and a number, which I wrote down on a notepad decorated with pink bunnies. "I'll be there as soon as I can. Put my wife back on the line."

When I went back into the TV room the children had quieted down.

"Saul wants to talk to you, Doreen," I said and she took up the phone.

"Daddy!" George cried.

"Dada," Simon echoed.

Miriam watched her mother's eyes. So did I.

We both saw Mrs. Lynx's expression change from attentive interest to fear. Instead of answering she kept nodding her head. She reached for her pocketbook on the coffee table.

"I wanna talk to Daddy," George complained.

Doreen gave him one stern look and he shut right up.

"Okay," Doreen said. "All right. I will. Be careful, Saul."

She hung up the phone and stood in one fluid movement.

"Holiday time," she said in a forced happy voice. "We're all going to Nana's cabin in Mammoth."

"Yah," George cried.

Simon laughed but Miriam had a grim look on her face. She was getting older and understood that something was wrong.

"Saul said that he'd be at the meeting place by nine tonight," Doreen told me. "He's in San Diego but he said that he'd drive straight there."

"What meeting place? He just gave me a number."

"Call it and they will tell you where to go."

"Is Daddy okay, Mommy?" Miriam asked.

"He's fine, sweetie. Tonight he's going to meet with Mr. Rawlins and then he's coming up to the cabin where we can go fishing and swimming."

"But I have my clarinet lesson tomorrow," Miriam said.

"You'll have to take a makeup," Doreen explained.

The two boys were capering around, celebrating the holiday that had befallen their family.

I LEFT DOREEN packing suitcases and keeping the children on track.

On the way down to the Pixie Inn I tried not to get too far ahead of myself. Saul's reaction to just a name increased my fears. I decided that Cinnamon had to be moved to a place where I knew that she'd be safe.

I parked down the block this time, just being cautious. There was a Mercedes-Benz parked on the motel lot. I didn't like that. I liked it even less when I saw the words *Fletcher's Mercedes-Benz of San Francisco* written on the license plate frame.

The door of Cinnamon's room was ajar. I nudged it open with my toe.

He was lying facedown, the six-hundred-dollar suit now just a shroud. I turned him over with my foot. Leonard Haffernon, Esquire, was quite dead. The bullet had entered somewhere at the base of the skull and exited through the top of his head.

The exit wound was the size of a silver dollar.

A wave of prickles went down my left arm. Sweat sprouted from my palms.

His valise was on the bed. Its contents had been turned out. There was some change and a toenail clipper, a visitor's pass to a San Francisco bank, and a silver flask. Any papers had been taken. The only potential perpetrator in evidence, once more, was me.

For a brief moment I was frozen there like a bug in a sudden frost. I was trying to glean from Haffernon's face what had occurred. Did Cinnamon kill him and run?

Probably.

But why? And why had he been there?

A horn honked out on the street. That brought me back to my senses. I walked out of that room and into the parking lot, then down the street to my loud car and drove away.

34

I drove for fifteen minutes, looking in the rearview mirror every ten seconds, before stopping at a gas station on a block of otherwise burned-out buildings. There was a phone booth next to the men's toilet at the back.

"Etta, is that you?" I asked when she answered on the ninth ring.

"Is it my number you dialed?"

"Have you heard from Raymond?"

"And how are you this evenin', Mr. Rawlins? I'm fine. I was layin' up in the bed watchin' *Doctor Kildare*. How 'bout you?"

"I just stumbled on a dead white man never saw it comin'."

"Oh," Etta said. "No, Ray haven't called."

"Shit."

"Primo did though."

"When?"

"'Bout a hour. He said to tell you that a guy came by an' left sumpin' for ya."

"What guy?"

"He didn't say."

"What did he leave?"

"He didn't say that either. He just said to tell you. You in trouble, Easy?"

"Is the sky blue?"

"Not right now. It's evenin'."

"Then wait a bit. It'll be there."

Etta chuckled and so did I. She was no stranger to violent death. She'd once shot a white man, a killer, in the head because he was about to shoot me. If we couldn't laugh in the face of death there'd be precious little humor for most black southerners.

"You take care, Easy."

"Tell Mouse I need his advice."

"When I see him."

I SPED OVER to Primo's place worried about having given his number to Philomena. Primo was a tough man, a Mexican by birth. He had spent his whole life traveling back and forth across the border and south of there. On one trip through Panama he'd met Flower, his wife. They lived in a house I owned and had more than a dozen kids. They took in stray children too, and animals of all kinds. Any grief I brought to them would cause pain for a thousand miles.

But Primo was sitting out in the large yard. He was laid back in a lawn chair, drinking a beer and watching six or seven grandchildren play in the diminishing light. Flower was up on the porch with a baby in her arms. I wondered if it was her baby or just a grandchild.

As I approached, half a dozen dogs ran at me growling and crying, wagging their tails and baring their fangs.

"Hi-ya!" Primo shouted at the animals.

The children ran forward, grabbing the dogs and pulling them back. A pure-bred Dalmatian eluded his child handler and jumped on me, pressing my chest with his forepaws.

"That's my guard dog," Primo said.

He put out a hand, which I shook as the dog licked my forearm.

"Love thy neighbor," I said.

Primo liked my sense of humor. He laughed out loud.

"Flower," he called. "Your boyfriend is here."

"Send him to my bedroom when you finish twisting his ears," she responded.

"I wish I had time to sit, man," I said.

"But you want them papers." Primo finished my sentence.

"Papers?"

All the children, dogs, and adults crowded through the front door and into the house. There was shouting and laughing and fur floating in the air.

While Primo went into the back room looking for my delivery, Flower came very close to me. She stared in my face without saying anything.

She was a very black, beautiful woman. Her features were stern, almost masculine, most of the time, but when she smiled she honored the name her father had blessed her with.

At that moment she had on her serious face.

"How is she, Easy?"

"Very sick," I said. "Very sick."

"She will live," Flower told me. "She will live and you will have a beautiful granddaughter from her."

I touched Flower's face and she took my hand in hers.

The dogs stopped barking and the children hushed. I looked up and saw Primo standing there, smiling at me.

"Here it is," he said, handing me a brown envelope large enough to contain unfolded pages of typing paper.

"Who left this?"

"A black boy. Funny, you know?"

Raphael.

"What did he say?"

"That this was what you wanted and he hopes you do what's right."

I stood there thinking with all the brown children and red-tongued dogs panting around me.

"Stay and eat," Flower said.

"I got to go."

"No. You are hungry. Sit. It will only take a few moments and then you will have the strength to do whatever it is you're doing."

THAT WAS A TOUGH PERIOD in my life. There's no doubt about it. I was on the run in my own city, homeless if I wanted to live. Feather's well-being was never far from my heart, but the road to her salvation was being piled with the bodies of dead white men. And you have to understand the impact of the death of a white man on a black southerner like me. In the south if a black man killed a white man he was dead. If the police saw him on the street they shot first and asked questions . . . never. If he gave himself up he was killed in his cell. If the constable wasn't a murdering man then a mob would come and lynch the poor son of a bitch. And failing all that, if a black man ever made it to trial and was convicted of killing a white man — even in self-defense, even if it was to save another white man — that convict would spend the rest of his days incarcerated. There would be no parole, no commutation of sentence, no extenuating circumstances, no time off for good behavior.

There was no room in my heart except for hope that Feather would live. Hovering above that hope was the retribution of the white race for my just seeing two of their dead sons.

But even with all of that trouble I have to take time to recall Flower's simple meal.

She gave me a large bowl filled with chunks of pork loin simmered in a pasilla chili sauce. She'd boiled the chilies without removing the seeds so I began to sweat with the first bite. There was cumin and oregano in the sauce and pieces of avocado too. On the side I had three homemade wheat flour tortillas and a large glass of lightly sweetened lemonade.

I felt like a condemned man but at least my last meal was a feast.

AFTER I ATE I made noises about leaving, but Primo told me that I could use his den to take care of any business I needed to attend to.

In the little study I settled into his leather chair and opened the envelope left by Raphael.

There were twelve very official sheets of parchment imprinted with declarations in French, Italian, and German. Each page had a large sum printed on it and a red wax seal embossed at one corner or another. There was a very fancy signature at the bottom of each document. I couldn't make out the name.

And there was a letter, a note really, written in German and signed H. W. Göring. In the text of the note the name H. Himmler appeared. The note was addressed to R. Tourneau. I didn't need to know what the letter said. At any other time I would have burned it up and moved on with my life. But there was too much I didn't understand to discard such an important document.

I had what Lee wanted but I didn't trust that Maya would pass on the information. I didn't know how much the bonds were worth but I did know that they were said to be Swiss and that my daughter was in a Swiss hospital.

I called Jackson and gave him all the information I could about the bonds. He asked a few questions, directing me to codes and symbols that I would never have noticed on my own.

"It'd be better if I could check 'em myself, Ease," Jackson said at one point.

But remembering his quandary over the TXT tape on his desk, I said, "I better hold on to these here, Jackson. There's some bloodthirsty people out there willing to do anything to get at 'em."

Jackson backed down and I made my second call.

He answered the phone on the first ring.

"Easy?"

"Yeah. Who's this?"

"Christmas Black," the man said. I couldn't tell one thing about him. Not his age or his race.

"I'm up in Riverside," Black said, "on Wayfarer's Road. You know it?"

"Can't say that I do."

He gave me precise instructions that I wrote down.

"What do you have to do with all this?" I asked.

"I'm just a layover," he said. "A place to gather the troops and regroup."

After talking to Christmas I called EttaMae and left the particulars with her.

"Tell Mouse to come up when he gets the chance," I said.

"What makes you think I'll be talkin' to him anytime soon?"

"Is the sky blue?" I asked.

35

I took Highway 101 toward Riverside. The fact that I had a destination relaxed me some. The thousands of dollars in Swiss bonds on the seat beside me gave me heart. Haffernon's body and Cinnamon's involvement with his death were on my mind. And then there was the Nazi high command.

Like most Americans I hated Adolf Hitler and his crew of bloodthirsty killers. I hated their racism and their campaign to destroy any people not their own. In '45 I was a concentration camp liberator. My friends and I killed a starving Jewish boy by feeding him a chocolate bar. We didn't know that it would kill him. How could we?

Even as a black American I felt patriotic about the war and my role in it. That's why I found it so hard to comprehend wealthy and white American businessmen trading with such villains.

Between Feather and Bonnie, Haffernon and Axel, Cinnamon and Joe Cicero, it was a wonder that I didn't go crazy. Maybe I did, a little bit, lose control at the edges.

CHRISTMAS BLACK had given me very good directions. I skirted downtown Riverside and took a series of side streets until I came to a graded dirt road that was still a city street. The houses were a little farther apart than in Los Angeles. The yards were larger and there were no fences between them. Unchained dogs snapped at my tires as I drove past.

After a third of a mile or so I came to the dead end of Way-farer's Road. Right where the road terminated stood a small white house with a yellow light shining over the doorway. It was the embodiment of peace and domesticity. You'd expect your aged, widowed grandmother to live behind that door. She'd have pies and a boiled ham to greet you.

I knocked and a child called out in some Asian language.

The door swung inward and a tall black man stood there.

"Welcome, Mr. Rawlins," he said. "Come in."

He was six foot four at least but his shoulders would have been a good fit for a man six inches taller. His skin was medium brown and there was a whitish scar beneath his left eye. The brown in his eyes was lighter than was common in most Ne-groes. And his hair was as close-cropped as you can get without being bald.

"Mr. Black?"

He nodded and stepped back for me to enter. A few steps away stood a small Asian girlchild dressed in a fancy red kimono. She bowed respectfully. She couldn't have been more than six years old but she held herself with the poise and attitude of the woman of the house. Just seeing her I knew that there was no wife or girlfriend in the black man's life.

"Easy Rawlins, meet Easter Dawn Black," Christmas said.

"Pleased to meet you," I said to the child.

"It is an honor to have you in our home, Mr. Rawlins," Easter Dawn said with solemnity.

To her right was a door open onto a bedroom, probably hers. On the other side was a cavernous sitting room that had a very western, almost cowboy feel to it. The girl gestured toward the sitting room and I followed her direction.

Behind Easter was a bronze mirror. In the reflection I could see the satisfaction in Christmas's face. He was proud of this little girl who could not possibly have been of his blood.

Feather came into my mind then and I tripped on the Indian blanket used as a throw rug. I would have fallen but Black was quick. He rushed forward and grabbed my arm.

"Thanks," I said.

The sitting room had a fifteen-foot ceiling, something you would never have expected upon seeing the seemingly small house from the road. Beyond that room was a kitchen with a loft above it, neither room separated by walls.

"Sit," Black said.

I sat down on one of the two wood-framed couches that he had facing each other.

He sat opposite me and flashed a brief smile.

"Tea?" Easter asked me.

"No thank you," I said.

"Coffee?"

"Naw. I would never get to sleep then."

"Ice water?"

"Are you going to keep on offering me drinks till you find one I want?" I asked her.

That was the first time she smiled. The beauty of her beaming face hurt me more than Bonnie and a dozen African princes ever could.

"Beer?" she asked.

"I'll take the water, honey."

"Daddy?"

"Whiskey and lime, baby."

The child walked away with perfect posture and regal bearing. I had no idea where she could have come from or how she got there.

"Adopted daughter," Black said. "I got her when she was a tiny thing."

"She's a beautiful princess," I said. "I have a girl too. Nothing like this one but I'm sure they'd be the best of friends."

"Easter Dawn doesn't have many friends. I'm schooling her here at home. You can't trust strangers with the people you love."

This felt like a deeply held secret that Christmas was letting me in on. I began to think that his bright eyes might have the light of madness behind them.

"Where you from?" I asked because he had no southern accent.

"Massachusetts," he said. "Newton, outside of Boston. You ever been there?"

"Boston once. I had a army buddy took me there after we were let go in Baltimore, after the war. Your family from there?"

"Crispus Attucks was one of my ancestors," Black said, nodding but not in a prideful way. "He was the son of a prince and a runaway slave. But most importantly he was a soldier."

There was a finality to every sentence he spoke. It was as if he was also royalty and not used to ordinary conversation.

"Attucks, huh?" I said, trying to find my way to a conversation. "That's the Revolutionary War there."

"My family's menfolk have been in every American war," he said, again with a remoteness that made him seem unstable. "Eighteen-twelve, Spanish-American, of course the Civil War. I myself have fought in Europe, and against Japan, the Koreans, and the Vietnamese."

"Here, Mr. Rawlins," Easter Dawn said. She was standing at my elbow holding a glass of water in one hand and her father's whiskey in the other.

Judging from her slender brown face and flat features I suspected that Easter had come from Black's last campaign.

She carried her father's whiskey over to him.

"Thanks, honey," he said, suddenly human and present.

"Easter here come from Vietnam?" I asked.

"She's my little girl," he said. "That's all we care about here."

Okay.

"What was your rank?" I asked.

"After a while it didn't matter," he said. "I was a colonel in Nam. But we were working in groups of one. You have no rank if there's nobody else there. Covered with mud and out for blood, we were just savages. Now how's a savage rate a rank?"

He shone those mad orbs at me and I believe that I forgot all the problems I came to his door with. Easter Dawn went to his side and leaned against his knee.

He looked down at her, placing a gigantic hand on her head. I could tell that it was a light touch because she pressed back into the caress.

"War has changed over my lifetime, Mr. Rawlins," Christmas Black said. "At one time I knew who the enemy was. That was clear as the nose on your face. But now . . . now they send us out to kill men never did anything to us, never thought one way or the other about America or the American way of life. When I realized that I was slaughtering innocent men and women I knew that the soldiering line had to come to an end with me."

Christmas Black could never hang out with the guys on a street corner. Every word he said was the last word on the subject. I liked the man and I knew he was crazy. The thing I didn't know was why I was there.

36

I was nursing my water, trying to think of some reply to a man who had just confessed to murder and gone on to his quest for redemption.

Lucky for me there came a knock at the door.

"It's Uncle Saul," Easter Dawn said. She didn't exactly shout but you could hear the excitement in her voice. She didn't exactly run either but rather rushed toward the front of the house.

"E.D.," Christmas said with authority.

The girl stopped in her tracks.

"What did I tell you about answering that door?" her father asked.

"Never open the door without finding out who it is," she said dutifully.

"Okay then."

She hurried on, followed by her father. I trailed after them.

"Who is it!" Easter Dawn shouted at the door.

"It's the big bad wolf," Saul Lynx replied in a playful voice he reserved for children.

The door flew open and Saul came in carrying a box wrapped in pink paper.

Easter Dawn put both hands behind her back and gripped them tightly to keep from jumping at him. He bent down and picked her up with one arm.

"How's my girl?"

"Fine," she said, obviously trying hard to restrain herself from asking what was in the box.

Christmas came up to them and put a hand on Saul's shoulder.

"How you doin'?" the black philosopher-king asked.

"Been better," Saul said.

By this time the girl had moved around until she had snagged the box.

"Is it for me?" she pleaded.

"You know it is," Saul said and then he put her down. "Hey, Easy. I see you made it."

"That reminds me," I said. "I gave Ray this address too. He should be by a little bit later."

"Who's that?" our host asked.

"Friend'a mine. Good guy in a pinch."

"Let's go in," Christmas said.

Easter ran before us, opening the present as she went.

SAUL SAT next to the war veteran and I sat across from them with my water.

"Joe 'Chickpea' Cicero" were the first words out of Saul's mouth. "The most dangerous man that anybody can think of. He's a killer for hire, an arsonist, a kidnapper, and he's also a torturer —"

"What's that mean?" I asked.

"It's widely known that if someone has a secret that you need to get at, all you have to do is hire Chickpea. He promises an answer to your question within seventy-two hours."

I glanced at Christmas. If he was frightened it certainly didn't show on his face.

"He's bad," Black agreed. "But not as bad as his rep. It's like a lot of white men. They can only see excellence in one of their own."

Excellence, I thought.

"That might be," Saul said. "But he's plenty dangerous enough for me."

Easter Dawn brought in a beer, which she offered to her Uncle Saul.

"Thanks, honey," Saul said.

"Easter, this is man talk," Christmas told the girl.

"But I wanted to show Mr. Rawlins my new doll," she said.

"Okay. But hurry up."

Easter ran out and then back again with a tallish figurine of an Asian woman standing on a platform and stabilized by a metal rod.

"You see," she said to me. "She has eyes like mine."

"I see."

The doll wore an elaborate black-and-gold robe that had a dragon stitched into it.

"That's a dragon lady," Saul told her, "the most important woman in the whole clan."

The child's eyes got bigger as she studied her treasure.

"You're spoiling her with all those dolls," Christmas said.

I was thinking about the assassin.

"No he's not, Daddy," Easter said.

"How many do you have now?"

"Only nine, and I have room for a lot more on the shelves you made me."

"Go on now and play with them," her unlikely father said. "I'll come say good night in an hour."

Decorum regained, Easter left the room and the men went back to barbarism.

"What's Cicero got to do with this?" Christmas asked.

"I don't know." Saul was wearing a tan suit with a brown T-shirt.

Christmas Black raised his head as if he'd heard something. A moment later there was a knock at the door.

"Stay in your room, E.D.," Christmas called.

We all went to the door together.

I had my hand on the .38 in my pocket.

Black pulled the door open and there stood Raymond.

"Christmas Day," Mouse hailed.

"Silent Knight," our host replied.

They shook hands and gave each other nods filled with mutual respect. I was impressed because Mouse's esteem was an event more rare than a tropical manifestation of the northern lights.

On our way back to the couches I felt my load lighten. With Raymond and someone he considered an equal on our side I didn't think that anyone would be too much for us.

I revealed as much of the story as I dared to. I told them about the state of Axel's house but not about finding his corpse. For that I relied on their imaginations when they heard about the meeting between Chickpea and Axel. I told them about Maya's calls and about finding Haffernon in Philomena's room. I told them about the existence of the bonds and the letter, but not that I had them.

"How much the bonds worth?" Raymond wanted to know.

"I don't know," I said. "Thousands."

"You think this Haffernon's the top man?" Christmas asked.

"Maybe. It's hard to tell. But if Haffernon was the boss, then who killed him? He is the one hired Lee. I'm sure of that."

"Lee has at least twenty operatives at his beck and call," Saul said.

"And if anybody's behind Haffernon," I added, "they'll have a whole army at their disposal."

"What's the objective, gentlemen?" Christmas asked.

"Kill 'em all," Mouse said simply.

Christmas's lower lip jutted out maybe an eighth of an inch. His head bobbed about the same distance.

"No." That was me. "We don't know which one of them it is."

"But if we do kill 'em all then the problem be ovah no mattah which one it was."

Christmas laughed for the first time.

Saul gave a nervous grin.

I said, "There's still the money, Ray."

"Money don't mean much if they put you in the ground, Ease."

"I can't go out killing people for no reason," Saul said.

"There's a reason," Christmas replied. "They suckered you in and now your life's on the line. The cops wouldn't touch this one and if they did they'd put you in jail. There's your reason."

"Yeah," I said, because once you invited men like Christmas and Mouse into the room Death had to have a seat at the table too. "But not before we find out what's what."

"An' how you plan to do that, Easy?" Mouse asked.

"We go to the horse's ass. We go to Robert E. Lee. He's the one brought us in. He should be able to find out what the problem is."

"What if he's the problem?" Christmas asked.

"Then we'll have to be smart enough to fool him into showing us that fact. The real problem is getting to him. I got the feelin' that Maya doesn't want that conversation to come about."

"That's easy," Saul told us. "Call him now, when she's not at work."

AFTER A SMALL STRATEGY discussion Saul dialed the number. It rang five times, ten. He wanted to hang up but I wouldn't let him. After at least fifty rings Lee answered his business phone.

"It's Saul Lynx, Mr. Lee. I'm calling you at this late hour because I have some fears that Maya may not be trustworthy. . . . The way I feel right now, sir, I wouldn't want to work for you again. . . . But you have to understand we believe . . . Mr. Rawlins and I believe that Axel Bowers was murdered and that Mr. Haffernon was too. . . . Yes . . . Easy has talked with Maya a few times since that initial meeting and he told her that he located Miss Cargill and that he'd spoken to Axel. Did she tell you about that? . . . I assume that she hasn't. . . . Sir, we need to meet . . . No, not at your house . . . Not in San Francisco. . . . There's a bar called Mike's on Slauson in Los Angeles. Easy and I want to meet you there."

There was a lot of argument about the meeting but Lee finally gave in. The way we figured it, if there was a problem between Maya and Lee he would have some inkling of it beyond our insinuations. If he doubted her loyalty he'd have to take the meeting.

As if she could read the vibrations in the air Easter Dawn made tea and brought it to us just when the call was over. Her father didn't chastise her for leaving her room.

I took the child on my lap and she sat there comfortably, listening to the men.

"I'll go with you and Raymond back to L.A.," Saul said.

"No. Go to your family, man. Ray and me can see to this."

"What about you?" Christmas asked Mouse.

"Naw, man. It ain't no war. Just one white boy think he bad. If I cain't take that then I'm past help."

Easter brought out her dolls after that and we all told her how beautiful they were. She basked in the attention of the four men and Christmas was glad for her. After he put her to bed we all left. Mouse asked Christmas could he leave his red El Dorado there for a few days. He wanted to be able to strategize with me on the ride.

When we approached my flashy Pontiac I felt that I was leaving something, a fellowship that I'd not known before. Maybe it was just sadness at leaving a home when I was homeless.

37

In the front yard Saul came up to us, shook Mouse by the hand, and then drew me away.

"Easy, I know I got you into this mess," he said. "Maybe I should come along."

"No, Saul, no. Neither you or me got the stomach for a man like this killer. Really Mouse would be better on this alone."

"Well then why don't you grab Jesus and come up and stay with us at the cabin?"

"Because EttaMae would kill me if I let her husband get shot out there. It already happened one time. I got to cover his back and you got to go to your family."

Saul gave me his hangdog stare. He was a homely man, there's no doubt about that. I held out a hand and he grabbed on to it.

"I'm sorry," he said.

"Don't be. I asked you for the job and you came through for

me. If I'm very lucky I'll come out of this alive and with the money for Feather's doctors. If I'm just plain old lucky I'll just get the money."

Saul nodded and turned to leave. I touched his arm.

"Why'd you want me to come out here?" I asked him. I thought I knew but I wanted to see what he had to say.

"I did Christmas a favor once. He's the kind of guy that takes a debt seriously. I wanted you to know him if you got into a bind. He'll do whatever it takes to make things right."

IT WAS LATE on the highway ride home. After my accident and two near misses I was paying close attention to the road and the speedometer. Mouse and I smoked with the windows down and the chilly breezes whipping around us.

After quite a while I asked, "So what's that Christmas Black's story?"

"What you mean?" Mouse asked. He understood my question; he was just naturally cagey.

"Is that his real name?"

"I think it is. All the kids in his family named after holidays. I think that's what he told me once."

"What's his story?" I asked again.

"He a terror," Mouse said.

"What's that supposed to mean?"

"He kilt a whole town once."

"A what?"

"Whole town. Men, women, chirren. All of 'em. Every last one." Mouse sneered thinking about it. "He kilt the dogs and the water buffaloes an' burnt down all the houses an' half the trees an' crops. Mothahfuckah kilt every last thing 'cept a couple'a chickens an' one baby girl."

"In Vietnam?"

"I guess it was. He didn't give the town a name. Maybe it was Cambodia or Laos maybe. Shit, the way he tell it, it could'a been anywhere. They just put that boy in a plane an' give him a parachute an' a duffel bag full'a guns an' bombs. Wherever he land people had to die."

"How do you know him?"

"Met once down in Compton. There was some guys thought they was bad messin' wit' a friend'a his. The dudes called themselves my friends an' so I looked into it. When I fount out what they was doin' I jes' smiled at Christmas. He taught 'em a lesson an' we went out to eat sour pork an' rice."

I was sure that there was more to the story but Raymond didn't brag about his crimes much anymore.

"So he left the army after killin' that village?"

"Yeah. I guess if you do sumpin' like that it's a li'l hard to live wit'. For him."

"You wouldn't take it hard if you had to kill like that?"

"I wouldn't never have to kill like that, Easy. I ain't never gonna be in no mothahfuckah's army, jumpin' out no plane, killin' li'l brown folk. If I kill a town it'a be for me. An' if it's for me then I'ma be fine wit' it."

I rolled up my window then, the chill of Raymond's words being enough for me.

For a long while I remained silent, even in my mind.

When we got to L.A. I asked Raymond where he was going.

"Home," he said.

"With Etta and LaMarque?"

"What other home you evah hear me talk about?"

That was how I learned that his exile was over.

"You know what to do at Mike's?"

"What, now I'm stupid too?"

"Come on, Ray. You know how serious I am about this."

"Sure I know what to do. When you get there we gonna be ready for Mr. Lee."

I dropped him off at maybe three in the morning. He gave me the keys for his place on Denker. I went there, scaled the stairs, and climbed into bed, fully dressed. The sheets smelled of Georgette. I inhaled her tomato garden bouquet and was suddenly awake. Not the wakefulness of a man aroused by the memory of a woman. Georgette's scent had aroused me but I had Christmas Black's story in my mind.

I was so close to death at that time that my senses were attuned to its intricacies. My country was sending out lone killers to murder women and children in far-flung nations. While I slept in the security of Mouse's hideaway innocent people were dying. And the taxes I paid on my cigarettes and the taxes they took out of my paycheck were buying the bullets and gassing up the bombers.

It was a state of mind, sure, but that didn't mean that I was wrong. All those years our people had struggled and prayed for freedom and now a man like Christmas, who came from a whole line of heroes, was just another killer like all those white men had been for us.

Is that what we labored for all those years? Was it just to have the right to step on some other poor soul's neck? Were we any better than the white men who lynched us in the night if we killed Easter Dawn's mother and father, sister and brother, cousins and friends? If we could kill like that, everything that we fought for would be called into question. If we became the white men we hated and who hated us, then we were nowhere, nowhere at all.

The sorrow in my heart finally came to rest on Feather. I thought about her dying and so I picked up the phone and called the long-distance operator.

"Allo?" Bonnie said in the French accent that came out whenever she was on the job in either Europe or Africa.

"It's me."

"Oh . . . hi, baby."

"Hey . . . how's Feather doin'?"

"The doctors say that she's very, very sick." She paused for a moment to hold back the grief. I took in a great gulp of air. "But they believe that with the proper transfusions and herbs, they can arrest the infection. And you don't have to worry about the money for a few months. They'll wait that long."

"Thank Mr. Cham for that," I said with hardly any bitterness in the words.

"Easy."

"Yeah?"

"We have to talk, honey."

"Yes. Yes we do. But right now I got my hands full with tryin' to get Feather's hospital bills paid without havin' medical bills of my own."

"I, I got your message," she said, not identifying the man who answered the phone. "Is everything okay?"

"All you got to do is call EttaMae before you come back to the house. There's a man I got to talk to first."

"It's been hard on me too, Easy. I had to do what I've done just to get —"

"Is Feather there?"

"No. She's in the hospital, in a room with three other children."

"There a phone in there?"

"Yes."

"Can I have the number?"

"Easy."

"The number, Bonnie. Whatever we feelin' it cain't touch what's goin' on with her."

"HELLO?"

"It's your daddy, sugar," I said.

"Daddy! Daddy! Where are you?"

"At Uncle Raymond's. How are you, baby?"

"The nurses are so nice, Daddy. And the other girls with me are very sick, sicker than me. And they don't speak English but I'm learning French 'cause they're just too tired to learn a new language. One girl is named Antoinette like the queen and one is Julia . . ."

She sounded so happy but after a short while she was tired again.

"HELLO?"

"It's me, Jackson."

"Easy, do you know what time it is?"

It was four forty-seven by my watch.

"Were you asleep?" I asked. Jackson Blue was a night owl. He'd party until near dawn and then read Voltaire for breakfast.

"No, but Jewelle is."

"Sorry. You made any progress on those bonds?"

"I put the numbers through a telex in the foreign department. They good to go, man. Good to go."

"How much?"

"The one you told me about is eight thousand four hunnert eighty-two dollars and thirty-nine cent. That's before fees."

A hundred thousand dollars, maybe a little more. I couldn't

see Haffernon putting his life on the line for money like that. So it had to be the letter.

"Jackson."

"Yeah, Ease?"

"You ever hear of a guy name of Joe Cicero? They call him Chickpea."

"Never heard of him but he got to be a literate son of a bitch."

"Why you say that?"

"'Cause the first Cicero, the Roman statesman, was called Chickpea. That's what Cicero means, only in the old Latin they had hard c's so you called it 'Kikero.'"

"Yeah. He got a kick all right."

38

I dreamed that I was a dead man in a coffin underground. Down there nobody could get to me but I could see everything. Feather was playing in the yard, Jesus and Benny had a child that looked like me. Bonnie lived with Joguye Cham on a mountaintop in Switzerland that somehow overlooked the continent of Africa. Across the street from the cemetery there was a jail and in it were all the people, living and dead, who had ever tried to harm my loved ones.

I'd fallen asleep on my back with my hands on my thighs. I woke up in the same position. I was completely rested and happy that Mouse's dreams infected mine.

It was after two. I had no job so the calendar and the clock lost meaning to me. It was like when I was a youngblood, running the streets hunting down love and the rent.

My passion had cooled in that imagined grave. The cold earth had leached out the pain and rage in my heart. Feather had a chance and I had a hundred thousand dollars in pay-on-demand bonds. Maybe I'd lost my woman. But, I reasoned, that was like if a man had come awake after a bad accident. The doctors tell him that he's lost an arm. It's a bad thing. It hurts and maybe he sheds tears. But the arm is gone and he's still there. That's some kind of luck.

MIKE'S BAR was in a large building occupying what had once been a mortuary. It had one large room and four smaller ones for private parties and meetings. In the old days, before I ever moved to L.A., the undertakers had a speakeasy behind their coffin repository. Mourners would come in grieving and leave with new hope.

Mouse knew about the old-time club because people liked talking to him. So we took the private room that used to store coffins and he secreted himself behind the hidden door. From there he could spy on the meeting with Lee.

This plan had a few points to recommend it. First, if Lee got hinky Mouse could shoot him through the wall. Also Mouse had a good ear. Maybe Lee would say something that he understood better than I. But the best thing was to have Mouse at that meeting without Lee seeing him; there might come a day when Raymond would have to get close to Lee without being recognized.

I got to the bar at six-twenty, ten minutes before the meeting was to take place. Sam Cooke was singing on the jukebox about the chain gang. Mike, a terra-cotta-colored man, stood statuelike behind his marble-top bar.

"Easy," he called as I came in the door.

I looked around for enemies but all I saw were men and

women hunched over small tables, drinking and talking under a haze of tobacco smoke.

"He in there," Mike told me when I settled at the bar.

"He say anything?"

"Nope. Just that you was comin' an' that a tiny little white man was comin' too. Told me that there might be another white guy in snakeskin, that if I saw him to give him a sign."

"When the little white guy gets here make sure he's alone," I said. "If he is then send him in."

"I know the drill," Mike said.

Mouse had done the bartender a favor some years before. Mike once told me that he was living on borrowed time because of what Raymond had done.

"Any favor he ask I gotta do," Mike had said. "You got to die one day."

I remembered those last words as I walked into the small room that had once held a few dozen coffins.

IT WAS A BRIGHT ROOM with a square pine table that had been treated with oak stain. The chairs were all of one general style, but if you looked closely you could see they weren't an exact match. Mouse was bunged up in the back wall, behind white plasterboard. I wondered if Lee would appreciate the poetry of our deception. He had watched me from behind a similar wall in his own house.

Raymond didn't talk to me. This was business.

I lit a cigarette and let it burn between my fingers while searching the room for living things. There were no plants in the sunless chamber, of course. But neither was there a solitary fly or mosquito, roach or black ant. The only visible, audible life in that room was me. It was more solitary than a coffin because at least in the ground you had gnawing worms for company.

There came a knock and before I could reply the door swung open. Red-skinned Mike stuck his head in and said, "He's cool, Easy." Then he moved back and Robert E. Lee entered.

Lee wore a big mohair overcoat and a black, short-brimmed Stetson. He looked from side to side and then stepped up to the table. His footsteps were loud for such a small man.

"Have a seat," I said.

"Where's Saul?"

"Hiding."

"From you?"

I shook my head. "Me'n Saul are friends. He's hiding from our enemies."

"Saul told me that he'd be here."

"You're here, man. Have a seat and let's talk some business."

He knew he would have to hear me out. But the white man hesitated, pretending that he was weighing the pros and cons of my request.

"All right," he said finally. Then he pulled out the chair opposite me and perched on the edge.

"I got the bonds," I said. "Bowers is most likely dead. So's Haffernon."

"Haffernon was my employer," Lee told me. "Turn over what you've got and we'll both walk away."

"What about my ten thousand?"

"I have no more employer," he said by way of explanation.

"Then neither do I."

"What do you want from me, Rawlins?"

"To make a deal. I get a piece of the action and you call Cicero off my ass."

"Cicero? Joe Cicero?"

The honesty of his fear made me understand that the situation was far more complex than I thought.

"I'd never do business with a man like that," Lee said with incantatory emphasis, like he was warding off an evil spell I'd cast.

"How do you know the guy if you don't work with him?" I asked. "I mean he's not in the kind of business that advertises."

"I know of him from the newspapers and some of my friends in the prosecutor's office. He was tried for the torture and murder of a young socialite from Sausalito. Fremont. Patrick Fremont."

"Well he's been runnin' around lookin' for that briefcase you hired me to find. He told me that he killed Haffernon and Axel and that me and my family are the next ones on his list."

"That's your problem," Lee said. He shifted as if he might stand and run.

"Come on, man. You the one hired me. All I got to do is tell Chickpea that you the one got the bonds, that Maya picked 'em up someplace. Then he be on your ass."

"Saul said something about Maya on the phone," Lee said. "Do you know anything about that?"

"A few days ago she fired me," I said.

"Nonsense."

"Then she hired me again when I told her that I'd found Philomena but refused to share my information."

"How can I believe anything you say, Mr. Rawlins? First you tell me that Joe Cicero is after the bonds, then you say that my client and your quarry are dead, that you have the bonds we were after, and that Maya has betrayed me. But you don't offer one shred of evidence."

"You never told me about no bonds, Bobby Lee," I said, falling into the dialect that gave me strength.

"Maybe you heard about them."

"Sure I did . . . from the woman had 'em — Philomena Cargill. She gave 'em to me to keep Cicero from makin' her dearly departed."

Somewhere in the middle of the conversation Lee had changed from a self-important ass to something much closer to a detective — I could see it in his eyes.

"So you have these bonds?" he asked.

"Sure do."

"Give them to me."

"I don't have 'em here, an' even if I did you'd have to take 'em. Because you didn't tell me about half the shit I was gettin' into."

"Detectives take chances."

"An' if I take 'em," I said, "then you gonna take 'em too."

"You can't threaten me, Rawlins."

"Listen, babe, you just named after a dead general. With the shit I got I could threaten Ike himself."

It was the certainty in my voice that tipped him to my side.

"You say Maya fired you?"

"Said that you'd concluded the case and that my services would no longer be needed."

"But she didn't tell you about the bonds?"

"No," I said. "All she said was that we were through and that I could keep the money I already had."

"I need proof," Lee said.

"There was a murder at the Pixie Inn motel this afternoon. The man found there is Haffernon."

"Even if that's so it doesn't prove anything," Lee said. "You could have killed him yourself."

"Fine. Go on then. Leave. I tried to warn you. I tried."

Lee remained seated, watching me closely.

"I know some federal officials that could look into Cicero," he said. "They could get him out of the action until the case is resolved. And if we can pin these murders on him . . ."

"You sayin' that we could be partners?"

"I need proof about Maya," he said. "She's been with me for many years. Many years."

"When it's over we could set her up," I offered. "Agree to give her the bonds or put her with Cinnamon and record what she says. I think those two would like each other. But I need you to do somethin' about Cicero. That mothahfuckah make a marble statue sweat."

Lee smiled. That gave me heart about him. In my many years I had come to understand that humor was the best test for intelligence in my fellow man. The fact that Lee gained respect for me because of a joke gave me hope that he would come to sensible conclusions.

"He really came to you?" Lee asked.

"Right up in my office. Told me to give up Cinnamon or else my family would be dead."

"He mentioned her name?"

I nodded. "Philomena Cargill."

"And you have the bonds?"

"Sure do."

"How many?"

"Twelve."

"Was there anything else with them?"

"They were in a brown envelope. No briefcase or anything."

"Was there anything attached?"

"Like what?" I was holding back a little to see how much he was willing to give.

"Nothing," he said. "So what do we do now?"

"You go home. Gimme a way to get in touch with you and I will in two days. In that time figure out what you need on Maya and talk to who you need to about J.C."

"And what do you do?"

"Keep from gettin' killed the best I can, sit on those bonds while they accrue interest."

He gave me a private phone number that only he answered.

He rose and so did I. We shook hands.

He was sweating under that heavy coat. He was probably armed under there. I would have been.

39

Thirty seconds after Lee left, a section of the wall to my left wobbled and then moved back. Mouse came out through the crack wearing a red suit and a black shirt. He was smiling.

"You didn't tell me you had the bonds, Ease."

"Sure I did. The same time I told Lee."

The smile remained on Raymond's face. He never minded a man holding his cards close to the vest. All that mattered to him was that in the end he got his proper share of the pot.

"What you think?" I asked as we emerged into the barroom.

"I like that dude. He got some nuts on him. An' he smart too. I know that 'cause a minute after he walked in I figgered I'd have to shoot the mothahfuckah in the head he mess around."

That was sixty seconds after Lee had left the room. We made

it halfway to the bar. Mouse ordered scotch and I was about to ask for a Virgin Mary when six or seven cracks sounded outside.

"What was that?" Mike shouted.

I looked at Raymond. He had his long barreled .41 caliber pistol in his hand.

Then two explosions thundered from the street. Shotgun blasts.

I headed for the door, pulling the pistol from my pocket as I went. Mouse was ahead of me. He threw the door open, moving low and to his left. A motor revved and tires squealed. I saw a car (I couldn't place the model) fishtailing away.

"Easy!" Mouse was leaning over Robert Lee, ripping open his overcoat and shirt.

There was a sawed-off shotgun next to the master detective's right hand and blood coming freely from the right side of his neck. When Mouse tore the shirt I could see the police-issue bulletproof vest with at least five bullet holes.

Mouse grinned. "Oh yeah. Head shot the only way to go."

He clasped his palm on the neck wound. Lee looked up at us, gasping. He was going into shock but wasn't quite there yet.

"She betrayed me," he said.

"Get the car, Easy. This boy needs some doctor on him."

I SAT WITH LEE in the backseat while Mouse drove Primo's hot rod. I had the general's namesake's head and shoulders propped up on my lap while holding his own torn shirt against the wound.

"She betrayed me," Lee said again.

"Maya?"

"I told her that I was coming to see Saul."

"Did you say why?"

His eyes were getting glassy. I wasn't sure that he heard me.

"She doesn't know, but if what you said, you said, you said . . ."

"Hold on, Bobby. Hold on."

"She knew. She knew where we were meeting. I didn't tell her what Saul said. I didn't, but she betrayed me to that snake, that snake Cicero."

He never closed his eyes but he passed out still and all. I couldn't get another word out of him.

IT WAS A SLOW NIGHT in the emergency room. Lee was the only gunshot wound in the place. Maybe it was because of that, or maybe it was his being white that got him such quick service that day. They had him in a hospital bed and hooked up to three machines before I had even finished filling out the paperwork.

Five minutes after that the cops arrived.

When I saw the three uniforms come in I turned to Mouse, intent on telling him to ditch his gun. But he was nowhere to be seen. Mouse knew that those cops were coming before they did. He was as elusive in the street as Willie Pepp had been in the ring.

"Are you the man that brought him in?" the head cop, a silver-haired sergeant, asked me right off.

The other uniforms performed a well-rehearsed flanking maneuver.

"Sure did. Easy Rawlins. We were meeting at Mike's Bar and he'd just left. I heard shots and ran out . . . found him lying on the ground. There was a car racin' off but I can't even say for sure what color it was."

"There was a report of a sawed-off shotgun on the ground. Who did that belong to?"

"I have no idea, Officer. I saw the gun but I left it . . . for evidence."

I was too cool for that man. He was used to people being agitated after a shooting.

"You say you were having a drink with the victim?" he asked.

"I said I was having a meeting with him."

"What kind of meeting?"

"I'm a detective, Sergeant. Private. Mr. Lee — that's the victim — he's a detective too."

I handed him my license. He studied the card carefully, made a couple of notes in a black leather pocket notebook, and then handed it back.

"What were you working on?"

"A security background check on a Maya Adamant. She's an operative who works with him from time to time."

"And why did you flee the scene?"

"You ever been shot in the neck, Sergeant?"

"What?"

"I hope not, but if ever that should happen I'm sure that you would want somebody to take you to a doctor first off. 'Cause you know, man, ain't no police report in the world worth bleedin' to death out on Slauson."

The sergeant wasn't a bad guy. He was just doing his job.

"Did you see the shooter?" he asked.

"No sir. Just what I said about the car."

"Did the victim . . ."

"Lee," I said.

"Did he say anything?"

"No."

"Did the shooter get shot?"

"I don't know."

"They found blood halfway up the block," the sergeant said. "That's why I ask."

He peered into my face. I shook my head, hoping that Joe Cicero was dying somewhere.

A young white doctor with a pointy nose came up to us.

"Your friend is going to be fine," he told me. "No major vascular damage. The shot went through."

"Can I speak to him?" the policeman asked the doctor.

"He's in shock and under sedation," the doctor said. He wouldn't meet the policeman's eye. I wondered what secrets he had to hide. "You won't be able to talk to him until morning."

Blocked there the cop turned back to me.

"Can you tell me anything else, Rawlins?"

I could have told him to call me mister but I didn't.

"No, Sergeant. That's all I know."

"Do you think this woman you're investigating might have something to do with it?"

"I couldn't say."

"You say you were investigating her."

"My findings were inconclusive," I said, falling out of dialect.

The cop stared at me a moment more and then gave up.

"I have your information. We may be calling you."

I nodded and the police took the doctor somewhere for his report.

EVERYTHING CALMED DOWN after half an hour or so. The police left, the doctor went on to other patients. Mouse was long gone.

I stayed around because I knew that someone wanted Lee dead, and so while he was unconscious I thought I'd watch over him. This wasn't as selfless an act as it might have seemed. I still needed the haughty little detective to run interference with Cicero. I didn't know if Lee had actually seen Cicero shoot at him, if Lee had shot him, and, if he had, if the wound would ultimately be fatal. I had to play it as if Cicero was still in the game and as deadly as ever.

The only thing worth reading in the magazine rack in the waiting room was a science fiction periodical called *Worlds of Tomorrow*. I found a story in it called "Under the Gaddyl." It was a tale about man's future, the white man's future, where all of white humanity was enslaved under an alien race — the Gaddyl. The purpose of the main character, a freed slave, was to emancipate his people. I read the story in a kind of wonderment. Here white people all over the country understood the problems that faced me and mine but somehow they had very little compassion for our plight.

I was thinking about that when a shadow fell over my page. I knew by the scent who it was.

"Hello, Miss Adamant," I said without looking up.

"Mr. Rawlins."

She took the seat next to me and leaned over, seemingly filled with concern.

"He knows you set him up. He told the cops that," I said.

"What are you talking about?"

"He knows that you sent Cicero down to blow him away."

"But I . . . I didn't."

She was good.

"If you don't know nuthin' about tonight then what the fuck you doin' here? How the hell you know to find him in this emergency room?"

"I came down because I knew you or Saul would tell him about our conversations. I wanted to talk to him, to explain."

"So you were outside the bar?" I asked. "Watchin' your boss get shot down?"

"No. I was at the Clarendon Hotel. I heard on the news about the shooting. I knew where the meeting was."

"What about Cicero?" I asked.

Her face went blank. I could tell that this was her way of going inward and solving some problem. I was the problem.

"He called me," she said.

"When?"

"After you came to see us. He wanted to talk to Mr. Lee but I told him that all information had to go through me. He said that we had interests in common, that he wanted to find Philomena Cargill and a document that Axel had given her."

"And what did you say?"

"I told him that I didn't know where she was."

If she could have, Maya would have stopped right there. But I moved my hands around in a helpless manner like Boris Karloff's Frankenstein's monster did just after he murdered the little girl.

"He said that he wanted to meet with you and did I know where you were," she added.

"Me?"

"He said that if anybody could find Philomena that you could."

"How did he know about me?" I asked.

"He didn't say."

"You didn't tell him?"

"No."

"How did he know how to call you in the first place?"

"I don't know."

"Did you tell anyone that I was working for you?" I asked.

"No."

"Did your boss?"

"I do all the talking about business," she said with a hint of contempt in her voice.

"And so you told Cicero where I was?"

"I didn't know. But when Mr. Lee said that he was coming down to meet Saul I called Cicero. I had been trying to get in touch with Mr. Lynx but he didn't answer his phones. I told Cicero where Saul would be, thinking that he might help him find you."

"And what would you get out of that?"

"Cicero has a reputation," she replied.

"Yeah," I said. "Assassin. Torturer."

"That may be. But he is always known to meet his side of a bargain. I told him what I wanted for the information and he agreed."

"You wanted the bonds," I said.

"Yes."

I didn't say anything, just stared at her.

"That little bastard pays me seven dollars an hour with no benefits. He makes more than a quarter million a year," she said in defense from my gaze, "and I do almost everything. I'm on duty twenty-four hours a day. He calls me home from vacations. He makes me talk to everybody, do the books, do all the business. I make all of the major decisions while he sits behind his desk and plays with his toy soldiers."

"Sounds like a good enough reason to kill him," I said.

"No. If I got the bonds I could cash them in and set up a retirement fund. That's all I wanted."

"Is that why you and Lee were feuding when Saul and I were there?"

"Yes. Mr. Lee didn't want to take the case but . . . but I hoped to be able to get hold of the bonds, and so I had talked him into it. He was looking for a way out of it, he didn't like the smell of Haffernon. When you demanded to meet him he almost let it go."

"So why would Cicero want to kill Lee?"

"I don't know but I would suspect that whatever job he was working on, Lee's death had to be part of it."

"Maybe yours too," I suggested.

She blanched at the notion.

40

After our chat I asked Maya to come up with me to the nurses' station. There I introduced her to the pointy-nosed doctor and to Mrs. Bernard, the bespectacled head nurse.

"This is Miss Maya Adamant," I said. "She'll tell you that she's a friend of Mr. Lee's, but the police suspect her in his shooting. They don't have proof, but you probably shouldn't let her run around here unsupervised."

The stunned look on their faces was worth it.

Maya smiled at them and said, "It's a misunderstanding. I work for Mr. Lee. At any rate I'll wait until he's conscious and then you can ask him if he wants to talk to me."

THE MORNING WAS CHILLY but I didn't feel so bad.

I missed having Bonnie to call. For the past few years I'd been able to talk to her about anything. That had been a new experience for me. Never before could I fully trust another human being. If it was five in the morning and I'd been out all night I could call her and she'd be there as fast as she could. She never asked why but I always explained. Being with her made me understand how lonely I'd been for all my wandering years. But being alone again made me feel that I was back in the company of an old friend.

I was worried about Feather's survival but she had sounded good on the phone and there was already new blood flowing in her veins.

Blood and money were the currencies I dealt in. They were inseparable. This thought made me feel even more comfortable. I figured that if I knew where I stood then I had a chance of getting where I was going.

I PARKED ACROSS THE STREET from Raphael Reed's apartment building a little after seven. I had coffee in a paper cup. The brew was both bitter and weak but I drank it to stay awake. Maybe Cinnamon was with the young men. I could hope.

Sitting there I went over the details I had. I knew more about Lee's case than anyone, but still there were big holes. Cicero was definitely the killer, but who held his reins? He couldn't have been a player in the business. He could have worked for anybody: Cinnamon, Maya, even Lee, or maybe Haffernon. Maybe Bowers hired him back in the beginning. It would be good to know the answers if the police came to see me.

Near nine Raphael's friend Roget came out the front door of the turquoise building. He carried a medium-sized suitcase. He could have had a change of underwear in there, could have been going to visit his mother, but I was intrigued. And so when the high-yellow freckled boy climbed into a light blue Datsun I turned over my own engine.

He led me all the way to Hollywood before parking in front of a boxy four-story house on Delgado. He walked up the driveway and into the backyard. After a moment I followed.

He went to the front door of a small house back there. He knocked and was admitted by someone I couldn't see. I went back to the car. When I sat down exhaustion washed over me. I lay back on the seat for just a moment.

Two hours later the sun on my face woke me up.

The blue Datsun was gone.

SHE WAS WEARING a T-shirt, that's all. The soft outline of her nipples pressed against the white cotton. The dark color pressed against it too.

After answering my knock she didn't know whether to smile or to run.

"What do you want from me now?" she asked. "I gave you the bonds."

"Can I come in?"

She backed away and I entered. It was yet another cramped cabinlike room. The normal-sized furniture crowded the small space. There was a couch and a round table upon which sat a portable TV. A radio on the window shelf played Mozart. Her musical taste shouldn't have surprised me but it did.

On the table was an empty glass jar that once held nine Vienna sausages, a half-drunk tumbler of orange juice, and a depleted bag of barbecue potato chips.

"You want something to drink?" she asked me.

"Water be great," I said.

She went through a tiny doorway. I heard the tap turn on and off and she returned with an aqua-colored plastic juice tumbler filled with water.

I drank it down in one gulp.

"You want more?"

"Let's talk," I said.

She sat down on one end of the golden sofa. I took the other end.

"What do you want to know?"

"First — who knows you're here?"

"Just Raphael and Roget. Now you."

"Do they gossip?"

"Not about this. Raphael knows someone's after me and Roget does whatever Raphael says."

"Why'd you kill Haffernon?" It was an abrupt and brutal switch calculated to knock her off track. But it didn't work.

"I didn't," she said evenly. "I found him there and ran but I didn't kill him. No. Not me."

What else could she say?

"How does that work?" I asked. "You find a dead man in your own room but don't know how he got killed?"

"It's the truth."

I shook my head.

"You look tired," she said, sympathy blending in with her words.

"How'd Haffernon get to your room?"

"I called him."

"When?"

"Right after I met you. I called him and told him that I wanted to get rid of the bonds. I asked him would he buy them off me for face value."

"And what about the letter?"

"He'd get that too."

"When was this meeting supposed to happen?"

"Today. This afternoon."

"So how does he show up dead on your floor yesterday?"

"After the last time I talked to you I realized that Haffernon could just send that man in the snakeskin jacket to kill me and take the bonds, so I went to Raphael and asked him to take the bonds to your friend."

"Why?"

"Because even though I hardly know you, you seem to be the most trustworthy person I've met, and anyway . . ." Her words trailed off as better judgment took the wheel.

"Anyway what?"

"I figured that you wouldn't know what to do with the bonds and so I didn't have to worry about you cashing them."

That made me laugh.

"What's so funny?"

I told her about Jackson Blue, that he was willing at that moment to cash them in. I could see the surprise on her face.

"My Uncle Thor once told me that for every one thing you learn you forget something else," I said.

"What's that supposed to mean?"

"That while they were teaching you all'a that smart white world knowledge at Berkeley you were forgetting where you came from and how we survived all these years. We might'a acted stupid but you know you moved so far away that you startin' to think the act is true."

Cinnamon smiled. The smile became a grin.

"Tell me exactly what happened with Haffernon," I said.

"It's like I said. I called him and made an appointment for him to meet me at the motel —"

"At what time?"

"Today at four," she said. "Then I got nervous and went to give the bonds to Raphael to give to your friend —"

"What time was that?"

"Right after I talked to you. I got back by about five. That's when I saw him on the floor. He'd been early, real early."

"But who could have killed him if you didn't?"

"I don't know," she said. "It wasn't me. But when I talked to him he said that he wasn't the only interested party, that what Axel planned to do would sink many innocent people."

I thought about the bullet that killed Haffernon. It had entered at the base of the skull and gone out through the top. He was a tall man. In all probability either a very short man or a woman had done him in.

"Did you give your real name at the motel?"

"No. I didn't. I called myself Mary Lornen. That's the names of two people I knew up north."

Proof is a funny thing. For policemen and for lawyers it depends on tangible evidence: fingerprints, eyewitnesses, irrefutable logic, or self-incrimination. But for me evidence is like morning mist over a complex terrain. You see the landscape and then it's gone. And all you can do is try to remember and watch your step.

The fact that Philomena had delivered those bonds to Primo meant something. It gave me doubts about her guilt. While I was having these thoughts Philomena moved across the couch.

"Kiss me," she commanded.

41

Cinnamon's kiss was a spiritual thing. It was like the sudden and unexpected appeasement between the east and west. A barrier fell away, forgiveness flooded my heart, and somewhere I was granted redemption for all my transgressions.

"I need this," she whispered. "It doesn't have to mean anything."

She pressed her breasts against me, positioning me so that I was leaning back on the arm of the sofa. Then she grabbed my ankles and pulled hard so that, with my help, she got me flat on my back.

She lifted the white T-shirt to straddle me. When she did so I caught a glimpse of her protruding pubic hair. I felt like a child seeing something that had been kept from him for what seemed like an eternity.

"Wh-what do you need?" I said, embarrassed by my stutter.

She moved down to my shins and reached up to catch the waist of my pants. With a quick tug she had both my pants and boxers down to my knees. Then she came up again.

Just before settling back down she said, "I need your warmth."

The feel of her hot sex sitting down on mine gave the hiss of her words a deeper meaning.

"Pull up your shirt," she said.

She began rocking gently back and forth and to the sides, doing things with my erection, which lay flat against my belly, that I would never have thought of on my own. I watched closely, looking for passion. But she was in control. The feeling was inside and she was keeping it there. She laid her hands upon my chest. I could see a finger against my erect nipple but I couldn't feel it.

"Was he your lover?" I asked. It was the last thing on my mind.

"Axel?"

"Sure."

"Sure," she repeated.

"What were you guys doing?"

"You mean how did we do it?"

"No. Those bonds. That letter."

"He loved me," she said. "He wanted to help me cross over from where everybody else was."

I understood every word, every inflection. She moved side to side and I felt her excitement down between my thighs even if it didn't show on her face.

"You love him?"

"If I tell you about him will you tell me something?"

I nodded and gulped.

"What do you want to know?" she asked.

"Do you love him?" I asked even though there was another question in my mind.

"It's more than that," she whispered with a sneer and an evil twist of her hips. "He reached out and saved my life. He took me in his house and then left me there with all those treasures. He introduced me to friends and family and never walked into a room where I couldn't go with him. And he never gave me a dime I didn't work for and he did what I told him to do."

The idea of a man obeying this woman brought a sound from my chest that I'd not heard before, not even from some infant that was all feelings and desire.

"He let me help him," she said. "He recognized that I was smart and educated and that I could understand him better than all those old white men and women that made him ashamed."

"Were you helping him with those bonds?" I asked, again a question I didn't care to ask.

"That was him. That was his devil."

She lifted off of me and cold concern rose in my face. She smiled and came back down.

"My turn," she said with a swivel.

"What?"

"What's making you so sad?" she asked.

In a flood of words I told her about Feather and about Bonnie, who was saving her while in the arms of an African prince in the Alps. It sounded like a bad movie but the words kept coming. It was almost as if I couldn't inhale before finishing the tale.

Her fingernail got caught on my nipple. A shock made me jump and press hard against her sex.

"Oh!" she said and then snagged the nipple again.

She'd found another way to pleasure us both. My breath was coming harder.

In between her rocking and snagging she said, "All men feel that women do them wrong. They feel like that all the time. But that's just silly. Here you got a woman givin' up everything to save your little girl and all you can think about is a passing fancy or even maybe another lover. What do you think they're doin' right now?"

I reached out and pinched one of her nipples and then the other.

She liked that but only showed it by inhaling deeply.

And to show me that it wasn't too overwhelming she began to speak again.

"It's like when Axel's older cousin Nina got jealous of me bein' in his bed. She loved him in another way; like Bonnie loves you. You shouldn't be jealous of her. You should be happy that she can give your little girl life."

Those were the words I had wanted to hear, needed to hear for days. I opened my mouth but she spoke first.

"No," she said, pinching my nipples hard and then pounding down, her sex against mine. "No. No more. Come to me."

I came all at once, before I was ready. She smiled but didn't slow the hammerlike rhythm against my erection. It hurt but I didn't throw her off or complain. And after a few seconds I had another orgasm. I guess that's what it was. It happened somewhere inside my body. All of a sudden there was a dam I didn't know about and it broke open and everyone in its path was drowned.

WHEN I AWOKE, the woman who might have been a murderer was lying along my side with her head nestled against my shoulder. I knew almost nothing about Philomena Cargill and yet she had touched me in a place I couldn't even have imagined on my own. Was she like this for all men? A fertility goddess come from Africa somewhere to bedevil mortal men with something they could never know without her? Her hand was on my limp sex. But as soon as I saw it I began to get hard again.

"We should get cleaned up," she said, awakening to my arousal.

"Yeah. Yeah."

There was a jury-rigged shower nozzle attached to the wall above the small bathtub in the restroom. We washed each other. Physically I was as excited as I had been on the couch but my mind was free.

"Where does Axel's cousin live?" I asked.

"Down in L.A. somewhere." In her mind she was still in Berkeley.

"And is she related to the family business somehow?"

"Nina's father was the man who started the company. He's Tourneau, Rega Tourneau."

"Was he part of the company before the war?"

"Oh yeah."

"Is he still alive?"

She began to lather my pubic hair, working deftly around the erection. "He's very old. Ninety I think. Nobody in the family likes him."

After the shower I was still straining with excitement. Cinnamon stood in front of me, smiling, and asked, "Are you going to leave now?"

I wanted to leave because I knew somehow that I'd lose something of my soul if I let her make love to me again.

"No," I said. "I'm not going anywhere."

42

I didn't leave Philomena's until early the next morning. It had been a long time since I'd spent a night like that. Georgette was wonderful and passionate but Cinnamon Cargill was the spice of sex with no impediments of love at all. Where Georgette kissed me and told me that she wanted to take me home forever, Cinnamon just sneered and used sex like a surgeon's knife. She never said one nice or kind thing, though physically she loved me like I was her only man.

When she'd leave the room to go to the toilet she seemed surprised, and not necessarily happy, to see me when she returned.

She told me all about old Rega Tourneau. He was the family patriarch, born in the last century. He had married Axel's father's aunt and so there was some family connection there — though not by blood.

"The old man had a sour temperament," Philomena said.

"When he was a boy he was caught in a boiler explosion that scarred his face and blinded his eye."

When he retired he became reclusive and removed.

He had a disagreement with Nina about the man she married. Rega didn't like him and so he disowned his daughter. As far as Philomena knew, Nina was still out of the will.

Nina Tourneau eventually separated from her husband and tried to become an artist down in Southern California somewhere. When that failed she became an art dealer.

Then we made love again.

Philomena would have married Axel if he'd asked her to. She would have had his children and hosted his acid parties with catered meals and champagne chasers.

"But you never said you loved him," I said.

"Love is an old-fashioned concept," she replied in university-ese. "The human race developed love to make families cohesive. It's just a tool you put back in the closet when you're done with it."

"And then you take it out again when someone else strikes your fancy?"

Then we made love again.

"Love is like a man's thing," she told me. "It gets all hot and bothered for a while there, but then after it's over it goes to sleep."

"Not me," I said. "Not tonight."

She smiled and the sun came up.

I forced myself to get dressed and ready to go.

"Do you have to leave?" she asked me.

"Do you love me?" I asked.

It is a question I had never asked a woman before that day. I had no idea that the words were in my chest, my heart. But that was the reply to her question. If she had said yes I would have taken a different path, I'm sure. Maybe I would have taken her with me or maybe I would have cut my losses and run. Maybe we would have flown together on the bearer bonds to Switzerland, where I would have taken a flat above Bonnie and Joguye.

"Sure I do," she said with a one-shoulder shrug. She might as well have winked.

I breathed a deep sigh of relief and went out the door.

I PARKED MY LOW-RIDER car across the street from an innocuous-looking place on Ozone, less than a block away from Santa Monica beach. It was a little after seven and there was some activity on the street. There were men in suits and old women with dogs on leashes, bicyclers showing off their calves in shorts, and bums shaking the sand from their clothes. Almost everyone was white but they didn't mind me sitting there. They didn't call for the police.

I drank my coffee, ate my jelly doughnut. I tried to remember the last good meal I'd had. The chili at Primo's, I thought. I felt clean. Cinnamon and I had taken four showers between our fevered bouts of not-love. My sex ached in my pants. I thought about her repudiation of love and my surprising deep need for it. I wondered if my life would ever settle back into the bliss I'd known with Bonnie and the hope for happiness I had discovered in Cinnamon's arms.

These thoughts pained me. I looked up and there was Jackson Blue walking out his front door, his useless spectacles on his face and a black briefcase dangling from his left hand.

I rolled down the window and called his last name.

He went down behind a parked car next to him. At one time seeing him jump like that would have made me grin. Many a time I had startled Jackson just because he would react like that. He dove out windows, skipped around corners — but that day I wasn't trying to scare my friend, I got no pleasure witnessing his frantic leap.

"Jackson, it's me . . . Easy."

Jackson's head popped up. He grimaced but before he could complain I got out of the car with my hands held up in apology.

"Sorry, man," I said. "I just saw you and shouted without thinkin'."

The little coward pulled himself up and walked toward me, looking around to make sure there was no trap.

"Hey, Ease. What's wrong?"

"I need help, Jackson."

"Look like you need three days in bed."

"That too."

"What can I do for ya?"

"I just need you to ride with me, Blue. Ride with me for the day if you can."

"Where you ridin'?"

"I got to find a white woman and then her daddy."

"What you need me for?" Jackson asked.

"Company. That's all. That and somebody to bounce ideas off of. I mean if you can get outta work."

"Oh yeah," Jackson said in that false bravado he always used to camouflage his coward's heart. "You know I'm at that place sometimes as late as the president. He come in my office and tell me to go home. All I gotta do is call an' tell 'em I need a rest day an' they say, *See ya.*"

He clapped my shoulder, letting me know that he'd take the ride.

"But first we gotta go tell Jewelle," he said. "You know babygirl gotta know where daddy gonna be."

We walked back to his door and Jackson used three keys on the locks. The crow's nest entrance of his apartment looked down into a giant room. It was like staring down into a well made up to be some fairy-tale creature's home.

"Easy here, baby," Jackson announced.

She was standing at the window, looking out into a flower garden that they worked on in their spare time. She wore a pink housecoat with hair curlers in her hair like tiny, precariously perched oil drums.

Jackson and I were in our mid-forties, old men compared to Jewelle, who was still shy of thirty. Her brown skin and long face were attractive enough, but what made her a beauty was the power in her eyes. Jewelle was a real estate genius. She'd taken my old manager's property and turned it into nearly an empire. The riots had slowed her growth some but soon she'd be a millionaire and she and Jackson would live with the rich people up in Bel Air.

Jewelle smiled as we descended the ladderlike stairs to their home. The walls were twenty-five feet high and every inch was covered in bookcases crammed with Jackson's lifelong collection of books.

He had eight encyclopedias and dictionaries in everything from Greek to Mandarin. He was better read than any professor but even with all that knowledge at his disposal he'd rather lie than tell the truth.

"Hi, Easy," Jewelle said. She loved older men. And she loved me particularly because I always helped when I could. I might have been the only man (or woman for that matter) in her life who gave her more than he took.

"Hey, J.J. What's up?"

"Thinkin' about buying up property in a neighborhood in L.A. proper," she said. "Lotta Koreans movin' in there. The value's bound to rise."

"Me an' Easy gonna take a personal day," Jackson said.

"What kinda personal day?" Jewelle asked suspiciously.

"Nobody dangerous, nothing illegal," I said.

Jewelle loved Jackson because he was the only man she'd ever met who could outthink her. Anything she'd ask — he had the answer. It's said that some women are attracted to men's minds. She was the only one I ever knew personally.

"What about your job, baby?" she asked.

"Easy want some company, J.J.," Jackson told her. "When the last time you hear him say sumpin' like that to me?"

I could see that they'd talked about me quite a bit. I could almost make out the echoes of those conversations in that cavernous room.

Jewelle nodded and Jackson took off his tie. When he went to the phone to make a call Jewelle sidled up next to me.

"You in trouble, Easy?" she asked.

"So bad that you can't even imagine it, J.J."

"I don't want Jackson in there with you."

"It's not like that, honey," I told her. "Really . . . he just gonna ride with me. Maybe give me an idea or two."

Jackson came back to us then.

"I called the president at his house," the whiz kid said proudly. "He told me to take all the time I needed. Now all you got to do is feed me some breakfast and I'm ret-to-go."

43

Jackson made us go to a little diner that looked over the beach.

The problem was that the place he chose, the Sea Cove Inn, was where Bonnie and I used to go in the mornings sometimes. But I made it through. I had waffles and bacon. Jackson gobbled French toast and sausages, fried eggs and a whole quart of orange juice. He had both the body and the appetite of a boy.

The waitress, an older white woman, knew Jackson and they talked about dogs — she was the owner of some rare breed. While they gabbed I went to the pay phone and called EttaMae.

"Yes? Who is it?"

"Easy, Etta."

"Hold on."

She put the receiver down and a moment later Mouse picked it up.

"You in jail, Easy?" he asked inside of a big yawn.

"At the beach."

"How's Jackson?"

"He's somethin'."

"Your boy Cicero is what a head doctor girlfriend I once had called a psy-ko-path. I think that's what she called me too. Anyway he been killin' an' causin' pain up an' down the coast for years. They say he was a rich kid but his folks disowned him after his first murder. I know where he been livin' at down here but he ain't been there for days. I got a guy watchin' the place but I don't think he gonna show."

"Crazy, huh?"

"Everybody say it. Mothahfuckah cover his tracks with bone an' blood. You know I be doin' the country a favor to pop that boy there."

"Yeah," I said, thinking that deadly force was the only way to deal with Joe Cicero. A man like that was dangerous as long as he drew breath. Even if he was in prison he could get at you.

"What you want me to do, Easy?"

"Sit tight, Ray. If you get the word on Cicero give me a call."

"Where at?"

"I'll call Etta tonight at six and tomorrow morning at nine. Leave me something with her."

"You got it, brother."

He was about to hang up when I said, "Hey, Ray."

"What?"

"Do you ever get scared'a shit like this?" I knew the answer. I just didn't want to get off the phone yet.

"Naw, man. I mean this some serious shit right here. It'a be a lot easier takin' down that armored car. That's all mapped out. All you gotta do is follow the dots on a job like that. This here make ya think. Think fast. But you know I like that."

"Yeah," I said. "It sure does make you think."

"Okay then, Easy," Mouse said. "Call me when you wanna. I'ma be here waitin' for you or my spy."

"Thanks, Ray."

WE HAD JUST FINISHED rutting on the cold tiles next to the bathtub when Philomena told me about the gallery where Nina Tourneau worked. She enjoyed giving me information after a bout of hard sex. The force of making love seemed to give her strength. By the time we were finished I don't think she was that worried about dying.

The gallery was on Rodeo Drive in Beverly Hills. I put my pistols in the trunk and my PI license in my shirt pocket. Even dressed fine as we were Jackson and I were still driving a hot rod car in the morning, and even though he had a corporate look I was a little too sporty to be going to a respectable job.

I parked in front of the gallery, Merton's Fine Art.

There was the sound of faraway chimes when we entered. A white woman wearing a deep green suit came through a doorway at the far end of the long room. When she saw us a perplexity invaded her features. She said something into the room behind her and then marched forward with an insincere smile plastered on her lips.

"May I help you?" she asked, doubtful that she could.

"Are you Nina Tourneau?"

"Yes?"

"My name's Easy Rawlins, ma'am," I said, holding out my city-issued identification. "I'm representing a man named Lee from up in San Francisco. He's trying to locate a relative of yours."

Nothing I said, nor my ID, managed to erase the doubt from her face.

"And who would that be?" she asked.

Nina Tourneau was somewhere in her late fifties, though cosmetics and spas made her look about mid-forty. Her elegant face had most definitely been beautiful in her youth. But now the cobwebs of age were gathering beneath the skin.

"A Mr. Rega Tourneau," I said.

The name took its toll on the art dealer's reserve.

Jackson in the meanwhile had been looking at the pale oil paintings along the wall. The colors were more like pastels than oils really and the details were vague, as if the paintings were yet to be finished.

"These paintin's here, they like uh," Jackson said, snapping his fingers. "What you call it? Um . . . derivative, that's it. These paintin's derivative of Puvis de Chavannes."

"What did you say?" she asked him.

"Chavannes," he repeated. "The man Van Gogh loved so damn much. I never liked the paintin's myself. An' I sure don't see why some modern-day painter would want to do like him."

"You know art?" she asked, amazed.

At that moment the chimes sounded again. I didn't have to look to know that the police were coming in. When Nina whispered into the back room I was sure that it was to tell her secretary to call the police. After the riots people called the police if two black men stopped on a street corner to say hello — much less if they walked into a Beverly Hills gallery with paintings based on old European culture.

"Stay where you are," one of the cops said. "Keep your hands where I can see them."

"Oh yeah," Jackson said to Nina. "I read all about them things. You know it's El Greco, the Greek, that I love though. That suckah paint like he was suckled with Picasso but he older than the hills."

"Shut up," one of the two young cops said.

They both had guns out. One of them grabbed Jackson by his arm.

"I'm sorry, Officers," Nina Tourneau said then. "But there's been a mistake. I didn't recognize Mr. Rawlins and his associate when they came in. I told Carlyle to watch out. He must have thought I wanted him to call you. There's nothing wrong."

The cops didn't believe her at first. I don't blame them. She seemed nervous, upset. They put cuffs on both Jackson and me and one of them took Nina in the back room to assure her that she was safe. But she kept to her story and finally they set us free. They told us that we'd be under surveillance and then left to sit in their cruiser across the street.

"Why are you looking for my father?" Nina asked after they'd gone.

"I'm not," I said. "It's Robert Lee, detective extraordinaire from Frisco, lookin' for him. He gave me some money and I'm just puttin' in the time."

Miss Tourneau looked at us for a while and then shook her head.

"My father's an old man, Mr. Rawlins. He's in a rest home. If your client wishes to speak to me you can give him the number of this gallery and I will be happy to talk with him."

She stared me in the eye while saying this.

"He disowned you, didn't he?"

"I don't see where that's any of your business," she said.

I smiled and gave her a slight nod.

"Come on, Jackson," I said.

He shrugged like a child and turned toward the door.

"Excuse me, sir," Nina Tourneau said to Jackson. "Do you collect?"

You could see the question was a novel thought to my friend. His face lit up and he said, "Lemme have your card. Maybe I'll buy somethin' one day."

THE POLICE were still parked across the street when we came out.

"Why you didn't push her, Easy?" Jackson asked. "You could see that she was wantin' to know what you knew."

"She told me where he was already, Mr. Art Collector."

"When she do that?"

"While we were talkin'."

"An' where did she say to go?"

"The Westerly Nursing Home."

"And where is that?"

"Somewhere not too far from here I bet."

"Easy," Jackson said. "You know you a mothahfuckah, man. I mean you like magic an' shit."

Jackson might not have known that a compliment from him was probably the highest accolade that I was ever likely to receive.

I smiled and leaned over to wave at the policemen in their prowler.

Then we drove a block south and I stopped at a phone booth, where I looked up Westerly.

44

"Why you drivin' west, Easy?" Jackson asked me.

We were on Santa Monica Boulevard.

"Goin' back to Ozone to pick up your car, man."

"Why?"

"Because the cops all over Beverly Hills got the description of this here hot rod."

"Oh yeah. Right."

ON THE WAY to the nursing home Jackson stopped so that he could buy a potted white orchid.

"For Jewelle?" I asked him.

"For a old white man," Jackson said with a grin.

He was embarrassed that he didn't pick up on why we needed to switch cars and so he came up with the trick to get us in the nursing home.

We decided to send Jackson in with the flowers and to see how far he could get. The ideal notion would be for Jackson to tell the old man that we had pictures of him in Germany humping young women and girls. Failing that he might find a way to get us in on the sly. Every mansion we'd ever known had a back door and some poor soul held a key.

I wasn't sure that Rega Tourneau was mastermind of the problems I was trying to solve, but he was the centerpiece. And if he knew anything, I was going to do my best to find out what it was.

Westerly was a big estate a few long blocks above Sunset. There was a twelve-foot brick wall around the green grounds and an equally tall wrought iron gate for an entrance. We drove past it once and then I parked a few woodsy blocks away.

For a disguise Jackson buttoned the top button of his shirt, turned the lapels of his jacket up, and put on his glasses.

"Jackson, you really think this is gonna work? I mean here you wearin' a two-hundred-dollar suit. They gonna know somethin's up."

"They gonna see my skin before they see anything, Easy. Then the flowers, then the glasses. By the time they get to the suit they minds be made up."

After he left I lay down across the backseat.

There was an ache behind my eyes and my testicles felt swollen. Back when I was younger that pain would have been a point of pride. I would have worked it into street conversation. But I was too old to mask pain with bluster.

After a few moments I fell into a deep slumber.

Haffernon was standing there next to me. We were locked in a bitter argument. He told me that if he hadn't done business with the Nazis then someone else would have.

"That's how money works, fool," he said.

"But you're an American," I argued.

"How could you of all people say something like that?" he asked with real wonder. "Your grandparents were the property of a white man. You can't ever walk in my shoes. But still you believe in the ground I stand on?"

I felt a rage growing in my chest. I would have smashed his face if a gun muzzle hadn't pressed up against the base of his skull. Haffernon felt the pressure but before he could respond the gun fired. The top of his head erupted with blood and brain and bone.

The killer turned and ran. I couldn't tell if it was a man or woman, only that he (or she) was of slight stature. I ran after the assassin but somebody grabbed my arm.

"Let me go!" I shouted.

"Easy! Easy, wake up!"

Jackson was shaking my arm, waking me just before I caught the killer. I wanted to slap Jackson's grinning face. It took me a moment to realize that it was a dream and that I'd never find a killer that way.

But still . . .

"What you got, Jackson?"

"Rega Tourneau is dead."

"Dead?"

"Died in his sleep last night. Heart failure, they said. They thought that I was bringing the flowers for the funeral."

"Dead?"

"The lady at the front desk told me that he'd been doin' just fine. He'd had a lot of visitors lately. The doctors felt that maybe it was too much excitement."

"What visitors?"

"You got a couple'a hunnert dollars, Easy?"

"What?" Now awake, I was thinking about Rega Tourneau dying so conveniently. It had to be murder. And there I was again, scoping out the scene of the crime.

"Two hunnert dollars," Jackson said again.

"Why?"

"Terrance Tippitoe."

"Who?"

"He's one'a the attendants up in there. While I was waitin' to see the receptionist we talked. Afterwards I told him I thought I knew how he could make some scratch. He be off at three."

"Thanks, Mr. Blue. That's just what I needed."

"Let's go get lunch," he suggested.

"You just ate a little while ago."

"I know this real good place," he said.

I flopped back down and he started the car. I closed my eyes but sleep did not come.

"YEAH, EASY," Jackson was saying.

I was stabbing at a green salad while he chowed down on a T-bone steak at Mulligan's on Olympic. We had a booth in a corner. Jackson was drinking beer, proud of his work at the Westerly Nursing Home. But after the third beer his self-esteem turned sour.

"I used to be afraid," he said. "All the time, day and night. I used to couldn't go to sleep 'cause there was always some fear in my mind. Some man gonna find out how I cheated him or slept wit' his wife or girlfriend. Some mothahfuckah hear I got ten bucks an' he gonna stove my head in to get it."

"But now you got a good job and it's all fine."

"Job ain't shit, Easy. I mean, I like it. Shoot, I love it. But the job ain't what calms my mind. That's all Jewelle there."

He snorted and wiped his nose with the back of his hand.

"What's the matter, Jackson?"

"I know it cain't last, that's what."

"Why not? Jewelle love you more than she loved Mofass and she loved him more than anything before he died."

"'Cause I'm bound to fuck it up, man. Bound to. Some woman gonna crawl up in my bed, some fool gonna let me hold onta his money. I been a niggah too long, Easy. Too long."

I was worried about Feather, riding on a river of sorrow and rage named Bonnie Shay, scared to death of Joe Cicero, and faced with a puzzle that made no sense. Because of all that I appreciated Jackson's sorrowful honesty. For the first time ever I felt a real kinship with him. We'd known each other for well over twenty-five years but that was the first time I felt true friendship for him.

"No, Jackson," I said. "None'a that's gonna happen."

"Why not?"

"Because I won't let it happen. I won't let you fuck up. I won't let you mess with Jewelle. All you got to do is call me and tell me if you're feelin' weak. That's all you got to do."

"You do that for me?"

"Damn straight. Call me anytime day or night. I will be there for you, Jackson."

"What for? I mean . . . what I ever do for you?"

"We all need a brother," I said. "It's just my turn, that's all."

TERRANCE TIPPITOE was a small, dark-colored man who had small eyes that had witnessed fifty or more years of hard times. He had told Jackson to meet him at a bus stop on Sunset at three-oh-five. We were there waiting. Jackson made the introductions (my name was John Jefferson and his was George

Paine). I set out what I needed. For his participation I'd give him two hundred dollars.

Terrance was pulling down a dollar thirty-five an hour at that time and since I hadn't asked him to kill anyone he nodded and grinned and said, "Yes sir, Mr. Jefferson. I'm your man."

A time was made for Jackson to meet Terrance a few hours later.

Before Jackson and I separated back in Santa Monica, he agreed to lend me the two hundred.

The world was a different place that afternoon.

45

I went back to the hospital and got directions at the main desk to Bobby Lee's new room. Sitting in a chair beside Lee's door was an ugly white man with eyebrows, lips, and nose all at least three times too big for his doughy face. Even seated he was a big man. And despite his bulky woolen overcoat I could appreciate the strength of his limbs.

As I approached the door the Neanderthal sat up. His movements were graceful and fluid, as if he were some behemoth rising from a primordial swamp.

"Howdy," I said in the friendly manner that many Texas hicks used. I didn't want to fight this man at any time, for any reason.

He just looked at me.

"Easy Rawlins to see Robert E. Lee," I said.

"Right this way," the brute replied in a melodious baritone. He rose from the chair like Nemo's *Nautilus* rising from the depths.

Opening the door he gestured for me to go through. He tagged along behind — an elephant following his brother's tail.

Lee was sitting up in the bed wearing a nightshirt that wasn't hospital issue. It had white-on-white brocade along the buttons and a stylish collar. Seated next to him was Maya Adamant. She wore tight-fitting coral pants and a red silk blouse. Her hair was tied back and her visage was nothing if not triumphant.

They were holding hands.

"You two kiss and make up after the little tiff and trifling attempt at murder?"

I felt the presence of the bodyguard behind me. But what did I care? It was gospel I spoke.

"I told Robert everything," Maya said. "I have no secrets from him."

"And you believe her?" I asked Lee.

"Yes. I've realized a lot of things being so close to death. Lying here I've come to understand that my life has had no meaning for me. I mean, I've done a lot of important things for others. I've solved crimes and saved lives, but you know if someone is on a path to hell you can't save them."

His mouth was still under the sway of the drugs they'd given him but I perceived a clear mind underneath the weave of meandering thoughts.

"She sent Joe Cicero to our meeting," I said. "Then Joe emptied a clip into your chest. He almost killed you."

"She didn't know that he'd do that. Her only desire was to get the bonds. She's a woman without a man. She has to look out for herself."

"Wasn't it your job to get the bonds and give them to Haffernon?"

"He only wanted the letter."

Those five words proved to me that Lee's mind was running on all six cylinders. If I had become used to the idea of that letter, then I might not have noticed him slipping it in there.

"What letter?" I asked.

Lee studied my face.

"It doesn't matter now," he said. "Haffernon is dead. I've received notice."

It was my turn to stare.

"The only problem now is Joe Cicero," Lee said. "And Carl here is working on that problem."

"Cicero can't be in this alone," I said. "He has to be working for someone. And that someone can always find another Chickpea."

Lee smiled.

"I must apologize to you, Mr. Rawlins. When you first walked into my offices I believed that you were just a brash fool intent on pulling the wool over my eyes; that you only desired to make me do your bidding because I was a white man in a big house. But now I see the subtlety of your mind. You're a top-notch thinker, and more than that — you're a man."

I can't say that the accolades didn't tweak my vanity, but I knew that Lee was both devious and a fool, and that was a bad combination to be swayed by.

"Can I speak to you alone?" I asked the detective.

He considered a moment and then nodded.

"Carl, Maya," he said in dismissal.

"Boss . . ." Big Carl complained.

"It's okay. Mr. Rawlins isn't a bad man. Are you, Easy?"

"Depends on who you're askin'."

"Go on you two," Lee said. "I'll be fine."

Maya gave me a worried look as she went out. That was more of a compliment than all her boss's words.

After the door was shut I asked, "Are you stupid or do you just not care that that woman sent an assassin after you?"

"She didn't know what he intended."

"How can you be sure of that? I mean you act like you can read minds, but you and I both know that there ain't no way you can predict a woman like that."

"I can see that some woman has gotten under your skin," he said, leveling his eyes like cannon.

That threw me, made me realize that Bonnie was on my mind when I was talking about Maya. I could even see the similarities between the two women.

"This is not about my personal life, Mr. Lee. It's about Joe Cicero and your assistant sending him after you, after me. Now you and I both know that he'd have taken the same shots at me if I'd gone through that door first. And I don't have no bullet-proof vest."

"If what you told me is correct he needed you to gather information."

"Then he'd have grabbed me, tortured me."

"But that did not happen. You're alive and now Joe Cicero will be under the gun. I shot him you know."

"How bad?" I asked.

"It's hard to say. He jerked backward and fired again. I let off another shell but he was running by then."

"Can't say that he's dead. Can't be sure. And even if you could, and even if Carl gets him or the police or anybody else — that still doesn't account for who's doing all this."

"The case is over, Mr. Rawlins. Haffernon is dead."

"You see?" I said. "You see? That's where you're wrong. You think life is like one'a those Civil War enactments you got up in your house. People gettin' killed here, Bobby Lee. Killed. And they're dyin' 'cause'a what Haffernon hired you for. They're not gonna stop dyin' just because you call the game over."

I have to say that Lee seemed to be listening. There was no argument on his lips, no dismissal in his demeanor.

"Maybe you're right, Mr. Rawlins. But what do you want me to do?"

"Maybe you could work the Cicero-Maya connection. Maybe she could pretend that she still wants to work with him. Somehow we get on him and he leads us to his source."

"No."

"No? How can you just say no? We could at least ask her if it makes sense. Shit, man, this is serious business here."

"It's too dangerous."

"What's dangerous is tellin' a hit man where your boss is goin' and not lettin' your boss in on the change of plan. What's dangerous is walkin' out of a bar and havin' some man you never met open fire on your ass."

"I can't put Maya in danger."

"Why not?"

"Because we're to be married."

46

I left the hospital in a fog. How could he do that? Get engaged to a woman who not forty-eight hours before almost got him killed?

"She almost took your life," I'd said to him, floundering for sense.

"But she's always loved me and I never knew. A beautiful woman like that. And look at the way I was treating her."

"She could'a quit. She could'a demanded a raise. She could'a taken her damn phone off the hook. Why the fuck does she have to send a killer after you?"

"She was wrong. Haven't you ever been wrong, Mr. Rawlins?"

ON THE DRIVE BACK to Santa Monica I was angry. Here I was so hurt by Bonnie, who with one hand was trying to save my little girl's life and with the other caressing her new lover. Now

Lee forgives attempted murder and then rewards it with a promise of marriage.

I opened all the windows and smoked one cigarette after another. The radio blasted out pop songs that had sad words and up beats. I could have run my car into a brick wall right then. I wanted to.

"HERE WE GO, Easy," Jackson said. "Here's all the names in the register for the last week."

Terrance Tippitoe hadn't been subtle in his approach. He'd torn out the seven sheets of paper in the guest log and folded them in four.

I perused the documents for maybe twenty-five seconds, not more, and I knew who the mastermind was. I knew why and I knew how. But I still didn't see a way out unless I too became a murderer.

"What is it, Easy?" Jackson asked.

I shoved the log sheets into my pocket, thinking maybe if I could implicate the killer in Rega Tourneau's death then I could call in the cops. After all, I was on a first-name basis with Gerald Jordan, the deputy chief of police. I could slip him those sheets and the police could do the rest.

"Easy?" Jackson asked.

"Yeah?"

"What's wrong?"

That made me laugh. Jackson joined in. Jewelle came to sit behind him. She draped her arms around his neck.

"Nuthin's wrong, Blue. I just gotta get past a few roadblocks is all. Few roadblocks."

Jackson and Jewelle both knew to leave it at that.

* * *

I WASN'T THINKING too clearly at that time. So much had happened and so little of it I could control. I had to have a face-to-face with Cicero's employer. And in that meeting I had to make a decision. A week ago the only crime I'd considered was armed robbery, but now I'd graduated to premeditated murder.

Whatever the outcome it was getting late in the evening, and anyway I couldn't wear the same funky clothes one day more. I figured that Joe Cicero had better things to do than to stake out my house so I went home.

I drove around the block twice, looking for any signs of the contract killer. He didn't seem to be there. Maybe he was dead or at least out of action.

I took the bonds from the glove compartment of my hot rod and, with them under my arm, I strode toward my front yard.

Tacked to the door was a thick white envelope. I took it thinking that it had to have something to do with Axel or Cinnamon or maybe Joe Cicero.

I opened the door and walked into the living room. I flipped on the overhead light, threw the bonds on the couch, and opened the letter. It was from a lawyer representing Alicia and Nate Roman. They were suing me for causing them severe physical trauma and mental agony. They had received damage to their necks, hips, and spines, and she had severe lacerations to the head. There was only one broken bone but many more bruised ones. They had both seen the same doctor — an M.D. named Brown. The cost for their deep suffering was one hundred thousand dollars — each.

I walked toward the kitchen intent on getting a glass of water. At least I could do that without being shot at, spied on, or sued.

I saw his reflection in the glass door of the cabinet. He was coming fast but in that fragment of a second I realized first that the man was not Joe Cicero and second that, like Mouse, Cicero had sent a proxy to keep an eye out for his quarry. Then, when I was halfway turned around, he hit me with some kind of sap or blackjack and the world swirled down through a drain that had opened up at my feet.

I LOST CONSCIOUSNESS but there was a part of my mind that struggled to wake up. So in a dream I did wake up, in my own bed. Next to me was a dark-skinned black man. He opened his eyes at the same time I opened mine.

"Where's Bonnie?" I asked him.

"She's gone," he said with a finality that sucked the air right out of my chest.

THE MORNING SUN through the kitchen window woke me but it was nausea that drove me to my feet. I went to the bathroom and sat next to the commode, waiting to throw up — but I never did.

I showered and shaved, primped and dressed.

The bonds were gone of course. I figured that I was lucky that Cicero had sent a proxy. I was also lucky that the bonds were right there to be stolen. Otherwise Joe would have come and caused me pain until I gave them up. Then he would have killed me.

I was a lucky bastard.

After my ablutions I called a number that was lodged in my memory. I have a facility for remembering numbers, always did.

She answered on the sixth ring, breathless.

"Yes?"

"That invitation still open?"

"Easy?" Cynthia Aubec said. "I thought I'd never hear from you again."

"That might be construed as a threat, counselor."

"No. I thought you didn't like me."

"I like you all right," I said. "I like you even though you lied to me."

"Lied? Lied about what?"

"You acted like you weren't related to Axel but here I see that you signed into the Westerly Nursing Home to visit Rega Tourneau. Cynthia Tourneau-Aubec."

"Tourneau's my mother's maiden name. Aubec was my father," she said.

"Nina's your mother?"

"You seem to know everything about me."

"Did you know what Axel was trying to do?"

"He was wrong, Mr. Rawlins. These are our parents, our families. What's done is done."

"Is that why you killed him?"

"I don't know what you're talking about. Axel told me that he was going to Algeria. I don't have any reason to think that he's dead."

"You worked in the prosecutor's office when Joe Cicero was on trial, didn't you?"

She didn't answer.

"And you visited your grandfather only a few hours before he was found dead."

"He was very old. Very sick. His death was really a blessing."

"Maybe he wanted to confess before he died. About trips to the Third Reich and pornographic pictures of him with twelve-year-olds."

"Where are you?" she asked.

"In L.A. At my house."

"Come up here . . . to my house. We'll talk this out."

"What is it, Cindy? Were you in your grandfather's will? Were you afraid that the government would take away all of that wealth if the truth came out?"

"You don't understand. Between the drugs and his crazy friends Axel only wanted to destroy."

"What about Haffernon? Was he getting cold feet? Is that why you killed him? Maybe he thought that dealing with a twenty-year-old treason beef would be easier than if he was caught murdering Philomena."

"Come here to me, Easy. We can work this out. I like you."

"What's in it for me?" I asked. It was a simple question but I had complex feelings behind it.

"My mother was disowned," she said. "But the old man put me back in the will recently. I'm going to be very rich soon."

I hesitated for the appropriate amount of time, as if I were considering her request. Then I said, "When?"

"Tomorrow at noon."

"Nuthin' funny, right?"

"I just want to explain myself, to help you. That's all."

"Okay. Okay I'll come. But I don't want Joe Cicero to be there."

"Don't worry about him. He won't be bothering anyone."

"Okay then. Tomorrow at twelve."

I WAS ON A FLIGHT to San Francisco within the hour. I rented a car and made it to an address in Daly City that I'd never been to before. All of this took about four hours.

It was a small home with a pink door and a blue porch.

The door was ajar and so I walked in.

Cynthia Aubec lay on her back in the center of the hardwood floor. There was a bullet hole in her forehead. Standing over her was Joe Cicero. His right arm was bandaged and in a sling. In his left hand was a pistol outfitted with a large silencing muzzle. He must have been killing her as I was walking up the path to her door.

My pistol lay impotent in my pocket. Cicero smiled as he raised his gun to point at my forehead. I knew he was thinking about when I had the drop on him; that he wouldn't make the same mistake that I had.

"Well, well, well," he said. "Here I thought I'd have to chase you down, and then you come walking in like a Christmas goose."

With my eyes only I glanced to the sides. There was no sign of the man who had sapped me the night before.

Beyond the young woman's corpse was a small coffee table upon which sat two teacups. She'd served him tea before he shot her. The thought was grotesque but I knew I wouldn't have long to contemplate it.

"Lee is going to put the cops on you for the Bowers killing and for Haffernon," I said, hoping somehow to stave off my own death.

"I didn't kill them. She did," he said, waving his pistol at her.

"But you were at Bowers's house," I said. "You threatened him."

"You know about that, huh? She hired me to get the bonds from Bowers. When I told her what he'd said she took it in her own hands." He coughed and I glanced at the teacups. A tremor of hope thrummed in the center of my chest.

"Haffernon too?"

He nodded. There was something off about the movement of his head, as if he weren't in full control.

"Why?" I asked, playing for time.

"He was getting weak. Didn't want to do what they had to do

to keep their nasty little secret. That's why I had to kill her. I knew that" — he coughed again — "sooner or later she'd have to come after me. Nobody could know or the whole house of cards would fall. That's why I work for a living. A rich family will take your soul."

"Why not?" I asked, as bland as could be. "Why couldn't anybody know?"

"Money," he said with a knowing, crooked nod. "Sometimes it was just that she wanted her inheritance. Sometimes she was angry at the kid for taking all that wealth for granted when she and her mother had been living hand to mouth."

He straightened his shooting arm.

"And she knew you from your trial about the torture?"

"You do your homework, nigger," he said and then coughed. Blood spattered out onto his lips, but because he had no free hand he couldn't rub it off to see.

I leaped to the left and he fired. He was good. He was a right-hander and dying but he still hit me in the shoulder. I used the momentum to fall through a doorway to my left. Screaming from the pain, I made it to my feet. I was halfway down the hall when I heard him behind me. He fired again but I didn't feel anything.

I fell anyway.

As I looked back I saw him staggering forward, shooting once, and then he fell. He didn't move again.

I was on the floor next to a bathroom. I went in, trying not to touch any surface. I got a towel from the rack next to the tub and used it to staunch the bleeding from my shoulder.

When the blood was merely seeping I checked Cicero. He was dead. In his jacket pocket was an envelope containing twenty-five thousand dollars. In a folder on the coffee table I found the bonds and the letter.

There were many photographs on the shelves and window-sills. Some were of Cynthia and her mother, Nina Tourneau. One was Cynthia as a child on the lap of her beloved grandfather — pornographer, child molester, and Nazi traitor.

I took the bonds, leaving the letter for the cops to mull over. The teacups had the same strong smell that the cup had at Axel's house. Only one had been drunk from.

47

I drove my rental car for hours, but it seemed like several days, bleeding on the steering wheel and down my chest. I drove one-handed half the time, using the stiffening fingers of my right hand to press the towel against the shoulder wound.

It was a minor miracle that I made it to Christmas Black's Riverside home. I don't remember getting out of the car or ringing the bell. Maybe they found me there, passed out over the wheel.

I came to three days later. Easter Dawn was sitting in a big chair next to my bed, reading from a picture book. I don't know if she knew how to read or if she was just interpreting the pictures into stories. When I opened my eyes she jumped up and ran from the room.

"Daddy! Daddy! Mr. Rawlins is awake!"

Christmas came into the room wearing black jeans and a drab green T-shirt. His boots were definitely army issue.

"How you doin', soldier?" he asked.

"Ready for my discharge," I said in a voice so weak that even I didn't hear it.

Christmas held up my head and trickled water into my mouth. I wanted to get up and call Switzerland but I couldn't even lift a hand.

"You bled a lot," Christmas said. "Almost died. Lucky I got some friends in the hospital down in Oxnard. I got you medicine and a few pints of red."

"Call Mouse," I said as loudly as I could.

Then I passed out.

The next time I woke up, Mama Jo was sitting next to me. She had just taken some foul-smelling substance away from my nose.

"Uh!" I grunted. "What was that?"

"I can see you gonna be okay, Easy Rawlins," big, black, handsome Mama Jo said.

"I feel better. How long have I been here?"

"Six days."

"Six? Did anybody call Bonnie?"

"She called Etta. Feather's doin' good, the doctors said. They won't know nuthin' for eight weeks more though. Etta said that you and Raymond were doing some business down in Texas."

Mouse sauntered in with his glittering smile.

"Hey, Easy," he said. "Christmas got all yo' money an' bonds and shit in the draw next to yo' bed."

"Give the bonds to Jackson," I told him. "Let him cash 'em and we'll split 'em three ways."

Mouse smiled. He liked a good deal.

"I'll let you boys talk business," Jo said. She rose from the chair and I watched in awe, as always impressed by her size and bearing.

Mouse pulled up a chair and told me what he knew.

Joe Cicero made the TV news with his murder of Cynthia Aubec and her poisoning of him.

"They say anything about a letter they found?" I asked.

"No. No letter, just mutual murder, that's what they called it."

That night Saul Lynx arrived in a rented ambulance and drove me home.

Benita Flag and Jesus were there to nurse me.

Two weeks after it was all over I was still convalescing. Mouse came over and sat with me under the big tree in the backyard.

"You don't have to worry about them people no more, Ease," he said after we'd been gossiping for a while.

"What people?"

"The Romans."

For a moment I was confused, and then I remembered the accident and the lawsuit.

"Yeah," he said. "Benita showed me the papers an' I went ovah to talk to 'em. I told 'em about Feather and about you bein' so tore up. I gave 'em five thousand off the top'a what Jackson cleared and told 'em that you was a good detective and if they ever needed help that you would be there for 'em. After that they decided to drop that suit."

There weren't many people in Watts who wouldn't do what Ray asked. No one wanted to be on his bad side.

THEY FOUND AXEL Bowers in his ashram and tied Aubec to that crime too. The papers made it an incestuous sex scandal. Who knows, maybe it was. Dream Dog was even interviewed. He told the reporters about the sex and drug parties. In 1966 that was reason enough, in the public mind, for murder.

A few days later I received a card from Maya and Bobby Lee.

They were on their honeymoon in Monaco. Lee had connections with the royal family there. He said that I should call him if I ever needed employment — or advice. That was the closest Lee would ever come to an offer of friendship.

I sent the twenty-five thousand on to Switzerland. Feather called me once a week. Bonnie called two times but I always found an excuse to get off the line. I didn't tell them about my getting shot. There was no use in worrying Feather or making Bonnie feel bad either.

I lived off of the money Jackson got from the bonds and wondered who at Haffernon's firm bought off the letter. But I didn't worry too much about it. I was alive and Feather was on her way to recovery. Even if the moral spirit of my country was rotten to the core at least I had played a part in her salvation — my beautiful child.

IT WAS A MONTH after the shooting that I got a letter from New York. With it was a tiny clipping saying that an inquiry had opened concerning the American-owned Karnak Chemical Company and their dealings with Germany during the war. Information had come to light about the sale of munitions directly to Germany from Karnak. If the allegations turned out to be true a full investigation would be launched.

The letter read:

Dear Mr. Rawlins:

  Thank you for whatever you did. I read about our reptilian friend in the Bay Area. I just wanted you to see that Axel had an ace up his sleeve. He probably gathered the information in Egypt and Germany and sent it to the government before he told anybody about

the Swiss bonds. I think he wanted me to have
them if anything happened to him. He couldn't
know how slow the government would work.
    It was nice meeting you. I have a low-level
job at an investment firm here in New York.
I'm sure that I will get promoted soon.
    If you're ever out here come by and see me.

"love"

Cinnamon

There was a dark red lipstick kiss at the bottom of the letter.

I sent her the two books I had taken from her apartment and a
brief note thanking her for being so unusual.

FIVE WEEKS LATER Bonnie and Feather came home.

Feather had been a little butterball before the illness. She was
just a wraith when she got on that plane to Switzerland. But now
she was at least four inches taller and dressed like a woman. She
was even taller than Jesus.

After kissing me and hugging my neck she regained her com-
posure and said, "Bonjour, Papa. Comment ça va?"

"Bien, ma fille," I replied, remembering the words I learned
while killing men across France.

WE ALL STAYED UP late into the night talking. Jesus was
even animated. He had learned some French from Bonnie over
time and so now he and Feather conversed in a foreign language.
Her recovery and return made him almost giddy with joy.

Finally there was just Bonnie and me sitting next to each
other on the couch.

"Easy?"

"Yeah, honey?"

"Can we talk about it now?"

There was fever in my blood and a tidal wave in my mind but I said, "Talk about what?"

"I only called Joguye because Feather was sick and I knew that he had connections," she began.

I was thinking about Robert E. Lee and Maya Adamant.

"When I saw him I remembered how we'd felt about each other, and . . . and we did spend a lot of time together in Montreux. I know you must have been hurt but I also spent the time making up my mind —"

I put up my hand to stop her. I must have done it with some emphasis, because she flinched.

"I'm gonna stop you right there, honey," I said. "I'm gonna stop you, because I don't wanna hear it."

"What do you mean?"

"It's not either me or him," I told the love of my life. "It's either me or not me. That's what I've come to in this time you were gone. When we talked at the airport you should'a said right then that it was always me, would always be. I don't care if you slept with him or not, not really. But the truth is he got a footprint in your heart. That kinda mark don't wash out."

"What are you saying, Easy?" She reached out for me. She touched me but I wasn't there.

"You can take your stuff whenever you want. I love you but I got to let you go."

JESUS AND BENITA moved her the next day. I didn't know where she went. The kids did. I think they saw her sometimes, but they never talked to me about it.

All Orion/Phoenix titles are available at your local bookshop or from the following address:

Mail Order Department
Littlehampton Book Services
FREEPOST BR535
Worthing, West Sussex, BN13 3BR
telephone 01903 828503, *facsimile* 01903 828802
e-mail MailOrders@lbsltd.co.uk
(Please ensure that you include full postal address details)

Payment can be made either by credit/debit card (Visa, Mastercard, Access and Switch accepted) or by sending a £ Sterling cheque or postal order made payable to *Littlehampton Book Services.*
DO NOT SEND CASH OR CURRENCY

Please add the following to cover postage and packing:

UK and BFPO:
£1.50 for the first book, and 50p for each additional book to a maximum of £3.50

Overseas and Eire:
£2.50 for the first book, plus £1.00 for the second book, and 50p for each additional book ordered

BLOCK CAPITALS PLEASE

name of cardholder ....

address of cardholder ....

delivery address
(if different from cardholder)
....
....
....

postcode ....   *postcode* ....

☐ I enclose my remittance for £............................

☐ please debit my Mastercard/Visa/Access/Switch (delete as appropriate)

card number ☐☐☐☐☐☐☐☐☐☐☐☐☐☐☐☐

expiry date ☐☐☐☐   Switch issue no. ☐☐

signature ....

prices and availability are subject to change without notice